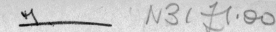

Elizabeth McGregor was born in Warwickshire and now lives in Dorset with her daughter, Kate. An award-winning short story writer, she is also the author of eleven novels, including six psychological thrillers and two comedies under the pseudonym Holly Fox. Her last two novels, *The Ice Child* and *A Way Through the Mountains*, are also published by Bantam. She is currently working on a new novel.

Also by Elizabeth McGregor

AN INTIMATE OBSESSION
YOU BELONG TO ME
LITTLE WHITE LIES
OUT OF REACH
SECOND SIGHT
THE WRONG HOUSE
THE ICE CHILD
A WAY THROUGH THE MOUNTAINS

(and as Holly Fox)

THIS WAY UP
UP AND RUNNING

The Girl in the
Green Glass Mirror

Elizabeth McGregor

BANTAM BOOKS

LONDON • TORONTO • SYDNEY • AUCKLAND • JOHANNESBURG

THE GIRL IN THE GREEN GLASS MIRROR
A BANTAM BOOK: 0 553 81605 5

First publication in Great Britain

PRINTING HISTORY
Bantam edition published 2005

1 3 5 7 9 10 8 6 4 2

Copyright © Elizabeth McGregor 2005

Set in 11/13pt Sabon by
Falcon Oast Graphic Art Ltd.

Bantam Books are published by Transworld Publishers,
61–63 Uxbridge Road, London W5 5SA,
a division of The Random House Group Ltd,
in Australia by Random House Australia (Pty) Ltd,
20 Alfred Street, Milsons Point, Sydney, NSW 2061, Australia,
in New Zealand by Random House New Zealand Ltd,
18 Poland Road, Glenfield, Auckland 10, New Zealand
and in South Africa by Random House (Pty) Ltd,
Endulini, 5a Jubilee Road, Parktown 2193, South Africa.

Printed and bound in Great Britain by
Cox & Wyman Ltd, Reading, Berkshire.

Papers used by Transworld Publishers are natural, recyclable
products made from wood grown in sustainable forests. The
manufacturing processes conform to the environmental
regulations of the country of origin.

For R, the magician

Prologue

He held up the magnifying-glass to the light.

It was smaller than a crown piece, and had a thick ebony edge, rubbed smooth, as smooth as the glass itself. He looked at it for a moment, at the grain within the wood, the silky rim. He lifted it to his face and saw the world change again inside the glass, reducing to flurries of shade.

Richard Dadd leaned against Bedlam's upper window.

This part of London's greatest lunatic asylum, in 1844, was a long corridor, filled with people, and there were only two windows, at each end. Between lay a hundred feet of squalling darkness, a storm of indistinct faces. There must have been a hundred and twenty men crammed into the space. A hundred and twenty in the dark, and only two windows. A place of madness and fright. Someone close to him was sitting on the floor, their possessions huddled into their side, an arm sheltering them against the shuffling feet of the crowd.

Dadd looked at the face, that of a boy of perhaps

fourteen. His skin was dirty close to the roots of his hair, but he had been washed by one of the attendants, a rag taken swiftly round his face, leaving the tidemark of grime. Dadd looked down on this stranger, seeing the bone, the eye socket, the mouth, the eyes. Most of all the eyes. The hand without the magnifying-glass twitched, the second finger and thumb pressing together. He needed a pencil, or a piece of charcoal. But not colour. There was no colour in those eyes, or in any eyes he saw now.

He saw only an eye leached of pigment, with reflections hurrying within it. And deeper still, beyond the surface of the eye, the alternative landscape of thought. Inside the thought, instinct. Inside the instinct, creation. Here was God in the eye of a bewildered boy sitting on a filthy floor. Here was God, forcing the fuse into the explosive, priming the weapon. Here was God, painting light on darkness, fashioning the stars and breathing creation into ashes.

Dadd turned back to the window, to the crane-fly caught in a web against the bars.

He brought the magnifying-glass to it, searching the dry, convulsing thorax, watching the brittle leg pulling in the spider's silk. The fly became a monster, but audaciously beautiful. It was formed of opaque segments, faint spindles of carbon. In the tissue, he could see mountains. He could see open sky. He could see mouths and grasses and insects and instruments and folds of fabric and sailing ships and hands. He could see Bacchanalia and Diadonus, a vine seat, the blade of a knife, bridges, moorland, clusters of ferns, and the magician with his arms outstretched.

He leaned back, gasping.

There was another world, and another world, and another world.

One

It was only a week after her husband had left her that Catherine Sergeant went to a wedding. It was a cold, bright spring day, a blue sky, frost on the deep grain of the church door. She arrived late purposely, to avoid the conversations, but she couldn't avoid them afterwards when the congregation emerged.

The photographer took the bridal couple close to the trees, to be photographed in the sunlight, under a thin veil of blackthorn blossom.

'Catherine,' a voice said.

She turned. It was Amanda and Mark Pearson.

'Why didn't you tell us you were invited?' they demanded. 'We could have come together.'

'I didn't decide until the last minute,' she said.

'Where's Robert?' Amanda asked.

'He's gone away.'

'Working?'

There was a moment. 'Yes,' she said.

She moved from person to person, friends of friends. Thankfully, this was not a family wedding; Catherine was a peripheral guest. There were some people whom she didn't know, and who asked her nothing.

She moved to the very edge of the crowd, and leaned on the wall. She was wearing red, and she thought suddenly how inappropriate it was, this celebratory colour, this colour of triumph. She felt anything but triumphant. She felt disoriented. It seemed incredible to her now that she had come at all; got dressed this morning – got into the car. Driven here, in a new red suit, wearing new shoes. Incredible that she had even gone out this week and bought the shoes. Sat in a shop, written a cheque. Incredible that she had gone through the motions.

The routine things. Working, driving, buying, eating, sleeping.

Had she slept? Four hours, perhaps. Never more each night in the last seven.

As she stared out over the valley, a country valley folded in with pasture, dissected by one road, which passed through what seemed now to be a grey cloud of leafless beech on the hill, she felt excruciatingly tired.

She looked down at the wall. The corrugated pale green, acid yellow and grey, of the lichen on the limestone: that was animation of sorts. She focused on the colours. Beyond the wall, the graves. The angle of the April light against them. *Alexander Seeley, born 18 November 1804, his wife Claudia Anne.*

The snowdrops forming a white square. The blackbird eyeing her from the neighbouring plot, perched on a stone angel with great folded wings, feather upon feather.

Some people nearby were distributing drinks while the photographs were taken.

Beyond them, Amanda was beckoning her, holding up a glass.

It's not difficult at all, Catherine told herself. Your husband is away, working – it's a simple explanation, plausible – so you've come on your own. But tomorrow, or the next day, he'll be home.

This is just a piece of time with a flaw in it and for a while had become unfathomable, like the experience of a dream, where days and weeks had become mixed. Living through this was just a matter of coming to terms with the change. Hours that buck and race, or slow to a crawl.

Tomorrow, or the next day, he'll come home.

Repeat it, repeat it.

Saying it makes it so.

Two

It was eight a.m. when she got to the auction rooms on Monday morning.

Pearsons was an independent firm and, as such, an idiosyncrasy, which had appealed to Catherine from the first. It occupied a huge barn of a building in a country town that, two centuries before, had been known for its silk weaving. Now all that was left of the silk was the single row of cottages on the main street, lavishly embellished above the doors with a scroll bearing the initials of the old company, and the Pearsons hall behind, with its pink-yellow brick.

Behind the town were the chalk hills, open downland with shadows of old hedges, even of medieval fields. Sometimes in the last light of a winter day, as she drove over the tops towards the town, she could see the ghosts of those old furrows.

Catherine passed now under the archway of the front door: Georgian columns, a tiled floor of white acanthus on blue. She took off her coat as she went, glad to be inside. It was still bitterly cold. Just as she draped it over her arm, she felt for the mobile phone in the pocket. She took it out to check that it was turned on. No messages. No text. She put it back.

Beyond the acanthus floor, Pearsons was far more prosaic: two small offices to either side, and past them, a vast ceilingless room, the timber joists of the roof revealed. The hall was packed this morning, with barely an inch of floor showing. 'Victorian and General' was the sale title, and it encompassed a vast variety of objects, the remains of scores of lives. Dealers were already in, eyeing the goods: she recognized the usual faces, the diehards already scribbling in their catalogues.

She paused to study the variety of objects. Nearest the door was a metamorphic library chair of modest beauty, decorated with floral inlay, its steps stored beneath the seat; beside it, in contrast, was a peeling chest of drawers that had never been beautiful even on the day it had been made. She edged down the narrow aisle, past desks and porcelain, empty frames, Lloyd Loom, ivory and silver locked in one glass-fronted cabinet; the skeletons of clocks, the grey-on-sepia of faded watercolours. As she passed a cardboard box full of vinyl records, she glanced down at the cover of the first disc. Tchaikovsky's second piano concerto. The illustration was a damask rose. She turned her head.

It was then that she saw the painting.

It was a familiar portrait of a young woman seated on a chair in a white dress, her left hand holding the edge of her seat, the right curled in her lap. Behind her, the draped curtains were yellow, and there was a suggestion of a street. Muted blues.

14

Catherine's eye ranged over it again. If you regarded it critically, much was anatomically incorrect. The right arm was foreshortened, the fingers only outlined. The left hand was almost bulky. Neither was the frame of the chair right: the back curved awkwardly, as if added by chance. And yet, stepping back, the picture was perfect. Something in the failings made it wonderful.

Mark Pearson was behind the desk at the furthest end of the hall. 'Catherine,' he called.

'It's here.' She pointed at the painting.

He got up and walked towards her. 'He brought it in himself.'

'Mr Williams?' she asked, astonished.

'Yes. On Saturday. I couldn't turn it down.'

No one would. The portrait was by a Scottish watercolourist.

'It doesn't belong here,' she said. 'It should be in the arts sale next month.'

Mark waved his hand. 'I told him,' he said. 'You know the obstreperous old boy.'

'But he didn't want to sell it. He told me so.'

'I knew he would, though,' Mark said, 'calling you back to the house – what is it? Four or five times?'

She frowned. 'I can't believe it,' she murmured. 'I don't understand. He loved this painting.'

'Maybe he fell out of love with it,' Mark said. 'It happens.'

She shook her head, and walked away, back to the office. A dealer, seeing her coming, gave her his leering smile. She raised her eyebrows at him good-humouredly. He was sixty, around twenty stone, with grey hair combed over a bald spot.

'Hey, Catherine,' he said, looking her up and down.

'Hello, Stuart. How are you?'

'Fine display you've got.' He laughed.

She went into the office, threw her coat on to a table. 'Brad Pitt, eat your heart out,' she muttered.

She sat down and gazed at the door she had closed behind her. She pressed her hands to her face, and roses bloomed back at her. The rose from the record cover, with its velvet petals, that would be so sensuous to the touch. A bank of red roses in a garden, long ago. A bouquet of red roses in a Cellophane wrapper, not so long ago. Forty-two red roses of overpowering scent, of asphyxiating luxury.

Why did you send them?

Because I've known you forty-two days.

The door opened.

She took down her hands.

'What's the matter?' Mark asked.

'Nothing,' she said.

'What did Stuart say?'

'It wasn't Stuart. It wasn't anything,' she said.

He came round the side of the desk. 'Remind me what you look like when it is something.'

She opened the diary.

He put a cup of coffee in front of her. 'Take note of the cup,' he said. 'Minton.'

'Thanks. I'm touched. What's this?' she asked, pointing at a diary entry for the next morning.

He perched himself on the edge of the desk. 'A man who rang up yesterday.'

'Bridle Lodge?'

'Somewhere near West Stratford.' He peeled a yellow

post-it from the edge of the page. 'I wrote the directions down.'

'Don't you want me here?'

He drained his own coffee, and looked her in the eye. 'Not with a face like a wet weekend, thank you.'

She looked back at him. Mark, fifteen years her senior, was one of the kindliest men she had ever met. Kindly, not simply kind, in an old-fashioned way, with courtesy and sweetness.

'What is it, really?' he asked.

She ought to have been able to tell him, of all people. But she couldn't.

That night, she phoned Robert's mother. She hadn't seen her in over a year. She sat in the kitchen, the phone in her hand for some minutes.

All around there was still the evidence of him. His magazines piled in the basket on the edge of the work-top, his notes on the memo board: the chiropractor's appointment, the dry-cleaning receipt. The coffee cup he had used last Saturday night stood by itself on the board by the sink where he had left it. She was too superstitious to move it.

When she eventually summoned the courage to dial, the phone rang for ages. She was about to hang up, when at last Eva answered.

'It's Catherine,' she said.

'Hello, Catherine,' said Robert's mother.

'How are you?'

'I'm well, I suppose.'

'I know that this seems like a strange question,' Catherine said, 'but is Robert with you?'

'Robert? I haven't seen him for months.'

'He didn't ring you?' Catherine asked. 'Any time in the last week?'

'Robert doesn't ring me,' his mother said. 'For that matter, neither do you.'

Catherine pressed the fingertips of her left hand hard into the palm. 'There's been no letter?' she persevered.

'Catherine,' Eva Sergeant replied, 'what is going on?'

'I don't know,' Catherine said. 'He left home.'

'Left home?' Eva echoed. She sounded amused. 'Have you had an argument?'

'No. Nothing.'

'There must have been an argument.'

'There was nothing at all,' Catherine responded. 'I woke up on Sunday morning and he had gone. He left a note, just a short note saying that he must go. His clothes were gone, money, cards, chequebook. His phone. Everything.'

'You've tried his number?'

'Of course. I've tried it fifty times a day for the last five days. I've left messages.'

'There's no need to raise your voice to me.'

Catherine took a breath. 'I'm sorry,' she said.

There was a long silence.

Catherine imagined her in the five-storey house. She could see Eva now, sitting at the basement kitchen table, the cigarettes next to her, the lighter in her hand. The house was always shuttered and closed. The upper rooms were faded, as if the house had drained the colour from the furnishings. Robert's mother kept the blinds drawn to preserve the carpets and furniture that she and Robert's father had brought back from the

Far East but, despite that, they still had a bleached look.

The kitchen was a relic of the 1950s, yet she gravitated there, to the warmth. What time was it? Catherine glanced up at her own clock. Six fifty.

'What is he doing?' Eva asked.

'I'm sorry?'

'Robert. What is he doing?'

'He's not at work . . .'

'But it's still the same job?'

'Yes.' How could it be otherwise? Robert was wedded to his work. He was an accountant for a national company, based in a regional office in Salisbury. Every day he drove for an hour each way. He would set off at seven in the morning, always wanting to be first in. Regularly, she suspected, he was the last to leave. She scoured her memory for some fragment from the last few weeks. Some mention of a client. But there was nothing.

But perhaps it was otherwise. Perhaps he had left his job. This possibility had not occurred to her until now. The firm had told her that he was on leave, but they might have been covering for him.

'Well, at least he hasn't been spirited away,' Eva commented.

'What do you mean?'

Catherine heard her lighting a cigarette, the intake of breath. 'If he took everything, he intended to leave,' Eva replied.

Catherine replaced the phone in its cradle, stood up and went upstairs. Only when she got to the bedroom did the full weight of Eva's insouciance hit her. She took off her clothes with a kind of savagery, got into the shower and let the water pour over her, turning up the temperature. She scrubbed at her skin, washed her hair. How could a mother not care where her son had gone? Eva had treated it as if it was a joke. And then the final insult, the hint that Robert's leaving had been no accident but planned. Not a word of comfort, no trace of sympathy.

Soap got into Catherine's eyes, and she rubbed at them with her knuckles. Eva's tone had suggested that such behaviour was inconsequential, almost to be expected. But Robert did not do such things. Robert was ruled by time. He was dependable. It was one of the things that had first attracted her to him, his air of security and reliability. Eva was wrong. But, then, Eva did not care. Eva and Edward – Robert's father, who had died some years ago, of a stroke – had sent their son to boarding-school when he was tiny. Eva had shown not a particle of emotion on Catherine and Robert's wedding day. Robert had considered it a minor miracle that she had come at all.

Catherine got out of the shower now, and caught sight of herself in the mirror, flushed, hollow-eyed. She dried herself, then walked into the bedroom, lay on the bed and pulled the covers over herself.

She was too angry to cry.

With her eyes closed, the truth rushed up at her.

This was how she had felt about Robert for at least a year.

Three

Her life – what she thought of as real life – began in paintings.

It had been one day in an interminable summer when London was full of asphyxiating heat, when the white Portland stone looked bleached, washed out, aching to the eye like faltering neon, that Catherine had discovered the galleries. Tired of touring Oxford Street, pushing through tourists, her first visit had been prompted by an argument with her best friend. They had fought on the corner of Millbank over something too trivial to remember; Catherine had caught the first bus she saw, got off by the Tate and walked in, up the Cinderella-sweep of steps, idly imagining herself in full ball-gown regalia. Her thoughts were turned inwards, to herself, to all the obsessive circularity of being fourteen. She couldn't have been less interested in art.

She had found herself in a wide, empty space where the floor was cool. She sat down, right in the centre, and looked up, dwarfed by the paintings, the Raphael cartoons. She looked at the figure of Christ, and the reflections in the Sea of Galilee, so cleverly made in negative to bring the correct perspective to the finished tapestries. A thrill – the thrill of its ingenuity.

Right until that moment, Catherine had been following her parents into a scientific career. A chemist. She had this blueprint plan for herself, to research something, to become famous for some discovery. To astound the world. She had opted for science because it seemed like a fast track to the unknown. When she put her eye to a microscope lens, she liked the invisible detail, the silent explosion of life that carried on every day without any human witness. She liked the thought that she – that everything – was built on these indestructible threads that re-formed themselves after apparent annihilation. Life triumphant wriggling in a mirror, in a piece of glass.

But this was the day – the day of the dwarfing Raphaels – that she had first seen Richard Dadd's painting.

She had come away from the giants and wandered into a smaller room. There, on the wall in the corner, tucked away almost out of sight, she found him. The painting was small, perhaps only twelve inches by ten. It was intensely green. It was called *The Fairy Feller's Master Stroke*. Just below the centre of the picture was a man, his back to the viewer, with an axe raised over his shoulders. In front of him on the ground was a dark oval, and the blade of the axe formed a gold rectangle above it, one of the few bright patches in a complicated sea of green and brown. All that Catherine noticed at first was the man, and the crowd around him, and that he was in some sort of clearing; then it dawned on her that the man was standing not between trees but between tall grasses, and that the crowds around him were not ordinary people but extraordinary ones. There were pirates, and dwarfs, and dragonflies. Misshapen faces and hands. Tiny feet above grossly distorted calves; wings folded behind backs. Satyrs crawled in the weedy undergrowth; an old man sat almost below the axe. Courtiers of all kinds – insects, humans – surrounded a crowned couple. Under them, crouching under a daisy bank, his arms extended left to right across the picture, was a robed magician, his finger raised as if commanding the moment of execution.

She looked again at the title. *The Fairy Feller's Master Stroke.*

She wondered for a second if the old man was the victim of the axe; then she looked again at the dark shape on the ground. It was a hazel or beech nut, stood on end to take the blow that would split it in half. A master stroke, to cut the whole in one clean movement.

Catherine felt a great temptation to touch the paint. It was thick – each tiny leaf, each petal exactly rendered. The grasses cut across the painting like cords, raised up from the paint. Every fraction of a millimetre – even the eyes, the fingernails – was accurate, tiny as it was: each crease of clothing and fold of skin. The exacting, almost painful detail. Everything in the detail.

At last she walked away from it, out into the brilliant gaze of the Victorians and pre-Raphaelites of the main display. She walked on past Sargent, and out again to Frith's *Derby Day*; as her gaze ran over the crowds in Frith's painting, she saw echoes of the goblin faces of

Dadd, and the vibration of colour of the axe hanging in mid-air.

It was several weeks later that she found out more about Dadd: that he had been hailed as a genius. That he had gone to Syria and Egypt, and fallen ill there. That he had come home in the first throes of schizophrenia. And that he had murdered his father, cut the old man's throat with a pocket-knife, and spent over forty years imprisoned, and that the painting she couldn't put out of her mind – along with all the other paintings that had started to inhabit her waking moments – *The Fairy Feller's Master Stroke*, had been painted in Bedlam, the hospital whose name had become a byword for fear.

Her parents couldn't understand her. They judged her obsession with art to be a passing phase. They made light of it, even laughed about it, as if indulging a childish whim.

They worked abroad so she only saw them every month or so. They were sociable, generous people, working in Brussels for Médecin Libre. Their life was talk: they negotiated aid-agency funding; they crossed frontiers. For two whole years when she had never seen them – lonely years of being nine and ten, and farmed out to friends' families at Christmas and in the holidays – they were in Somalia. Each a scientist, each an administrator, each with two feet firmly on the ground, they caught the Richard Dadd story only as a passing half-truth.

'Is that real?' her father had asked her, laughing, as he drove at a suicidal speed out of London. 'A painter? Some crazy painter?' He'd looked over his shoulder, smiling.

'I'm going to change courses,' she'd replied.

Her mother had then turned to look at her. 'To do what?'

'Fine art,' she'd said.

'Heaven help us all,' her mother had said, smiling, as if Catherine had made a joke.

'Not real, my love,' her father had repeated. She could still see his tanned hands on the steering-wheel. He was so glamorous, this loud-voiced man, almost a caricature of the ruddy red-faced Englishman. He had a life planned for his daughter, a life of research and exploration, a factual life. That was it exactly: a life of fact, a life in fact.

'Fine Art History,' she'd told them. The headlights of the car were dancing through the hedgerows. Pale blue light was stretched on the sky even though the ground was dark. Threads and filaments of stars and cloud were inappropriately visible in the blue. Dadd was whispering in her ear, a nail scratching on glass, a burr in cloth pressed to her skin.

Her school was on the fringes of Hampstead; each day Catherine passed a white clapboard house on the Heath. It had a curved bay window facing the road directly, so that if you couldn't see over the white-painted wooden gates you might think that the house was very narrow, like a white shoebox. One day not long after she had seen the Richard Dadd painting, she had stopped to look at the blue plaque on the wall of the clapboard house. 'George Romney,' it said. '1734–1802.'

When she had looked him up in a textbook, she discovered that Romney had been an artist who had tried to set up a little academy and been bankrupted for his trouble. She had sat back from the reference book in the school library, and thought of magnified threads, and Dadd's cordlike grasses, and Romney's brush on the canvas in the narrow, boarded house at the corner of the street, and the detail – all the complicated detail – of observation in Frith and Dadd. And she had wondered again, for a long time, about Dadd's obsession with the minute and unnoticed things in life. Things that pass like frames in a film, a flash of the moment.

As she sat forward again over the book, Catherine's eye had run down the page, and a list of artists who had lived in London. Constable was on the same index page as Dadd. John Constable, moving to Hampstead to end the 'sad, rambling life my married life has been', and finding his wife dead just a little while later: tuberculosis after the birth of their seventh child.

When she turned the page, she saw Constable's painting of Hampstead Heath: a rural idyll with a blue-shaded London far in the distance; and, later still, his pencil and watercolour drawn two years after his wife died. It was so full of dancing light, sun pushing rain from the canvas, a huge overarching ceiling of white light pressing from the left of the picture. She found that he had kept a scientific diary of the sky: *September 21st 1822, looking south, Brisk wind to East . . . S.E.5 O'clock Wind East.*

It was the pinpointing of light on a certain day, at a certain time, that bewitched her. The carefulness of it, the way that art stopped time, framing a moment on canvas, in rock or bronze. Frith freezing a London train station to a moment of the late nineteenth century; Constable scratching his observations to seal a few seconds of an afternoon that would otherwise have been lost. She opened the reference book wider and let the pages flip over. Other days, other moments, were sealed for ever by the brush. The uncovering of the Sphinx, recorded by Henry Salt; the Duke of Wellington, captured by Lucientes, pursed and disapproving over his shelf of medals.

Other faces and people, too, pinned eternally in place; Marie Antoinette, absurdly flushed and rouged, some time in 1783; the Melbourne and Milbanke families with their horses in the same decade, prancing about in Stubbs's hands; Richelieu by Champaigne, seemingly pained and saddened by the orgy of ochre and red satin he was swathed in.

It was the *seeing*. The artists saw the world, but something else too: a part of them transmitted itself to the picture, the canvas. She had closed the book and put it away, got up and gone out of the library.

But the paintings, their sights and insights, their other worlds, followed her.

Tossit's *The Last Evening*, and *The Birth of Venus* by Bouguereau, Venus lifting her long, heavy hair from her back, occupied by secret lust. The soft explosion of Whistler's *Nocturne*, Frost's *High Yellow*. She began looking in second-hand bookshops for volumes on painting. She found Gaddi and Gainsborough, Siberechts and Sickert. The style didn't interest her particularly, or the age of anything: it was detail. It became a preoccupation. The drooping lily and anemone in Ruysch's *Still Life*; the twist of silk braid below the plain face of Pisanello's anonymous fifteenth-century girl.

That weekend with her parents. Spring, fifteen years ago. Her mother had had a cold, and was curled up on the window-seat at the cottage, staring glumly at the rain. Her hands around the coffee cup were roughened with salt. They had been to a freshwater project, an estuary in Israel. They still had temporary flower tattoos on the back of their hands that a kibbutz girl had given them. Catherine remembered the complicated circular patterns of petals.

Her mother had reached out an arm to embrace her. Catherine had sat with her in the window-seat, watching the rain run down the windows.

'Such a dismal country,' her mother had whispered.

'Do you think so?' Catherine asked.

'Absolutely,' she told her daughter. 'That's why I always come back here.' The broad smile faded; she tilted her head. 'Will you tell me what's the matter?'

Catherine had laid her head in the crook of her mother's shoulder, running her finger over the tattoo. 'I don't know,' she'd murmured. 'Take me with you when you go.'

That had forced her mother truly to sit upright, and move her body so that she was angled to face Catherine. She put down her cup. Catherine had looked into her eyes and seen concern, and everything else her mother was: clever, courageous, outrageous, and – to a teenager – insufferably calm. 'You do such interesting things,' Catherine had complained.

'But you must finish school.'

'I know,' Catherine said. 'But when I was little I always went with you.'

And so she had, pre-school. Her early years had been full of colour. She often wondered in adulthood if the sight and senses of those years had fixed her future occupation. She had all kinds of countries in her head, each without a name. Too young to retain the exact location, she could remember nevertheless the taste of coffee drunk from her father's cup on a bare roof terrace; a view of white, near-white and cream houses, roofs falling, a spilled pack of playing cards, down a long hill, allied curiously and indivisibly with the sweet tastes of tomatoes, more like a sugary fruit than the acidic ones she knew at home. And other random memories: the sound of ripe oranges hitting a tin roof, waking her first thing in the morning at a farm they had stayed at in Jamaica, and of the red soil creeping between her toes as she collected the fallen fruit in a bucket before anyone else was awake; of lemons lying rotting on the ground because the old man who owned the farm was too arthritic to bend to retrieve them; the carpet of orange and yellow and red earth, and the smell of the fly-blown pith and flesh under her heel.

And the seemingly endless procession of ports and airports; of a boatman who took them across the Bosphorus into Istanbul, the inside of the tiny ferry cabin all mahogany polished like glass; and a woman who had accepted a lift from them outside Kuşadasi and was still there at Marmaris, silent, wrapped in a striped brown dress that folded and folded over her knees, and inside which she tucked her brown arms, and who had given Catherine frightening stares of appreciation.

And the one named place in her mind, Pamukkale, the wedding-cake hillside with its calcified pools catching the evening sun, orange-pink against a fading blue sky.

'We'll be home for six months after this project's finished,' her mother told her now, trying to reassure her. 'All summer, all autumn. We'll go riding. We'll get a cottage in the Lakes. How about that? Would you like that?'

Catherine had felt a rush of guilt. All her life she had understood the worthiness of what they did. But she had this feeling – she had had it since she saw the Dadd – some premonition. Of things that needed to be captured rushing away from you, of the necessity of holding on to the unseen, the unspoken. She had gazed into her mother's light brown, hazel-flecked eyes, seen her open expression, the smile.

'We'll make the time,' her mother had promised.

And when they were both gone, and Catherine was alone, she fixed them in the entire experience of that winter and spring, which had begun with the Raphaels and *The Fairy Feller's Master Stroke*.

Walking alone, walking down the sudden grief, so violent it hurt her like the residue of a physical assault, she could soothe herself only with light: the way light refracted in water, in mirrors and windows, and the way it was diluted, pinpointed or subdued by oils, pastels and watercolours. She wanted, in those weeks, actually to be a painter, to be able to submerge herself in that or some similar creative occupation. Anything to deflect the oppression of her feelings. But she knew that she couldn't paint. She could only look.

And she would find herself staring into the heart of a picture, into Ford Madox Brown's *An English Autumn Afternoon*, into the shadows, into the startling brilliance of detail, the trees, the inclination of a woman's face, the distance of a church tower, the scrupulous delicacy of hands or wings or leaves against the green of a garden, longing to blunt the blade of unhappiness that she felt was pressed against her throat, cutting off her air.

Saturday morning. Catherine was still in her dressing-gown, on her hands and knees, looking through the drawers of the study desk. She hadn't slept until three or four, and when she had woken four hours later, this thought was in her head.

That there would be a clue. There would be something – there *must* be something – that she had overlooked. The note said so little – 'I must go. I'll be in touch.' There must be light, she had added to herself. A light to shine. And the images – Romney, Jennings, Constable, with their lucidity – vibrated distantly. There would be a detail. A detail she had overlooked. Everything in the detail.

She had gone straight to the room where Robert had spent most of his time in the past month or so. He had been closeted in the study, accounts spread all around him. Once she had looked over his shoulder, and seen that they were their own household accounts, and not a client's, as she had supposed. 'Anything the matter?' she'd asked.

'No,' he'd told her.

She had never queried it. Robert always liked to

check. He was a meticulous person. It was another of the things that had first attracted her, in a screwed kind of way: that he was so careful.

'I'm your walking safety-net,' he had once joked, when they were first together.

She opened the first drawer. It was full of stationery: his business foolscap white envelopes; paper clips, staples, postcards. She took out the postcards and looked at them. Mark Raven's postcards from Amsterdam, bought in the Van Gogh Museum shop. They had gone there last autumn for the weekend – it had been her idea.

'It seems a lot of money for just a weekend away,' he'd protested.

'But it's only two hundred pounds,' she'd replied. 'It's a special offer.'

'Even so,' he'd murmured. But they had gone.

She spread out the images on the floor. Robert had bought them. Raven's colours: black, white, grey, green. Subdued. Had Robert bought them because he felt subdued? Shabby psychology, surely. Guesswork. Probably meaningless guesswork at that, she told herself.

Here was another of his. A lovely Ghirlandaio portrait, this time, of a young girl in profile, dressed in a gold embroidered gown. She looked beautifully calm and composed. A choice, she wondered. An accident? She imagined Robert leafing through the postcards while she looked at the art books. Picking up anything. Nothing. Something of significance? She doubted it. Just a handful of postcards as he stood near the till, waiting wordlessly for her.

She looked again in the drawer.

Catalogues of the Pearsons sales. A dozen or more. One was folded open at a particular page. She glanced at it. '*Lot 543, a Victorian style yellow gold necklace with stylized foliate panels . . .*' Her eye ran down the page. A pendant, a pebble pin, an enamel chatelaine. An aquamarine butterfly brooch. She frowned at the list. She couldn't remember if this page had any significance to her. She didn't recall being asked to bid on behalf of a client. She had no interest in the items themselves: she never wore necklaces or brooches. She only had one bracelet.

She looked at the dragonfly, composed of cabochon rubies alternating with brilliant-cut diamonds; an expensive piece. She put her hand on the page and felt how it had been folded open for some time, how it resisted being turned back to show its cover.

She put it to one side and looked in the next drawer.

Disks for the computer, a roll of parcel tape, scissors, print cartridges.

And the next. The bank statements. She had looked at these on the first day he had been gone, feeling sure that Robert would have left a reason hidden there, in the language he spoke most fluently. She had scanned the pages for the obvious: unusual debits, unusual amounts. She had looked at the credit-card bills, received last week. No hotels. No travel companies. Nothing out of place.

She dropped from her hunched position, half squatting, and lay down on the cards, the catalogues, and pressed her face into the floor, her hands to her head; her body curled in on itself. 'Where are you?' she whispered. 'Where are you?'

* * *

By midday, she was driving to Bridle Lodge. She hadn't intended to do so; she hadn't rung the owner to say that she was on her way. She had just snatched up the car keys and her coat, and slammed the door. Only when she got to the edge of town, and looked down at the map beside her, did she grasp that she was panting, in the grip of panic.

She was only at the wheel to escape the waiting that hung behind her in the house. It was impossible to focus on anything but this persistent circular thought: *I'm waiting for him.* It had assumed a presence, a body, a weight. After drinking her coffee – she couldn't eat, but she was persistently thirsty – she had stood indecisively in the hallway; she must have stood there for at least fifteen minutes. She couldn't go out. She had to wait. What if he came back while she was out? What if he rang?

She had stared at the silent phone. She ought to go. Hanging over the phone would not make it ring. Staying in the house would not bring him back to it. She ought to occupy herself. She ought to drive over to Amanda and Mark, confess to them what had happened. It made no sense to keep this secret.

'Why on earth didn't you say anything?' they would ask. 'Are you crazy? How long has he been gone? Nearly two weeks! Catherine . . .'

I've been waiting, she would say.

And it sat next to her now in the car, the waiting, like an inanimate shadow that she couldn't understand or get hold of, or lever against. And she felt a violent resentment towards him for doing this to her, for throwing her into this helplessness.

She sat at the road junction until a driver behind her leaned on his horn. Eventually he got out and came and rapped on her window. It was a narrow lane, at traffic lights. No other car could get past her.

'What's up?' he yelled. He was her own age. He rapped on the window again, frowning.

I can't help it, I'm sorry, she wanted to say. *I'm waiting*.

'Oh, God,' she whispered. She held up a hand, an apology.

She put the car into gear and her foot on the accelerator and sped out from the junction, without even checking the road.

Flight out of Egypt, 1849–59

Since they had brought him to Bedlam, all Dadd had been able to think of was flight.

At first it was simply the flight of escape: he had hardly recognized that he was truly imprisoned – time had lost shape, compressed or elongated into dreams – and he had entertained a notion that to change his landscape would be as easy as putting a brush to paper.

But he no longer thought like that.

He had passed five years in the cages, as if he were a species of carnivore at the zoological gardens. Sometimes Mr Monro came, the physician in charge of his case. Munro had told him that he was not only the son of a doctor, and a grandson of a doctor, but that all three – son, father, grandfather – had been physicians to Bedlam, the monstrosity of an asylum in Moorfields. One day he had told Dadd, trying to elicit a response from the silence, that he had been brought up in a house where Turner, Hunt and Cotman had been frequent visitors.

At the name Turner, Dadd had looked up at him.

'I am not indifferent to art,' Mr Munro had said.

And they had brought Dadd oils, and a canvas.

At first he painted what he remembered of his trips to Syria and Egypt, before the time that Osiris had captured him and shown him the point in the throat above the ridge of collarbone, the place where life was breathed into the body by God Himself, and the place where the blade must be put to release life. When Adam was filled with breath, God had put his mouth to this very spot above the clavicle. Osiris had shown him the place, in Egypt, in 1842, under a full moon, while the crew of the boat chanted in a circle on the sands.

When Dadd had seen his father standing before him in Cobham Park that fateful evening, he had known what he had been sent to do. The voices urged it: it was his divine instruction. It was not to end life, but to free it. Not to defy God, but to confirm Him and His creation. Only the few were brought this way. Only the few were shown the edge of life where creation and destruction trembled together and fought for dominance. Osiris had put the knife into his hand, the forearm on his father's shoulder, the blade against his father's throat.

Come Unto These Yellow Sands, he had called a painting that year. His siren call. A journey back to the sand-filled Nile, the silt making whorls in the water, his hand scoured by sand if he dipped it into the current.

On the canvas, half-naked and naked figures streamed through a rocky arch at the edge of the sea, threading like music realized in flesh through the sky, clefs and chords uncurling into bodies. From top to bottom of the picture, and from right to left, the figures ran in and out of shadows, in and out of blazing light. Entranced, exhausted, they streamed, ebbed and flowed. Come unto these yellow sands. Come to the edge of reason.

Inside the bellowing cages, the ranting galleries of corridors and cells, in the half-light afforded by tiny windows high in the walls, Dadd had painted Syria, Luxor and Damascus. He had filled notebooks with them all. He had tried to bring back the aching sunlight he had known; the heat, the intoxication of the senses. He had been bewitched by the villages then, and by Baalbeck, Nazareth, Carmel and Jerusalem. At Karnak, after Cairo, he was overcome by the size and strength of the temples; but passing from Alexandria to Malta, the old gods visited him, and sent pallid-faced demons to dance on his bed at night, and wrap themselves round the footboard where they sat to taunt him.

My mind is full of wild vagaries, he had told himself.

Outside in the greater world, men moved across the globe. Livingstone crossed the Kalahari Desert and reached Lake Ngami; the English colonized India; Paganini was approaching the last virtuoso ascension of his life; revolutions crossed Europe; Chopin struggled in the long closing journey of consumption; the speed of light in air and water was first measured by Foucault and Fizeau. And when Munro allowed the easel to be put before Dadd, he painted flight, and deserts of his own.

He painted a caravan halted by the seashore. Long ago, while still in Syria, he had written to Powell that he would have become rabid at the sight of the woman around the wells of the shore, with the overture of the *sea rolling in, the excitement of the scene enough to turn the brain of an ordinary weak-minded person like himself – he said this with easy calm, as if a storm was not gathering itself in his mind at that moment, like thunderheads of cloud, walls of indigo . . .*

And he had gone on to describe the women, dressed in loose blue garments with wide sleeves, carrying their pitchers of water on their heads, on little pads made for the purpose. He had painted a single naked child, a small boy, standing in the foreground, his arms crossed behind his back. No one paid attention to the child, more of a lost desire than a living human being.

And so he came, in the sixth year, to this great living image. The canvas was forty inches by fifty, a blaze of red, gold, white and green. The water-carriers, the women, were back, and the men seated on camels and horseback, and the blades: spears and curved scimitars, swords and daggers at the waist. The broadness of faces and foreheads was back, the emptiness of some eyes, the unfocused insignificance. Hands reached from the bottom left-hand side of the picture, devilish claws below the seemingly innocent image of a shawled girl bringing jars to the side of the stream. In the centre a warrior stood drinking, a leopardskin round his shoulders. To the right, a boy whispered in an old man's ear. There were dancing girls, merchants and soldiers, and, in the corner, at the foot of this bedlam, was the Christ Child at his mother's knee.

Dadd went over the painting again and again. He couldn't make the spear points go away, or the reflections of metal from the armour. Light picked up the spouts of drinking vessels, and coated them with silver.

Anywhere the mouth touched. Anywhere God had put His mouth to man, breathing life through the colour on the brush. They were created and ignited, all of them, all the girls, every child, all the women's faces, all the knowing broadness of the men, the strange ridged veins on the forearms, through the bleeding tip of the brush.

It exhausted him.

He had flown; he had disappeared for a while. He had vanished into a painted crowd.

But not for long. Not long.

Four

Robert was coming through the airport when he saw Amanda.

He supposed that it had been ridiculous of him to imagine that he might get away with becoming invisible, and as soon as he saw Catherine's business partner standing outside Departures – Amanda in all her full-blown finery, the white pashmina, the upraised arm as she waved to her retreating mother, the whole commanding Amanda – his heart did a lazy double-flip.

Well, so here it came.

'Robert!' she called.

He smiled, and pushed the luggage trolley in her direction.

She reached out and kissed him. 'Been away?'

'Yes.' Did she know? Was it possible that she didn't?

'Catherine mentioned it the other day.'

He stood still.

'Anywhere nice?'

A beat while he examined the bland expression on her face. 'Italy,' he told her. 'Rome.'

'How lovely!' She was already shepherding him out of the flow of arriving passengers, hand under his elbow. 'I must say, I approve of a company who sends one to Rome on business.' She sighed. 'I can't remember when Mark and I last went anywhere. The only time I see a bloody airport is when I bring Mother here.'

They were getting to the exit. He listened to her objectively, politely, wondering if he would ever see her again.

'She says she's perfectly capable, but, you know, she's seventy-seven. I imagine her going round and round the M25 in some taxi, forgetting where she's meant to be.'

'Is she well?' he asked. He didn't want to know. In fact, he didn't want to talk. He wanted to get away.

'Arthritis,' Amanda said. 'Mark will be breathing a prayer of thanks as we speak. She's awful to him. Awful.'

They stopped. 'Got your car here?' she asked.

'Yes.'

'Don't want a lift?'

'No. Thanks.'

There was the slightest of pauses. 'Catherine will be glad to have you back,' Amanda said.

Was there anything in the sentence? *Catherine will be glad to have you back*. No. Amanda would not have kept her temper if Catherine had confided in her. He would have been met with a stream of invective and demands.

'Well,' she said, 'I'm off, before the M4 disappears under a tide of Range Rovers heading west.'

'OK.'

'See you at home,' she told him. 'Why don't you come to supper on Sunday? You can tell us all about Rome.'

He smiled. 'Goodbye,' he said.

He watched her thread her way through the crowd. She walked at a rapid pace. She drove the same way, he knew. She would be back in three hours or so. Perhaps three hours or four before she spoke to Catherine.

Is Robert home yet? I saw him at the airport.

'Goodbye,' he murmured again, to himself.

Five

In February, the valley below Bridle Lodge had flooded. John Brigham had walked his dog right down to the water-meadows, and seen the river break its banks. It had been a Sunday morning. The weather was bright and cold after the week's downpour, but the force of the water from upstream had pushed the level too high. In a second, John had seen the meadows, with their Victorian irrigation ditches that so rarely filled, turn from a vivid green plain, intersected by low hedgerows and trees, into a lake.

He'd been coming down the path from Derry Woods; it was eight in the morning. Ahead of him, Frith was charging along the bridlepath, tail whipping about. John had stopped at the intersection of three paths, one that led deeper into the woods, one that led back to the lane, and a third that came down into the village by the bridge; he had looked at the valley below him, with streams of mist pouring off the river, and a faint wash of blue in the sky promising a sunny day. He had leaned on the stile for a long time.

At that point, he had been back in the country for just two weeks; lived in Bridle Lodge for just ten days. Frith was still cold, shivering at English frost after the Andalucían sun. In Aloro it would be mild now, the first heat coming to the mile upon mile of olive trees; there would be a curious opalescent haze along the coast, the harbinger of summer; the corrugated iron of the terrace roof would begin its spring percussion, cracking and expanding in the afternoon heat. They had lived in a farm near Aloro, in the mountains, for the last seven years. In January he had let it, packed his bags and come home.

Frith ran back to him as he leaned on the stile, one hand on his chest, knuckle pressing under the sternum. The spaniel watched with anticipation, a quizzical expression on its face.

John had got over the stile and walked on, and Frith kept close to his side along the narrower path, hedge on one side, field fence on the other. Sheep were on the pasture below the woods, on the slope of the hill; they bunched in one corner as dog and man passed. As they rounded the hill John saw the sudden influx of water on to the meadows below, and the strip of Tarmac lane, which barely allowed two cars to pass, vanished.

A man of fifty or so was standing outside his house as John and Frith emerged into the village. The bridge, a three-arched packhorse, four centuries old, was now just a brick strip with no road leading to or from it. The well-trodden river paths were gone, and the shallows where watercress grew impossibly thick in the summer. The river was a fantastic sight near the bridge:

contorted, swirling. A writhing grey mass. Further out, the grass had gone. The water flowed away almost serenely, in rippling shallows. Several other people had come out of their houses to watch.

'It just went like that,' the man had said to John, clicking his fingers. 'There was a car coming along the lane. They had to go in reverse. Elderly driver, too.'

'Where are they now?' John asked.

'Somebody come along behind them,' the man replied. 'They turned the car round for them.' John smiled. The man held out his hand. 'Peter Luckham.'

'John Brigham.'

'You're the new man in Bridle Lodge?'

'That's right.'

'You don't mind my saying . . .' Peter began.

'What?'

'Well, this might not happen if the weirs and channels were cleaned out at the Lodge.'

John had frowned. 'Weirs?' he said.

'Down below the house, where the rhododendrons are.'

John knew the patch, of course. Even as the hasty prospective buyer he had been in the autumn, on a flying visit from Spain, he could hardly have missed the giant rhododendrons and camellias below the tiered walkways. The garden close to the house was untidy and unloved; but where the lawn and box hedges ended, it fell away towards the stream in a series of zigzagged paths, whose gravel had been full of leaves and weeds when John had given them a cursory look. The rhododendrons climbed up beyond them, forty feet high.

'A wonderful sight in the spring,' the estate agent had commented.

And John had thought, A wonderful amount of work, and speculated if he would see it done.

He had looked back at Peter Luckham. 'There are weirs,' he said, flatly stating it.

'There used to be, when my father worked the garden,' Peter replied. 'A whole series of gates. You could regulate the water.'

'I haven't noticed anything,' John told him.

'There isn't much to see with all that muck,' Peter replied.

John had smiled. Muck was one way to look at it. A forest of uncut shrubs, the densely overhanging evergreens, the tangle of nettles and hellebores. A few days ago he had glimpsed the first shoots of blue between the trees, and realized that the ground would soon be awash with bluebells, flourishing in the dank shade.

But weirs on the stream? Irrigation gates? He hadn't seen them.

'Pettertons built the lodge in 1880,' Peter had continued. 'Planted out the gardens. Put in the weirs to make a lake. More a pond now. Choked with waterlily. All that stretch that looks like marsh.'

'All of that is man-made,' John had mused, seeing how it made sense. All winter it had simply been swamped with mud. A thick curtain of willows obscured what he had thought was a natural bank.

'Wants clearing out,' Luckham had said, hands in pockets, gazing at the bridge. 'If you don't mind my saying so.'

*   *   *

It was almost spring now. Or would be in another month. John had begun the crazy task himself, weeks ago, one evening in February. He had gone out as the light was fading, down to the lower garden. Dusk was ephemeral, barely fifteen minutes in that low, grey day. He had been sitting indoors, and the oppression of the flat sky, threatening rain but never delivering, had got to him. He had had to go for a breath of air.

Frith had been delirious, running in circles on the wet lawn, leaving muddy sprays where he skidded. John followed at a slow pace, feeling the immediate settling of damp on his clothes. The trees dripped moisture.

He had felt then, and for the remainder of that week, that he should not have come back, let alone bought the Lodge. And yet it had been an overwhelming conviction that had possessed him all that autumn, to come home. It wasn't that he felt the prognosis would be any better in England. He just wanted to be in England again, to be where he had grown up. And he had had to remind himself of that as he had walked down through the trees to where the lakes had once been. This was what he had come back for, he told himself; England in its underwater gloom of January and February, as the endless Atlantic rain swept in across the Somerset Levels.

He had stood under the rhododendrons and camellias and looked at the water that threaded down the slope. He was thinking of the last design job in London before he had left for Andalucía. He had been forty then. It was two years since Claire had died. Even when he had taken on the Hampstead job, he had known it would be his last in England. It had been his turning point: everything he had touched was full of change.

He had made that last house full of light.

The client had seen the Daryl Jackson beach house in Bermagui and wanted something exactly the same, with full-length wood-framed windows and a loose in-formality of styles. He couldn't provide Bermagui, of course. Hardly, in Hampstead, in an Edwardian terrace. But he did take out the back wall to two storeys, and extended the stone yard by fifty feet, and put in an open passage that was almost like a cloister running through the centre, with windows at either side, opening out into the garden.

'It's so light,' the couple kept saying. 'So light.'

And that was what he had given them: some of the light he could feel filtering slowly through himself after two years in the dark. Two years of sleepwalking through London from one project to another, fixated on stress structure and weight ratios and planning permissions; hunched over his drawing-board until the early hours of the morning because he dreaded the empty bedroom. Marking time only, in a kind of painted forest.

That was what London – that was what everything – had been to him then. A kind of moving fresco, pro-jected on to walls. Silhouettes only, with very little sound. After Claire had gone, and he had drowned himself in work, everything around him had possessed this two-dimensional quality. Plans in his head. Drawings of buildings. Renovations. The curious flat place where his life had ground almost to a halt.

And when houses were finished, had become

three-dimensional, and the flat spaces were filled with people, talking, moving people, families, animals and colours – the number of house-warmings, he went to, for Christ's sake, where the noise was almost too much – then, especially then, he lost interest. The houses had metamorphosed into breathing life. They had betrayed him. Taken up their beds and walked. More curious still, all the talking and animation had seemed to disgust him. He didn't want noise. He didn't want families and colour. He wanted to stay in the flat white world he had created.

But the last house, the Jackson-inspired house, was different. On the day the builders finished, he had drunk champagne with the owners, and felt their thrill. They were beginning something. And so was he. He was going to Aloro, in the Spanish mountains, to live in the light. He left his business in capable hands; he would keep on the office and the staff, returning only for the odd consultancy. He felt that the time had come. He was breaking away. His world was altering.

There was a flurry of movement. Frith came hurtling out of the bushes, a pheasant preceding him, with a clockwork whirring of wings. Surprised, John stopped. His thoughts of houses and light flashed past with the movement of the bird and the dog. He was suddenly back in the grey and dripping garden. The pheasant skirted the ground, hauling its body into the air above ground with obvious effort. Then, in the next second, Frith was gone.

The dog had vanished; at one moment he was on the edge of the path, the next, nowhere. John had run forward. At the next instant, Frith surfaced from under the mat of thick weed; spluttering and thrashing, he had tried to get back to the path.

'Here, Frith,' John called. He bent down. 'Get out of there.'

Soaked to the skin, liver-and-white coat plastered flat, Frith looked at him with almost human eloquence. He was getting nowhere. Only his front half was visible; he started clawing at the surface. His mouth gaped open with effort, and he whined. It was a sound John had not heard from him before: not the whine of excitement or impatience, but a kind of keening terror. Then, abruptly, he went under.

John had sat down on the path. He hesitated for a second, then swung his legs over the side and into the slush of mud and weed. He groped for purchase under the water, and felt a gravel edge. He stepped forward, feeling about with his hands for the dog. There wasn't a hint to show where Frith had been. The waterlilies, discoloured by frost, leathery and tattered remnants of summer laid over with rotted leaves, obscured everything. He gasped with the cold. He could feel blanket weed clinging to his legs and fingers. He started to sink: mud had replaced the gravel underfoot. He tripped on something heavy: a branch, lodged next to the bank. His boots filled with water.

'Frith,' he muttered, hands splayed beneath the water, feeling for the animal.

Suddenly the dog's whole bodyweight crashed into his leg. He could hardly get hold of him because, in panic, Frith was trying to lunge upwards. John stooped in the water, and put both arms around Frith's body. He pulled. The dog's head came out of the water, and his claws dug into John's shoulders. But John couldn't pull him any further. He felt down the body and his fingers fastened on thick weed wrapped round the back legs.

As Frith pulled, the weed tightened. John felt in his jacket for the pocket-knife he sometimes carried. It wasn't there. He sank a few inches deeper into the underfoot slime; Frith, seeing the bank, and safety, tried to wriggle out of his grasp, over his shoulder. He had to grab the scruff of the dog's neck and shake it. 'Stop,' he shouted. 'Keep still.'

He felt in the other pocket. Miraculously, a pair of secateurs. He got them out and, holding Frith with his right hand, felt about for the weed. Frith flopped against his shoulder, head against his neck. John could hear water rattling in the dog's chest.

It seemed hours before he had cut through the weed, but in reality it was no more than two or three minutes. As soon as Frith felt himself released, he lurched for the path, and John lost his footing. With a splash, kicking clumsily, he went under. As the water closed over his head, he had a second to feel himself into the murky green world below; then he surfaced. He lost a boot, climbed out of the water without it, then lay on the path gasping.

There had been no pain then, or when he had got up. He straightened, with mud and water streaming off his clothes. Frith stared up at him, wagging his tail slowly and apologetically. John went back to the water's edge, took hold of the nearest clump of lilies and wrenched them out of the pond. With them came the matted weed; he grasped another handful, dug his heels into the ground and tugged. It came up with a rush of suction; he flung it behind him. He knelt down and found the branch he had tripped against, pulled it to the side and yanked at it until it came free. Frith seized on it and dragged it away, pleased with this unexpected prize.

On his hands and knees, soaked to the skin, John had felt the breath scorch in his chest. He stopped, then stood up. He was shivering. Calling Frith, he set off for the house, and it was then, under the lavish greenery of the camellias, that the pain had struck. John knew better than to try to get to the house. He sat down while the garden tilted, and his view of it compressed into a narrow line. *He thought, No one will be here for days. Maybe a week. Maybe more.*

Eventually he lay down on the gravel, on his back, while the pain cruised through him, an out-of-control truck gathering speed along a highway. 'Shit,' he muttered. Frith came to look down at him. 'You'll have to bury me,' he told the dog, and laughed at the absurdity.

He waited, expecting the impact.

But it didn't come.

When the last of the light had gone he got up, and felt his way in the dark to the house.

The men came up at the beginning of March; and it was now a month since work had begun. A landscaper did the really heavy-duty stuff during the week; but at the weekend, it was just John, Peter Luckham and his two sons. The mesh of willow and reed had been taken away, and one of the willow trees, rotted beyond saving, had been cut down. Now, when John stood at the edge of the path, he could see right across the fields to the Sherborne road. They had found four little foot-bridges, and discovered that the first two ponds were almost circular. At either end of each bridge there was a stretch of brick in the ground, shaped like a fan. In the centre of each fan, lighter coloured brick described the intertwined letters L and H. They had all stood round and looked at the design.

'Who were L and H?' John asked.

'I don't know,' Peter told him.

They worked their way along the banks. A trailer attached to John's four-wheel drive towed away the debris, ploughing a furrow up the garden paths and across the lower part of the lawn.

It was Saturday morning; the sun was out. They had stopped to inspect the mechanism of an irrigation gate when Peter Luckham noticed a car turn off the road and move along the drive. 'You've got a visitor,' he observed.

John looked up as the small red car disappeared between the trees.

'Expecting anyone?' Luckham asked.

'No.'

They carried on with their work. Two minutes later, John's mobile rang. He took off his gloves, fished it out of his coat, looked at the display, didn't recognize the number. 'Hello?'

'Mr Brigham?' A woman's voice.

'Yes.'

'I'm Catherine Sergeant, from Pearsons. You asked us to call?'

'Is it you up at the house?' he asked. 'Driving a red car?'

'Yes,' she replied.

'You didn't make an appointment.'

'I'm sorry,' she said. It was a toneless reply.

He sighed with impatience. 'Wait there,' he told her finally. 'I'll be up in five minutes.'

He turned to Peter Luckham apologetically.

'Selling something?' the man asked him.

'Yes,' John replied. He shrugged off his coat, and threw down the heavy gloves.

'Hope it's worth something,' Luckham said, 'to pay for this lot.'

She was sitting in a patch of sunlight in the porch, on one of the wooden seats. With the tip of her shoe, she was tracing the tile pattern on the floor. He couldn't see her face, only the light brown hair and the slenderness of her hands, folded in her lap. A briefcase stood by her feet. She wore a pair of jeans and a sweater, not the usual business suit.

'Miss Sergeant?' he asked.

She looked up. He stopped in his tracks. *He knew her. This was the girl*. The shock at seeing her face took away his breath. He saw her unguarded expression for just a second: naked sorrow. It shook him. Then she stood up, and held out her hand. She seemed to pause, too, and hold his gaze. Then, 'It's the same pattern,' she said.

'I'm sorry?' he said. He looked away from her in case she thought his expression was strange.

'The floor here,' she said. 'It's exactly the same pattern as the entrance hall at Pearsons.'

'Is it?' he asked. They looked down at the yellow and green floor together. 'Acanthus,' he said.

'That's right.' And she smiled.

He released her hand. He had felt something from her: some tremor, like extreme fatigue. She had a lovely face but, *my God*, he thought. He had never seen anyone so pale.

'I'm sorry if I disturbed you,' she offered. 'You must be working in the garden – I saw the tree by the drive.'

They had put the carcass of the willow there for collection. 'Yes,' he told her, getting the key from his pocket. 'We're clearing the waterway.'

He opened the door that led into the shadowy hall. He wondered what her reaction would be. He hoped he wouldn't see her cast an insurance assessor's eye over the place. He hoped her attitude – which seemed to be quiet, taciturn – wouldn't change.

He ushered her inside. Their footsteps echoed a little.

Bridle Lodge had been built in 1880; from the first moment he had seen it, he had been touched by its style, the upper windows framed by their decorative columns and pediments, as if they were trying to be classical; the lower windows and doors were Gothic, arched and pointed. Whoever had designed the house had built a plain, substantial villa, a truly Victorian red sandstone pile. Then it was as if the owners had come into money: they had poured incredible embellishments all over the house, decorating every inch of stone with leaves and vines, putting elaborate ridge tiles on the roof, with shields and spearheads in the castellated pattern. But it was inside the house that they had excelled themselves.

The estate agent had been apologetic. 'It's been allowed to decay a bit,' he'd said, when they'd gone into this same hallway. And he'd stuck a finger in the panelling. 'Got a bit of worm,' he'd noted. 'Might as well point it out to you. Not a great deal to put it right, but all the same . . .'

By then John hadn't been listening: he'd been staring up into the enormous stairwell.

All the way up the stairs, alternate treads were topped by painted panels. They had once been gold; now the paint flaked. Here and there, they had simply been painted black. But those that remained were beautiful faded icons of William Morris and Edward Burne-Jones: each panel a picture of herbs, or fruits. Variegated sage, a chequerboard of pale green and white; oranges and their blossom; apricots, grapes, apples.

But the window. The amazing window.

Half-way up the stairs divided, going from a single wide flight into two, which each took a dog-leg turn and went up to the first storey on left and right. And at this half-way point there was an enormous stained-glass window. It was the most astonishing colour: pale sea green, the colour of a tropical sea just where it touches the sand. Hundreds of small circular discs made up this section, varying from turquoise to yellow and, combined, producing this watery effect. A pre-Raphaelite figure was right in the centre of the window: a girl, her fair hair braided modestly on her shoulders. She was holding the heavy fabric of her dress in deep folds.

He had walked straight up the stairs, and gazed at her.

'Lovely feature,' the estate agent had said. 'Very rare.'

John had been speechless. He'd been looking at her

face. She was from Holman Hunt's *The Awakening Conscience*, the girl starting up from her lover's lap to gaze at the transforming light from the garden. 'Who did this window?' he'd asked.

'I couldn't say.'

'Not a local artist.'

'I really don't know . . .'

John had looked down at the house details in his hand. For the hallway, it simply said, 'Panelled stair with stained-glass window.' He'd put his fingertips on the window. Some of the green glass discs were cracked, but the glass was thick here and there with very faint bubbles of air trapped inside.

Now, as John brought Catherine Sergeant into the hall, she said nothing. She didn't notice the window, which was behind her; she had walked ahead of him, her eyes on the floor. She stopped and waited for him, glancing at the boxes in the nearest room, and the alarm on the wall outside the drawing room.

'I haven't unpacked everything yet,' he told her, 'but the kitchen's habitable.'

'Is the dresser in there?' she asked, naming the piece of furniture that he wanted valued.

'Yes,' he said. He opened the kitchen door.

She walked forward, glancing to left and right. Then she turned back to look at him. 'The Astons owned this house,' she murmured.

'That's right,' he said. 'Did you know them?'

'Yes – not Colonel Aston. He had died by the time I joined Pearsons.'

'His wife lived alone, I believe.'

'For twenty years.'

'Nothing had been touched. There was even electrical wiring tacked to the plaster, running along the picture rails. When I lifted the floorboards . . .' he paused '. . . some of it was the original 1920s stock, like telephone cable.'

'I visited her in the nursing home, but only once or twice here.'

'So you don't know the house?' he asked.

'Not really. It was always rather dark.'

'I must show you one day,' he said. 'It's an Arts and Crafts museum.'

She said nothing. He wondered again at her soft, compliant attitude, which almost smacked of in-difference. She was hardly the saleswoman he had expected. 'This is the dresser,' he said.

She placed her hand on the satiny top, rubbed smooth by generations. 'French,' she said.

'Yes.'

'A family piece?'

'My wife's family.'

'It's lovely,' she told him. 'Why does she want to part with it?'

'She isn't here any more,' he told her. 'And, as you can see, it's really too large for this room.'

She looked directly into his eyes. 'Even so,' she said quietly, 'it's a shame to part with it. I'm afraid you won't get what it deserves here. You would raise more for it in London.'

'You don't want to take it on?'

'Oh, we'll take it, of course,' she told him. 'I only hope we can do it justice.'

He smiled at her. 'Would you like some tea?'

'Thank you,' she said. And again she gave him a lingering look, a duplicate of the one when she had first taken his hand.

He indicated a chair. She sank into it. Just as she did so, he noticed that he had left the miniature – his favourite, the one he had been looking at first thing this morning – on the dresser's lowest shelf. He reached up immediately and put it into his pocket, amazed at his forgetfulness, his carelessness.

Catherine Sergeant glanced at the movement, then back at the dresser, but said nothing. Her gaze drifted off to the side, to the window.

She didn't comment on the rest of the furniture: the large farmhouse table – which he loved, scrubbed to the colour of old ivory, scored by knife blades, and stained by coffee – and bentwood chairs, which had also belonged to Claire's mother, and had followed him from Spain.

However, as he got out the cups, she stood up and walked over to the window. Next to it, on the wall, hung the Wedgwood trials.

'What are these?' she asked.

He came over to her. 'Jasper trial pieces,' he said. 'From the Wedgwood factory.'

She looked closely at the little tongues of clay lined up in rows under the glass. 'What do the numbers mean?' she asked.

'Each one corresponds to an entry in the experiment book,' he said. 'They're test pieces, for colours, consistencies.'

'I've never seen anything like it,' she murmured. 'How old are they?'

'Eighteenth century.' He went over to the tea, poured it, and brought it to the table. When he glanced up, he saw that she was watching him with what looked like fascination. A smile flickered. 'Are you something to do with the porcelain industry?' she asked.

'No,' he said.

'A collector?'

'Yes.'

'And you're renovating the house?'

'I'm an architect.'

'Are you working on something now? Something else in this area?'

'No,' he said. 'Actually, I've retired.'

She raised her eyebrows. 'You're hardly retiring age.'

'I'm fifty.'

She sat down opposite him.

'I lived in Spain until last year,' he said. 'I worked there. Before that it was London.'

'Did you work on anything in London that I would recognize?'

'Well ... the Parbold house ... Green's restaurant ...'

She smiled back, a true smile. 'I worked near Green's.'

'Oh? Where?'

'At Bergen's.'

'As ...?'

'I specialized in nineteenth-century art.'

He hesitated. 'Nineteenth century?'

'Yes ...'

'And why did you leave them?' He held up his finger. 'Let me guess. You got married, and came here for the country idyll.'

The conversation, which had run so quickly until then, came to a resounding halt. She reddened.

'I'm sorry,' he said.

She was opening the briefcase, taking out a pen and paper. She laid a Pearsons form on the table, and began to fill it in. He watched his address being completed. She pushed a business card across the table, not looking at him, continuing to write. 'I'll give you our estimate,' she said. 'I'm going to say the Furniture Sale, not the General. Early-nineteenth-century French country dresser . . .' She glanced up. 'Is that right?'

'Yes,' he said.

'Early nineteenth . . . I would put a reserve on it . . .'

'All right,' he said.

'Two thousand pounds? I expect it to make much more, of course.'

'All right,' he repeated. He took the form, which she had now signed. She put the pen back into the case, locked it and got up, holding out her hand. 'Thank you so much for calling us,' she said. 'The rates of commission are on the notes on the reverse of your contract . . .'

'I'm sorry if I said something out of place,' he said.

'Not at all,' she replied, but he saw her feeling written in her face. He knew it too well to mistake it.

'The sale is next month,' she said. 'If you want someone to transport the dresser . . .'

She talked her way out of the door and walked rapidly up the hallway. Sunlight was pouring in through the porch. All down the stairs, green reflections shone through the window.

But she still didn't notice it. On the threshold she shook his hand again.

He watched her walk to her car, head down, face averted.

He locked the outer door, went back into the house and stopped outside the drawing room. He disabled the alarm and went in, the heavy oak door swinging back under the pressure of his hand. Once inside, he locked it behind him.

The room was not flooded with sunlight. He kept the blinds permanently drawn. They had been the first things to be fitted, long before his possessions arrived.

He walked into the centre of the room, and closed his eyes, took the miniature from his pocket, held it gently in one palm and covered it with the other. The painter whispered from the enamel disc.

He couldn't believe he had left it in full view of Catherine Sergeant. He couldn't believe he had forgotten it. The miniature had been resting on the dresser all the time he had been working down at the weir with Peter Luckham.

He walked slowly through the crowded space, opened the cabinet drawer, and put the miniature where it belonged, among its dozens of brothers and sisters.

Six

When his wife got home Mark Pearson was in the garden, digging the broad herbaceous borders. He watched the car pull into the drive, and then Amanda sat for a few moments, gesturing to him through the window that she was on her mobile. Eventually she clicked it shut and got out. 'Is Catherine at work?' she asked, meaning the offices. 'I'm trying to ring her.'

'On a Saturday?'

'OK, I'll try her mobile.' She considered the garden steadfastly for a moment. 'Where's that tree going?' she asked, nodding at the acer he had bought that morning.

'By the hedge.' He dug the fork into the soil, and dusted off his hands. 'Did you know there's mare's tail in here?' he asked.

'No,' she said. 'How long has Robert been gone?'

'It'll never come out,' he said. 'The bugger's been found in coal mines, you know. That's how deep the roots are.'

'Mark,' Amanda repeated, 'I've seen Robert at the airport.'

'Catherine's Robert?'

'Yes,' she said. 'At the airport.' She pronounced it with only half-comic deliberation for his benefit.

'So?'

'Did she say exactly where he was going?'

'No.'

She put her head on one side. 'He'd been to Rome. On business.'

Mark smiled at his wife. 'Isn't that allowed?'

Amanda turned on him a withering expression. 'I'm just surprised that she hasn't elaborated. Talked about where he was.'

Mark shrugged. 'I could do with some tea,' he said. 'I'm dying of thirst.'

Amanda didn't move. 'He looked peculiar,' she said. 'I've been thinking about it all the way home.'

'How peculiar?' Mark asked. 'Hand me the secateurs, darling.'

She did so absent-mindedly. 'I don't know,' she murmured. 'Has Catherine said anything to you?'

'About what?'

'Oh, for God's sake. About Robert. About them.'

'Why would she?'

'Well, you work together every day.'

'You work with her too.'

'I'm stuck in the office,' she pointed out. 'It's you two organizing the sales, seeing people.'

He was confused. 'Is something the matter?'

She shook her head as she turned away. 'Men,' she muttered to herself. 'Absolutely bloody useless.'

*   *   *

Amanda had first met Catherine when Mark engaged her as his partner. Charles Wellesley, his senior partner, had just retired. Catherine had come down from London.

Amanda recalled the day: Catherine coming into this garden, Robert following her. Amanda's first thought had been that Catherine was not as she had expected; she had had a mental image of someone from Bergen's as being much more forthright. Louder, if you like. Briskly confident, even overpowering. But as Catherine began to speak over pre-lunch drinks – they had brought their food out into the garden, which looked so much prettier in the summer – Amanda had approved of her. She liked her quietness. She could see that the woman was no fool: there was a sharpness in her eyes, especially when she was listening to others talk. Which had been something of a relief, since Mark was about to sink his money into her expertise.

They had walked down to the orchard together.

'Mark's been trying to get these apples to produce properly for years,' Amanda had said, as they paused under a tree and looked up through the sparsely laden branches. 'He's begun to take it personally that they won't.'

'My parents had a house in Sussex with a garden like this,' Catherine said. 'There were fruit trees there, too . . .'

'It must have taken all their time.'

'Actually, no,' Catherine had replied. 'They worked abroad. Someone came in to do it. They always said they would take it on when they retired.'

'And did they?'

'No,' Catherine told her. 'They died before they could.'

'Oh – I'm sorry.'

Catherine shrugged. 'Well . . . it was sudden . . .'

'They died together?'

'In a road accident.'

'My God.'

'They were in Nigeria. It was where they were working.'

'So they were relatively young?'

'Fifty. Forty-two.'

Amanda regarded her. 'And you were . . .'

'Still at school,' Catherine said, and walked on.

The day was hot. Robert came to join them for a while. Mark was cooking lunch. Amanda had taken to Catherine straight away; she couldn't say the same for her husband. He was much too formal, she thought at first. Then, later, she saw that it wasn't formality so much as coolness. Robert was rigidly polite, asking all the right questions about the house and themselves, but it was Catherine who, after her initial reserve, had engaged in the most interesting conversation. She gave a little of herself, unbent. And Amanda soon realized that she had almost given away her own life history before she returned to Catherine's.

They had been sitting back after lunch, gazing at the trees and the valley beyond.

'Mark tells me you've written a book,' Amanda said.

'That's right,' Catherine replied.

'Victorian painters . . . your subject?'

'Yes.'

'And one in particular.'

'Richard Dadd.'

At Mark's request, Catherine had brought a copy with her, but it took more prompting before she pulled it out of her bag and laid it on the table. Amanda lifted it and weighed it in her hand. It was slight, but rather beautifully done, with artwork on each chapter page: grasses and tiny figures.

'This is very nice,' Amanda said.

'It was for an exhibition at the Royal Academy.'

Mark smiled. 'I'm not sure we can live up to the heady glamour of the Academy, not at Pearsons. The most you'll see here is prints and pisspots.'

'How charming,' Amanda said, and threw a crumpled napkin at him. 'Just what we all wanted to know.'

Catherine laughed. 'It'll be nice to get into the real world,' she said. 'It'll be something different.'

That night, as they got ready for bed, Mark had referred back to this conversation. Standing half-dressed at the foot of the bed, Amanda had asked him what he was thinking about.

'Catherine,' he told her. 'Wonder if she'll stay.'

'She seems very straightforward.'

'She is,' he replied. 'Straightforwardly too good for us.' He had taken off his shirt and slung it into the laundry basket. 'She's quite well known. An expert. And she's only come here because of Robert.'

'Has she?'

'He wanted to be near his grandmother, apparently.'

She raised her eyebrows. 'Must be very close.'

'Bit of a come-down after Bergens. That's what I'm worrying about. Bit of a backwater.'

Amanda walked over to him and put her hands on his shoulders. 'Look,' she said, 'the woman's come down here to support her husband. She needs a job. And if she's an expert, that's all the more reason to snap her up. We could extend the paintings part of the business. Do more Fine Art sales.'

He had smiled at her. 'You like her,' he said.

'Yes,' she told him. 'I do.'

But she hadn't liked Robert.

The more they met him over the next few months, the more Amanda's misgivings grew. Robert did not make conversation; he didn't even try. He was the least sociable man she had ever met.

'What Catherine sees in him, I'll never know,' she told Mark one day, after Robert had come into the offices at lunchtime.

'What's the matter with him?' Mark had asked. 'Perfectly decent bloke.'

'Yes,' she'd murmured, half to herself, as she slotted more paper into the printer and watched Robert through the window as he walked out to his car. 'A perfectly decent bloody cold fish.'

And now today, at the airport.

Amanda watched Mark plant the acer, but her mind was elsewhere. She had seen something in Robert's gaze: a stubbornness, so deep it was almost aggressive, in the set of his mouth, and the straightness of his stance. It was as if she had been about to challenge him and he was ready to rebuff a threat, or field an answer. With a sudden lurch of anxiety, Amanda wondered what Robert had expected to be asked.

Seven

John Brigham had met his wife, Claire, when she was working in the West End.

She had only been in London for two weeks, after a year touring in the provinces. She was a set designer for a theatre company. She always joked that John had snatched her straight off the train. She had a beautiful voice, so beautiful with its soft Dumfriesshire burr.

For those first few dates, John would meet her when the theatres came out, in the crush on the corner of Wardour Street. For a while, they met only late at night and went to a restaurant in Chinatown. The first few times, he had got home at one or two in the morning, and spent the next hour or so too wired to sleep, looking out of the window at the castellated gable end of the house that faced his, absorbing every last detail of its white-on-grey pattern until the very texture of the bricks came to mean Claire, and the way that the lights from the street crept only into one corner while all the rest was hazily dark.

Then one night she came home with him.

He didn't go into the office the next day. He sat with her, watching her face with its sunny smile, her neat, practical hands fastened round a coffee cup; listening to the swing of her skirt against the stairs as she ran down them, late, to go to the theatre.

One night he went to the Apollo and saw the play.

He was at the end of a row. Directly behind him two women in their fifties were discussing the clothes and the amount of the surgery the actress was reputed to have undergone. His attention on the morose one-woman play had wandered; he tilted his head upwards and stared at the ornamentation of the boxes, the door-ways, the roof. He imagined Claire in the wings, hardly fifty feet from where he was sitting, and had a barely controllable urge to rush on to the stage and find her.

When they got home that night, she told him she was going away. 'She's taking the play to Broadway,' she said.

'Who?'

She named the actress.

'And you go with her?'

'That's what she's asked.'

He tried to absorb the information, what it meant to him. 'When?' he asked eventually.

'In the summer. It's a big deal.' She didn't meet his eye.

He felt as if the blood were draining out of his body. He had known her precisely three weeks.

'I have to go. It's my work,' she said. 'It's a dream chance.'

'Couldn't you work here with someone else?' he asked. She had said nothing, her eyes lowered. He wondered if he ought to dash the dream. He wondered if he could. 'Do you want to go?' he asked.

'I would like to see America,' she said.

Moments passed. He had lived a bachelor life until then, he had told everyone that he would never marry – he hadn't been able to imagine ever being in the frame of mind to commit his life to another person. 'I'll take you to see America,' he said.

She had given him a quizzical smile. 'Oh, yes?' she asked. 'When, exactly?'

'This summer,' he'd replied. 'On honeymoon.'

They bought a house in Rotherhithe, near the Tube, on a road that thundered all day long with lorries ferrying backwards and forwards from the new docklands houses half a mile away. Their own was not new. It wasn't appealing either. Not at first. Not until he had set to work on it. It had once been a pub, and had been boarded up for over a year. The window frames and the roof were rotted. He drew up plans that kept the anonymous face it turned to the road, and extended the house back, behind the nine-foot walls of the old delivery yard.

When they took out the windows, they found farthings that had been brand new in 1840, with the young queen's head on them. In the narrow chimney, among two centuries' worth of rubbish that rained down, were pewter buttons, a tattered shoe, the door of an iron birdcage. Under the floorboards there were more superstitious gifts to the house: horseshoes, plaited twigs, a comb, a cup and saucer wrapped in cotton, and, a kind of miracle, a wine-glass without a crack or a mark.

He sold his flat and he and Claire lived there, among piles of bricks and piping. The first night they had a mattress on the floor, no bed. He had never slept so well, and woke up to the sound of rain hammering on their newly secure roof, and blowing through the windows they had left open in the warmth of the evening. Claire had walked out to the bathroom, laughing at herself, shaking rain from her hands. He looked at the trail of wet footmarks on the dusty floorboards, saw the arch of her sole in the prints, the long area that barely touched the floor. He saw that imprint over and over again. He had seen it in Spain and here, at the Dorset house. Closed his eyes every time, waiting for it to vanish.

The following year, the year after they married, Claire changed her job. She began work at the Victoria and Albert Museum, in the costume department. She told him that she wished she'd done it long before. To be no longer at the mercy of a production, of whatever flavour, was like being released from prison, she said. He knew she was happy: she would go out of the house at more of a run than usual. Occasionally, she would accept a lift from him, fretting at his later start, or that he was apt to be distracted by something he wanted done in the house during the day.

His love for her never altered, not in a single direction. It felt fresh, newly minted, interesting, as if he were looking daily at something he had never seen before, and was surprised by it all over again.

That particular morning – that unforgettable morning – was cold. It was March, not a noteworthy day. Not bright. Not cold. A mild, grey day. As he turned the car in the yard, he saw her talking to the builders. She was wearing a long reddish coat. They said something to her, and she laughed. She nodded in John's direction, then added something. As she walked away, he saw the three men look at him, their faces betraying a mixture of reactions: envy, affection, surprise.

The traffic was bad. They got out of Rotherhithe, having crawled all the way down Salter Road towards the tunnel. Claire was putting on her makeup in the vanity mirror over the passenger seat. They'd argued about the route. She had a lecture to prepare, she said. She had an appointment that morning, at nine. She wanted to be early. 'I'm getting out at Bermondsey tube,' she'd told him, hand on the door. 'I can change at Westminster and be at South Kensington before you've got past this next set of lights.'

She was always impatient. It was pointless to try to dissuade her. With one eye on the road, he kissed her.

Her hand was still on the door. But her face wore a strange, abstracted expression.

'What is it?' he asked.

'Something's happened,' she said.

When he looked back at that day, he always wondered in what freakish split second she had managed to say those words. At the end of the sentence, her mouth stayed slightly open. Then she leaned to one side. Not slumped, leaned – almost a conscious movement, as if she was trying to avoid something coming towards her.

'Claire?' he said. 'Claire?'

He pulled the car to the side of the road. It was a bus stop. The queue all stared at him as he leaped out and came round to her side of the car. He opened the door. In those few seconds, she had closed her eyes. She was limp, like a toy, like a doll. He tried to prop her head up a little. A bus arrived. The driver blew his horn to get him to move the car.

A woman came out of the queue, and touched his arm. 'Is something wrong?' she asked. 'I'm a nurse at St Thomas's.'

They both bent down to Claire. A line of saliva was running out of his wife's mouth.

'Have you got a phone?' the woman asked.

'What?'

'A mobile phone.'

He was looking about for something to wipe Claire's face. In peculiar exasperation, he pulled at his wife's elbow. 'Wake up,' he said.

The woman reached behind him and grabbed his mobile from the dashboard. She took his hand off Claire's arm, and put the phone into it. 'Dial 999,' she told him.

He drove behind the ambulance, his eyes fixed on the rear doors. Nothing else. When the journey finished, he couldn't have told anyone how many sets of lights they had passed through or anything else about it. But he remembered the doors.

They took Claire inside, straight into a cubicle, and asked him to wait in Reception. He had to stand next to a ridiculously small glass window, and give Claire's details through the tiny pane. He couldn't catch what the receptionist was saying.

Then he stood in the centre of the corridor and waited.

After a minute, a nurse came along. 'Would you like to sit down?' she asked.

'No,' he said.

'Would you like a cup of tea?'

'No,' he repeated.

He watched as they took Claire away again, along the brightly lit corridor. He watched them go into the lift, watched the doors close.

'Where is she going?' he asked, more frightened than he could say by the obvious urgency with which they had brought her out of the room.

'She's going for a scan,' the nurse said. 'Sit down.' She guided him to a seat.

They were gone for forty minutes. In that time, a little boy was taken into the opposite cubicle; John could hear his mother saying that the child had fallen down during a game of football. Then the doctor's careful explanation that the cut needed stitches. 'It'll be all right,' the mother kept saying to her son. And later, when the tears subsided, 'We'll go for an ice-cream. You can tell Daddy you had a whole ice-cream, the big kind.'

John started to plan what he and Claire would do when this was over, when they got out of here. He would take her on holiday. They would go where they had been saving to go. Not save any more. Just go. They had been planning a holiday in Mauritius next year. They had the brochure. He would go straight from this hospital, he told himself, and book the flight. He would book the hotel she liked, the one with the little villas facing the sea.

And he kept repeating the other woman's words to himself: *It'll be all right. It'll be all right.*

His fingers flexed and unflexed. He saw himself turning the brochure pages in the shop. Giving them his credit card. He rehearsed it in minute detail, watching the clock above his head.

The mother and the boy passed him.

Someone else came along, an elderly man on a paramedics' stretcher. He was put into the same cubicle, then the paramedics came out and walked up to the nearest nurse, two burly men in fluorescent lime yellow jackets. He tried to make sense of what they were saying. Something about a stroke. Something about what they were doing after work. John tried to connect the two, the information about the patient, the plans for the evening.

The lift doors opened. The doctor who had been with Claire came out and walked towards him.

He knew before the man had uttered a word.

He walked a long way. He crossed the river. By then, it was lunchtime.

When he first came out of the hospital he had turned right and found himself in the curious labyrinth made for cars, not people, that led to Waterloo station. He had stopped, puzzled, trying to remember where he was headed; then he went back and walked over Westminster Bridge.

When he had first come to London, a newly qualified graduate, this view had thrilled him. All of this area. The Houses of Parliament, the Cenotaph, St James's Park, Horseguards. He had come down here maybe a hundred times just to walk it. Westminster Abbey, with the oldest garden in England; the Tate at Millbank, where the awesome Penitentiary had once stood, packed with industrial workshops and stables. He walked the route of the eighteenth-century builders, the Cubitts and Johnsons, Gibbs and Flew. He had walked right through Kensington, where the Rutlands and Chamberlains had once occupied the new Italianate villas, and down through Hammersmith, where speculators had thrown up five-storeyed terraces over the market gardens. Up again through Holland Park; back through what had once been piggeries and potteries. Fulham and Hammersmith, which had been once famous for spinach and strawberries, eaten up by builders of the railways. Ealing, with two hundred market gardens disappearing under tram lines and pavements.

He loved the city. He knew it. He could feel its organic growth beneath his feet. And yet that day, walking through Westminster, he felt that he had been put down in a foreign country. He couldn't recognize anywhere; even the street signs didn't make sense. He almost stepped out in front of a bus on the corner of Parliament Square. He looked up at the Abbey and felt nothing, except perhaps a dreamy fluidity, like the motion of waves.

He walked until he felt tired, and found himself in a square, with trees in the centre. It might have been anywhere in London. He glanced up to his left, and saw the long shallow steps of a house, and a sign on the door. It was familiar. He knew he'd been there before, and that it held some significance for him. He had the oddest conviction that, if he could get inside, he could rewind: replay the day, start it again. He would be safe.

His eyes ran over the lettering of the black and white sign without making any sense of it. It might as well have been in another language. He knocked on the green paintwork of the door, and a woman opened it. 'We close in fifteen minutes,' she said.

'That's OK,' he told her, and stepped inside.

'It isn't really enough time to see everything,' she warned him, taking his money in the dim hallway.

He wandered forward. Every inch of wall was crammed with objects; he walked into a dining room painted red and full of mirrors. Above the fireplace was a portrait of a man. He went on, into a narrow space with an ancient writing desk, that looked out past pale green panels into a courtyard. He passed a hand over his face. His skin was covered with a cold sweat. He felt dazed. There were architectural fragments everywhere, casts of cornices and capitals, statues, plaques, tiles, medallions. Fragments of a life. Fragments of his. The pieces reached right to the top of the walls and spilled over across the ceiling: hundreds, perhaps thousands.

Beyond the room he could see many more, all coloured by the light that filtered down through a far-off rooflight. He stepped into a three-storey shell of more stone, more statues, more paintings. There was a marble sarcophagus below him. Paintings crammed frame to frame. He looked up and saw implacable stone faces, carved leaves and vines, animal heads. And funeral urns.

'It's Seti the First,' said a voice beside him.

He swung round. There was an attendant in a green uniform. 'Thirteen hundred years before Christ,' the man said. 'It's carved out of a single piece of alabaster.

When Soane brought it here, he invited a thousand people to look at it, and he lit the rooms with three hundred oil lamps.'

John stared at the man. Then, at last, he realized where he was. 'It's Soane's house,' he said. 'Soane, the architect.'

The attendant looked back at him, frowning.

'It's Soane's house,' John heard himself repeat.

'Yes,' the man said.

'I saw his drawings,' John whispered. 'I did a paper on them. Six years ago. Seven.'

The man touched John's shoulder. 'Are you all right?' he asked.

John felt stifled and breathless. He wanted to get out, but he couldn't find the way. He tried to get back to the first red room, and found himself in another gallery, where the paintings were hung in movable racks as well as on the walls. It was a dead end.

Another attendant glanced at him.

'The way out,' John said.

He followed where the man pointed, brushing past the model of a tomb. *Made for his wife after her death*, said the printed label.

He gasped at it in the shadows.

Made for his wife after her death. St Pancras Gardens. 1815.

He got out somehow, into the dusty end of light in Lincoln's Inn Fields. He walked over to a bench, sat down on it heavily, trying to stop the pavement lurching under him; trying to stop the stone spinning drunkenly wherever he looked.

He got out his phone and dialled his sister's number,

hoping it was still the same. He hadn't spoken to her in a long time. All he could think was that he needed someone who had never met Claire. Even if that someone was Helen.

'Hello,' said a voice, inflected with a questioning note.

'It's me,' he murmured. 'Helen, can you help me?'

Columbine, 1854

There were no women in Bedlam – at least, none that Richard Dadd could see.

Sometimes, at night, he thought he heard their voices: he thought he heard screams so frightening that he would crawl into the corner of his cell and sit with his knees drawn to his chest, his head buried in them.

When he was a young man, in 1840, he had painted a girl in a white dress, holding a rose. It had been late spring. The magnolias had finished flowering; the roses were in first bloom. He had been twenty-three. Looking back on that part of his life was like putting a telescope to his eye, and seeing the years made inconsequentially tiny. He had been admired, then; he had been out in the roaring, peopled world; he had been adored and fêted. Admitted to the Schools of the Royal Academy at fifteen, he was thought a genius. His work was commissioned, bought. It was rumoured that he would not fail, or starve in a garret. He would rise to prominence; he would be famous. He would be courted. He would be loved.

He had had friends then, other artists, who had not been ashamed of his reputation or company, men who understood him, and came to see him. They had formed a group, to which others yearned to be admitted. They called themselves the Clique. Frith was one; Egg, Phillip and Ward were others. There was no animosity between them, no jealousy. They formed a committee to outdo the old academicians, to bring the light of new painters into the open, not have it suffocated by age.

Someone had once told him, in that time, that he was the brightest of them all. He had kept the letter, and wondered where it could be now. 'Sportive humour, innocent mirth . . . one of the kindest and the best, as well as the most gifted . . .'

She had written it to him, the girl in the white dress. She was Catherine, the wife of his eldest brother. He had persuaded her to sit for him one afternoon when the roses first came into bloom. He had picked the rose, a yellow one. Its name escaped him now, but his memory of her did not. She had sat on the bench outside the house, self-consciously holding the rose he had given her, the dark hair falling to her shoulders. Catherine and Robert had been married the year before his imprisonment: the year before his possession by demons, the year before the voices. He wondered if she had once come to see him, on the arm of his brother, or whether he had simply imagined her presence.

It was ten years now, a little more than ten years.

Lately he had been sketching a great deal. In January he had painted The Packet Delayed, *a child's game on a riverbank. He had been thinking of Robert then. Two boys hold on to a branch while trying to retrieve a toy* schooner from the water of the stream. He had painted the ship's masts so clearly, with such definition, that it was almost an engraving rather than a painting.

As winter progressed to spring, he painted David sparing Saul's life; and sketched the passions of brutality and pride; ambition; agony; raving madness. Drunkenness, avarice, melancholy. In the same week of June he painted two groups: all men conversing, settling disputes. One stood over a painting, inspecting it with a glass. Paint within paint within paint. Detail under detail. He sketched hands and mouths: hands extended, pointing and holding; mouths open in conversation. Faces turned to other faces, rapt in concentration.

When he sat back from A Curiosity Shop – done in such a hurry, from ten in the morning until three in the afternoon, missing luncheon, deaf to instructions to come to table – sadness swept over him.

He had no society of equals. He had no conversations. He could not make out liveliness or appreciation of intellect when others looked at him. He had lost it somewhere, by some action he could not fathom. He painted friendship, but he had none. He had been alone for over ten years, and never touched another human hand in admiration.

He took up the brush again, and painted Columbine, looking towards him over her right shoulder, the smile playing on her mouth. He completed it in a matter of minutes: it was not difficult. She inhabited his soul.

When it was over, he sat at the easel in the dying light of the afternoon, and wept for company. He was dying here, alone, forgotten, alive only in paint, in the *fantasies he created. And paintings were fragile. They did not last. He could destroy Columbine in a second, if he wished it. Even if she survived, she might be lost, torn, put away in the dark. She was not real. She was only a memory. In a flash of clarity, he wished violently for someone to talk to. Someone alive and substantial to love.*

For Frith, and Edward Ward, and John Phillip. For his own brother.

And for a girl in a white dress, holding a rose.

Eight

Two days after he had met Catherine at Bridle Lodge, John came out of the hospital, at eleven, and turned towards the town centre. It wasn't far to walk, and the day was lovely. He noticed as he came down East Walks – down the hill, with the water-meadows, woods and fields in the distance – that there was colour in the horse-chestnut trees. In another few weeks, those trees would be green towers, banked with white candles, he thought. Unexpectedly – or perhaps it was to be expected today – a lump came to his throat. He had the sudden conviction that he wouldn't see them flower, and he fought it all the way down the hill, an unseeing gaze fixed ahead of him. As he walked he told himself, *Don't be stupid*, over and over, a mantra keeping pace with his footsteps.

Almost as soon as he came into the main street by the church, he saw Catherine Sergeant.

'Hello,' he said, as he caught up with her.

She was walking slowly along the line of little shops and jumped. Colour rose in her face. 'Oh, hello.'

'Window shopping?'

She looked into his eyes only briefly. 'Yes,' she said.

'Not exactly busy in town today,' he observed.

'No one's here,' she agreed.

The act of saying this seemed to affect her. She began to frown, and put a hand to her face.

'Are you all right?' he asked.

She took a deep, gasping breath. In the same second, he remembered himself on the seat in Lincoln's Inn, and Helen at the other end of the line, repeating his name, 'John? . . . John?', while he tried to get air into his lungs.

He took Catherine's arm. 'Come with me,' he said.

'I'm all right,' she protested.

'I don't think so,' he said. 'Come and sit down for a minute.'

He walked her along the street. She did not resist. They turned up Colne Lane, a small cobbled alley that connected the two streets of the little town. She followed him, past clothes shops – frames of colour in plate-glass windows – past the cosmetics chain store with its familiar scent of fruit and incense washing out of the door. There was a florist's, where she paused briefly. Eventually he linked her arm and guided her to the café on the corner. He pushed open the door, and she walked to a table and sat down. Sitting opposite her, he was touched by the bewilderment in her expression.

The waitress came to the table; he gave her the order. When he looked back at Catherine she was leaning forward, elbow resting on the table, a hand raked through her hair, her head propped on it.

'You look tired,' he said.

She said nothing for some time. She seemed baffled. Then, abruptly, she asked, 'Where is your wife?'

He had been thinking of Claire so much lately, remembering her in the car, remembering her turning away from the builders, and their expressions as their eyes had followed her, remembering the wet imprint of feet, that he was shocked for a moment. It was as if Catherine had looked into him and asked the one question he never stopped asking himself.

'She died,' he told her, 'almost eleven years ago, of a brain haemorrhage.'

Catherine suddenly sat up. 'Oh, God,' she said. 'I didn't know.'

'It's all right.'

'No,' she told him. 'It isn't. I don't know why it occurred to me. I shouldn't have asked. I'm sorry.'

The drinks came. She stared down at her cup after the waitress had left. He watched her, not touching his own coffee, waiting.

'I thought perhaps you had parted,' she said. 'You seemed quite calm. I thought perhaps you had left her.'

'Left Claire?' he echoed. 'No.'

'No,' she repeated in agreement. 'No, of course not.' A kind of dull, bruised colour had come to her face. 'My husband left me two weeks ago,' she explained. She raised her eyes to him.

'I see,' John said. 'Now it's my turn to say I'm sorry.'

'I only want to know where he is,' she said. 'I only want an explanation.'

'And he didn't tell you where he was going?'

'I found a note.'

'That was all?'

'Yes.'

'There was no discussion beforehand?'

'No.'

'And the letter didn't explain or give a reason?'

'No,' she said. 'Just that he was leaving. Had already left.'

They sat still. Someone else came in at the door. There was a rattle of the bell, the clatter of another couple sitting down.

'And the stupid thing is . . . this is such a stupid thing, I mean, it doesn't really have any significance, I suppose . . .' She hesitated, then carried on: 'I found a catalogue, and this piece of jewellery, a necklace . . .'

'You mean some kind of sales catalogue?'

'For an auction.'

'He bid for this at an auction?'

'I don't know,' she said, then smiled crookedly. 'As I say, it's just stupid. It's meaningless.'

'Not if it's upset you,' he said.

'I've been wondering today if he's having an affair. If that's why he's gone.'

'Is that possible?'

'Anything's possible,' she said.

'But did you see any sign of it?'

'No,' she admitted. 'Well . . . maybe. With Robert, it's hard to tell.' She caught his puzzled expression. 'He's quiet,' she said, lamely. 'Very quiet.' Then a breath escaped her, hardly a smile. 'Silent, in fact.'

He waited a moment. 'Where could he be?' he asked. 'Do you have any theories?'

She looked up at him. Again, there was no direct

answer. She only said, 'I'm so angry, I can't sleep.'

'I would think that was normal.'

'I don't cry,' she said. 'I just rage. I'm so angry at wasting everything,' she said. 'The time.'

'You feel that time's been wasted?'

She picked up the coffee cup, then returned it, without drinking, to the saucer. 'Wouldn't you?' she asked. 'He's gone off somewhere – with someone, for all I know. I feel ridiculous. As if I didn't get the punchline to some cruel joke. As if I've been too dim to pick it up. Does that make sense?'

'Yes.'

'I'm just so angry.'

She seemed frozen in place. 'Catherine?' he prompted.

She closed her eyes briefly. 'I came down here five years ago to be with him,' she said. 'To be where he wanted. His grandmother lived in Milborne Port. It's about ten miles away. She was ill. He wanted to be near her.' She sighed. 'His mother wasn't terribly concerned,' she said. 'She tends to be unconcerned generally. About everything. Anything. Especially her own family.'

'And you came to live down here with him,' John said. 'You supported him. That was the right thing to do.'

She appeared not to hear him. 'His grandmother had died within the year,' she said.

She was far away, standing at a hospital gate next to her husband, who had been so affected by his grief, the first and last time that she had seen him so distressed. She had tried gently to pull him forward but Robert

90

had pulled away. His fingernails had caught her wrist, scratching her, raising a red weal. She didn't notice it until later. All she had wanted was to get him into the car, protect him from the gaze of passers-by.

'There was the house to clear,' she said quietly. 'She had all these objects ... Doulton figures ... and red Carlton. Rouge Royale.'

They had done the house together, the brutal task of going through all his grandmother's possessions. All the drawers and cupboards. Sorting through clothes. All the poignant paraphernalia of the elderly: the tablets lined up by the kettle, each bottle marked with different-coloured dots by a wavering hand. The half-bottle of brandy in the cupboard. The wooden tray of ironed silk scarves. The monogrammed towels, unused for decades. The camphor of mothballs between two ancient furs hanging in the satinwood wardrobe. The little travel clock, in a leather case, on the bedside table, and the parish magazine from the church, a small Bible with tiny print and gold-leaf-edged pages, which smelt astoundingly of lavender, as if it had been doused with scent.

The Rouge Royale was in the sitting room, in a glass-fronted cabinet.

There were about a dozen pieces: some little ornaments, small jugs and plates, then several large bowls. The colour, by which these were catalogued, was a deep scarlet, with a wonderful glaze that had a touch of opalescent blue, like oil in sunlit water.

They took them to Pearsons. It was Robert's decision.

Catherine had taken them from the wrappings

herself, and displayed them on an oak chest, far away from the door, close to the auctioneer's desk.

Robert had come in that same morning – there were a lot of his grandmother's things in the sale, chosen after agonizing hours of discussion as to what he wanted to keep and what he would sell – and, walking up the aisle, he had suddenly noticed the Carlton on the chest, blazing away in the daylight.

Even she had experienced a moment of anxiety when she had unpacked them. They had been so precious and so personal, collected over years, and looked so forlorn in public, as if Robert's grandmother herself were laid out for inspection. Even Catherine had thought it heart-rending, so the expression on Robert's face as he stood by them had not shocked her. She had expected him to feel desperately sad. But not what actually came. 'You're selling her,' he had said.

'What?' she said. She had tried to hold his hand.

He had stepped back. 'You're selling her,' he had repeated. 'And taking a bloody profit.'

Catherine looked up at John. He was waiting, his hands folded in his lap.

'There was so much that went wrong after that,' she said. 'And as time went on . . .'

Time. John wondered if she felt it as acutely as he did, its very essence slipping through her fingers, the impossibility of grasping it and making it stand still.

If only he could make it stand still. For a week. Or a month.

Abruptly she dropped her hands to the table. 'What

am I doing?' she asked herself loudly. 'Why am I wasting *your* time like this?'

He smiled. 'You're not.'

She glanced around. 'I am,' she said. 'I can't believe I've made you sit here . . .'

'It's no time at all,' he said.

She looked at him acutely.

'It will pass,' he said. 'I know it doesn't seem that way.'

She shook her head.

'You'll get an explanation, or you won't get an explanation,' he told her, 'and it will pass.'

Suddenly she slumped back in the seat, gazing at him, as if seeing him clearly for the first time. 'You're very patient,' she said.

He almost laughed. 'Actually, if there's one thing I'm not, it's patient,' he told her. 'Especially just now.'

'Just now?' she echoed.

He didn't want to go into details that even he couldn't face. He met her eyes; they exchanged a smile.

'Would you come out to dinner with me?' he asked. The question, which had not been in his mind, rushed out of his mouth. It astonished him: it had sprung from looking at her, from the tremor he had felt in her hand the other day, from her profile while she looked at the Wedgwood trials – something, perhaps not even any of those things, perhaps all of them – and, now that he had asked the question, he felt inept and unfeeling of her situation.

She had not responded.

'I'm really sorry,' he said. 'I just meant a dinner.' And he found himself laughing, in exasperation. 'Christ, that sounded crass. I just . . .' And he waved the subject away.

She began to smile and then, to his surprise, to colour. She didn't answer his question. Instead, she crossed her arms over her chest almost defensively. 'Time,' she murmured, regressing to the previous subject. 'It feels strange. Not normal, not as usual. It's all stretched out and distorted. Hours and hours.'

He took a breath, trying to follow the pattern of her thoughts. It wasn't difficult. He knew this curious, rootless sense of bafflement and abandonment so well. 'Circular hours,' he said, 'where nothing progresses, and you come back to the beginning.'

'That's right,' she said.

'It's all relative.'

'Is it?'

He could see that she doubted it. 'Of course. All time is relative,' he told her. 'Think about the endless days in a classroom, or behind a desk in a job you hated. Or the afternoon when you were a child, and playing, and the sun stopped in the sky and the trees never moved a leaf.' He smiled at her. 'You see?' he said. 'All time is relative.'

She considered him closely.

He looked out of the window at the traffic. 'If you think about it,' he mused, 'there's really no time at all.'

She was gathering her things together. 'Well,' she said, 'whether it exists or not, I've taken too much of yours.'

He stood up with her.

She put her handbag strap over her shoulder; pulled

on her gloves. He stepped past the table, and opened the door for her, ready to go back and pay the bill, let her walk away on her own.

Then she stopped on the threshold. 'Thursday,' she said. 'Perhaps Thursday?'

And she glanced back, just once, as she walked down the street.

Nine

As Catherine arrived home, pulling her car into the kerb, she saw that a man was standing on the doorstep. His hand was just dropping from knocking at the door. 'Mrs Sergeant?' he asked as she got out of the car.

'Yes.' She had never seen him before.

He held out his hand. She noticed that he was carrying a briefcase.

'If you're selling something,' she said, 'I'm afraid the answer's no.'

He smiled. 'I'm not selling anything,' he said. 'I've been asked to call on you. My name is Styles.' She considered him. He was about fifty, brown-haired, florid-faced, in a suit too small for him by at least one size. He looked hot, despite the day's temperature. He handed her a card. *Wade and Charleton*, it read. *Solicitors*.

'Do I know you?' she asked.

'I'm working for your husband,' he told her.

* * *

Sitting in her kitchen, Michael Styles looked even larger. Catherine made tea, almost holding her breath, knowing that there would be no good news. She opened the window on to the small courtyard garden she had planned so meticulously last year. The star magnolias were just coming out, white flowers on bare branches. They were only shrubs. She had discussed with Robert – only recently . . . was it only recently? Was it only in October or November? – that she might have to move them when they were a little larger. They had stood at this window and discussed something they would do together in four or five years' time.

The kettle boiled. She laid a tray. All the while she fought down another image, of Robert long ago, in some other tiny garden in London, before they had ever come here. Robert moving behind her, passing his arms round her waist.

She closed off the memory, turned with the laden tray, and put it on the table.

'That's nice,' Styles said.

'I'm sorry?'

'A teapot,' he said, indicating it with a nod. 'People don't bother, do they? It's nice to see a proper pot of tea.' He blushed as he spooned sugar into his cup.

She sat down opposite him, pitying his obvious discomfort. 'Where is he?' she asked.

'I'm afraid I can't tell you that,' he said.

She put her hands into her lap, hid them under the table so he wouldn't see her balled fists. 'What does he think I'm going to do?' she asked. 'Run after him with an axe?'

Styles looked at her.

'It was a joke,' she told him.

He opened his briefcase. 'I've been instructed to bring these to you.' He pushed three or four sheets of paper across the table towards her.

She looked at them upside down. 'In the County Court,' she read. There was a circular red stamp at the top of the page. Robert's handwriting filled the sheet. She turned them round. There was a date, the date of their marriage. And the place. 'The petitioner and respondent last lived together as husband and wife . . .' And then the address. This address. Their home address.

She looked up at Michael Styles. 'Robert filled these in?'

'Yes.'

'And left them with you . . . when?'

'A month ago.'

She was trying to work out the details. 'He filled these in, delivered them to you, and told you . . . what? To bring them to me?'

'Yes.'

'Today? Specifically today?'

Styles spread one hand in a faint semblance of apology. Or embarrassment. 'We had an instruction to bring them to you at a time to be notified.'

'And he's now notified you.'

'That's correct.'

'You mean he's been in touch with you?'

'Yes.'

'He phoned you, wrote to you . . . this week?'

Styles didn't reply.

She looked down at the sheet in front of her. 'There

are no children of the family living . . . no child has been born to the respondent during the marriage . . .' Robert had put a black line through both clauses. She turned the page. 'The said marriage has broken down irretrievably . . .'

She read twice the reasons he had given for the divorce, and something rushed through her: not anger, or any specific emotion, but more a physical reaction, a kind of rushing feeling inside her, as if her body had gone into overdrive. Blood raced through her heart while she bent over the pages. Eventually, she managed to stare back at Styles. 'You've read what it says?' she asked. 'About the grounds, the cause?'

'I have.'

'You accept what it says?'

He met her gaze. 'It isn't my business to accept it,' he told her.

'Only to deliver it,' she said. 'Is it true, what it says here?' She prodded the paper with her fingertip, making it slide across the polished table top.

'I couldn't say.'

'You mean you won't say.'

'I mean that I don't know the facts, but I accept them as my client's word,' he replied. He was measured, she would give him that. But, then, it was easy for him to be calm.

She pushed back her chair and got up. 'Do you do this all the time?' she asked. 'Do you often go to someone's home with stuff like this?'

'No,' Styles said. 'It's unusual.'

She glared at him. It wasn't his fault – she was well aware of that – but she felt she could have struck him, hurt him, for sitting there, opening his briefcase and putting this outrageous insult on the table.

'I don't suppose he told you what he was doing,' she said.

'The divorce?' Styles asked, perplexed.

'I don't mean the fucking divorce,' she retorted. 'Did he tell you that he was leaving without telling me beforehand? That he was going to walk out in the dark one morning, before I was awake, without discussing any of this with me?'

Styles remained silent, looking increasingly awkward.

'I mean,' Catherine said, aware now that her voice was rising, that it was running away from her with an hysterical pitch. She sounded unlike herself, like the typical hysterical woman, and Styles would be thinking, *So this was what he was running away from* . . . She couldn't help it. 'I mean, is it reasonable?' she demanded. 'Is that what a reasonable man does? What did I do that he couldn't speak to me? He didn't say a word, not a word . . .'

The doorbell rang.

Styles stood.

'I haven't finished,' Catherine said.

He looked at the door.

'I haven't finished talking to you,' she repeated.

It rang again.

'Oh, shit,' she muttered. She went out of the room, up the hallway, and wrenched open the door.

Amanda was standing on the step. 'What is it?' she said. 'What's the matter?'

Catherine held the door wide for her. 'You might as

well come in and join the party,' she said. 'The more the merrier.'

Styles had come out of the kitchen, and was hovering in the hall, briefcase in hand.

'This is Mr Styles,' Catherine said. 'Robert sent him.'

'Robert?' Amanda echoed.

'Mr Styles is a solicitor,' Catherine added. 'Did you know that they did house calls?'

'No,' Amanda said. And she gave Styles a sympathetic look.

'Neither did I,' said Catherine. 'Wonderfully good of him, isn't it? Apparently Robert asked him to come here. You know, just to dot the i's and cross the t's . . . like – like it's something Robert just thought of at the last minute,' she floundered. 'You know, as you're going out of the door on holiday or something, and you suddenly realize you've forgotten to stop the papers? You grab something – a scrap envelope – and you scribble down your instructions, and leave it on the side and ask a friend to drop it in for you. Just drop in this bloody note to say you're going away, and, oh, by the way, you won't be coming back.'

Amanda and Styles stood stock still.

Amanda put a hand on Catherine's arm. 'Where is he?' she asked. 'What's he done?'

Catherine nodded grimly at the man in front of them. Styles took a step forward. 'I've left the papers on the table,' he said, in a low voice, half to Catherine and half to Amanda, who was now holding her friend's shoulder protectively. He edged past Catherine, got to the door, and said, 'Thank you very much for the tea,' then went out on to the street.

'Shit,' Catherine muttered.

Amanda waited. 'Any way you want to start me at the beginning?'

Catherine let out a long breath. Together, they went back to the kitchen. Catherine dropped into the nearest chair. Amanda picked up the papers and read them slowly, carefully. She put them down on the table again, went to the cupboard, took out an extra mug, replenished the teapot with hot water, and sat down opposite her.

'I knew,' she said.

Catherine's head jerked up. 'What?'

'I saw Robert in the airport on Saturday,' she said.

'You *knew*?' Catherine echoed. 'You knew about *this* all along?' And she waved at the divorce papers.

'No, no,' Amanda reassured her. 'I didn't know a thing. But I saw him, I spoke to him, and he had this strange expression on his face . . .'

'You spoke to him?'

'Yes.'

'What did he say?'

'Nothing. At least, nothing of any consequence. He said he'd been to Rome on business.'

'Rome!'

Amanda looked at Catherine acutely. 'I take it that was a lie, then,' she said.

Catherine was breathing heavily. 'I don't know what's a lie and what isn't. Rome . . .'

'Have you spoken to his office?'

'They said he's on leave.'

'And how long has he been gone?'

'Two weeks . . . nearly three.'

A slight colour heightened in Amanda's face. 'He left you three weeks ago, and you've been on your own here, and you never said a word to us?'

Catherine leaned forward on the table, and rested her forehead on both palms.

'I can't believe it,' Amanda said, 'that you wouldn't say a thing to us.'

'It's just been surreal,' Catherine murmured. 'I kept telling myself he would come back.' She took down her hands and laid a finger on the divorce papers. 'Now this,' she said. 'How could he do it? Why would he do it?'

Amanda picked up the papers and read them again. When she came to the reason quoted for the divorce, she put a hand to her mouth. 'Is this really true?' she asked. 'There's someone else?'

'I don't know.'

'He didn't tell you?'

'He didn't tell me a thing. Not even that he was going. He disappeared one morning and left me a letter.'

'Jesus Christ!'

'It didn't say anything about another woman.'

Amanda took a moment to digest this information.

Catherine let out a gasping laugh. 'You see what he did? He filled in the whole bloody sheet for me to sign. Divorce on the ground of his adultery. Good of him, don't you think?'

The two women regarded each other levelly. Amanda sipped her tea, then put down her mug and said, 'Look, I'm not defending him. God knows, there isn't any bloody defence in the world for acting this way. But it's so out of character. Someone like Robert doesn't do this. Is he all right?'

'What do you mean, "all right"?'

'Well, has he been stressed about anything?'

'You think he's had a breakdown?'

'I don't know what to think, Cath. It's all so incredible.'

There was a long silence. Eventually Catherine broke it. 'Christmas,' she said. 'There was something just before Christmas.'

Three months. In the week before they broke for the holiday. She tried to recall it exactly. In the normal course of things, it might not have had any significance but, at the time, it had bothered her briefly. Not enough to mention. Not enough to argue about. But she had been puzzled. Robert coming home late, but not tired, wired-up somehow, as if he was coming down from a high. In any other man she might have guessed he was drunk, but Robert was not drunk: he was fired by some inner victory or revelation. She remembered wondering if he was going to be ill. He had gone to bed, and when she had come upstairs he had been sound asleep, unwakeable, the sleep of the dead or the just.

Or the adulterer, she thought now, stringing Robert's sleeping look, that of an exhausted child, with the colours of Christmas, and the sale that Pearsons had had that week, the paintings and jewellery sold, the unusually good-natured talk of the dealers, the Christmas trees strung on brackets above each shop in the town, and the white lines of lights criss-crossing the street above her. She thought of Robert now, and the images ran together, Robert fragmented in light and a mixture of voices.

'The necklace,' she said.

Amanda frowned. 'What necklace?'

Catherine got up and went upstairs, found the catalogue. When she came down, she threw it on to the table. 'Lot 543,' she said. 'It was in the drawer,' Catherine said, 'with the page folded back.' She glanced again at the illustration.

'Pretty,' Amanda commented.

Catherine sat down again on her chair. 'We had a telephone bidder,' she said. 'The only telephone bid in that section.'

'And you think this was something to do with Robert?'

'Why else would it be in his drawer?' She saw Amanda's doubt and snatched away the catalogue. 'It doesn't matter,' she said.

'Not in the greater scheme of things right now,' Amanda said.

Catherine's eyes were on the tabletop. 'Who is she?' she murmured. 'Are you sure he wasn't with anyone at the airport?'

'No one I saw.'

'You're sure?'

'I can't be sure. Certainly there was no one standing with him or even near him.' She paused. 'But . . .'

'But what?'

'I said to Mark when I came home that Robert had looked peculiar. I couldn't place his expression. Perhaps he was nervous – because I had seen him.'

'Guilty?'

Amanda considered. 'No,' she decided. 'Just wary.'

'And this was last Saturday.'

'That's right.' Amanda propped her elbows on the table. 'Couldn't you have told us?' she asked. 'Didn't you trust us?'

'It wasn't a case of trusting you. I just . . . hoped it would solve itself somehow.'

'By his coming back?'

'I suppose so.'

'And that's what you'd have wanted? That's what you still want?'

'No,' Catherine said. 'Not now.' Colour flooded her face. 'Are you joking?' She pushed back her chair, but made no move to get up. The two sat facing each other, the divorce papers still between them. Catherine's face gave nothing away. She was feeling nothing. She was blank, empty. She closed her eyes, and the afternoon she had spent etched itself on her mind. She had been to see Mr Williams, the man who had owned the painting of the girl. Mr Williams, who had so loved the painting because the subject resembled his wife. He lived alone in a great stone house at the end of a drive of overgrown laurels, two villages away. It was next to the church on the hillside, and was decaying slowly behind its huge walls, weeds growing in the gravel paths and over the old tennis court. 'I went to see a man today,' she observed.

'About this?' Amanda asked. 'About Robert?'

'No,' Catherine said. 'About a painting he sold. I went to see why he had brought it in when for months he's held on to it, selling other things in preference to it. It hung on his landing. You saw it when you came into the house and as you climbed the stairs. But he sold it.'

'Perhaps he needed the money,' Amanda said.

'He did,' Catherine agreed. 'He lives at Sandalwood.'

'That monster?'

'Yes.'

Amanda was watching her. 'What made you think of him?' she asked.

The first time Catherine had visited Mr Williams, he had told her that he and his wife had lived all over the world. He had been posted to Burma, when it was still Burma before the war, and travelled in Malaya. When war had broken out, he had enlisted in the Navy. He had been on the Arctic convoys. He had described Riga to her, a black outpost in a white-grey world. There, he had traded American dollars for Tsarist porcelain, cigarettes for Fabergé. After the war, he and his wife had settled in France.

He had auctioned his life to pay for repairs to the house: the porcelain, the surrealist sketch by Delvaux, the Balinese figures, the dancer's bracelets hung with Sri Lankan silver dollars, silkwork from Paris, and two bronzes he had brought out of Berlin.

Catherine had known him for the five years she had been in the area. A lonely old man living in what had once been a house full of the past, a house he had consistently stripped of his memories. 'Why did you sell your painting?' she had asked him that afternoon, over the tea he had made for her. A gentle old man moving slowly about his kitchen, laying a proper tray, arranging it carefully on the table. He always had a sweet, polite smile and was the soul of old-fashioned civility.

'It was only a painting,' he had told her, and he had closed his eyes as he had stood on the doorstep. 'Things are no good to me now.'

She had thought he was crying, but she had been wrong. He had opened his eyes and shaken her hand as she had given him the cheque for the painting. A dry, businesslike shake, an unsettling touch of veined skin and bone. The same sweet, sad smile as he waved to her when she drove away.

And then she thought of John Brigham's hand. To her surprise, her heart turned over, one lazy flip of desire. She listened almost objectively to the increased beat. John Brigham's hand: practical, long-fingered, sensitive. The warmth of his palm. He had looked at her today with candid directness and humour; yet she had had the strongest feeling that he was not just giving away something he had loved, like Alec Williams, but preparing himself for some moment – readying himself at the edge of a precipitous leap. There was something intensely familiar in his surroundings, in his house. Something that had nagged at her over the last few days.

He had turned and taken it from the dresser.

That was it. That was the thing that nagged at her.

He had taken . . . She tried to remember what it was. She had seen the movement. The way the hand that had touched hers today, and lingered, had snatched something from the dresser. Something small enough to be put into John Brigham's pocket. She frowned now, irritated at the memory and its intrusion. She had not been concentrating, then; she had been sunk in apathy. She had seen it lying there. Yet her gaze had drifted over it.

She took herself through the house again, followed him along the hall. There were William Morris panels on the stairs . . .

There was the dresser, and the glass-framed trials . . .

And then she remembered.

She stared past Amanda, seeing in her imagination the enamelled disc that John had put into his pocket with such haste.

It was a tiny, infinitely delicate portrait of a child. There was a perfectly rendered chessboard spread on a table in front of him, and, by his outstretched hand, a walnut shell halved and turned into a sailboat. There was an unmistakable, unforgettable expression on the child's face.

Once seen, never forgotten.

She straightened in her chair.

'What is it?' Amanda asked.

But Catherine couldn't tell her. Robert had vanished, momentarily, from her mind. All she could think of, all she could see in her mind's eye, was the fantastic, the impossible. The child in the locket.

And the painter of the child, the engraver whose world had been reduced to those few lines on paper. Like the configuration of lines on the papers in front of her on the table. Just a few lines. So much significance.

'Oh, my God,' she whispered to herself, in amazement. 'Richard Dadd.'

Ten

As he climbed the stairs, Robert's fingers closed round the key in his pocket. He suppressed an almost childlike need to run up the flight, two steps at a time, and only the fact that the stairway was narrow, the landings and turning ill lit, stopped him.

He got to his door and opened it.

It was only three rooms: a bed-sitting room, bathroom and kitchen. He walked across the carpet and stood with his hands on the window-sill, looking out at the view of London.

There wasn't much to see: part of a wall, and some heavily netted windows to an office, a higher building that backed on to the apartment block. When he had been shown round, it had been getting dark, and he had seen people moving about across the narrow gulf: a grey-haired woman, a man at a desk. Fluorescent lighting behind them, and banks of VDU monitors. When he had passed the door in the street below, he had known it was a broker's office. Anonymous, like him.

He turned his back, relishing his namelessness. This was what he had wanted: to be left alone, to relinquish an identity, even if it was only for the relatively short times between work and sleep. The rooms belonged to the company he now worked for: the job he was about to start in a week's time. It was a courtesy flat until he found a house, or an apartment, of his own. Not that he would be in a position to buy anywhere until the divorce settlement came through.

At the thought of Catherine, his face clouded. She would have got the papers today. It was done, then. She would realize his intentions. Perhaps she would be angry enough not to oppose him. That was what he wanted. Not to be opposed. Not to be questioned. Just to be released.

He walked over to the two suitcases, still on the floor of the sitting room. So far he had only had time to take out a few clothes. Now he began in earnest. It was only when he got to the bottom of the case, some five or ten minutes later, that he thought of Catherine in any real depth, in any way other than as a convenient caricature of anger.

For some reason, he had brought a copy of her book.

Why he should have seized on this as a memento was beyond him. It was the book that most irritated him: the symbol of her success. Now he looked at the cover for some time, a glossy representation of a fairy scene: Richard Dadd's painting of the meeting between Oberon and Titania.

He found nothing attractive in it; he never had. He had never understood her obsession with the painter. And this was one of the least appealing female figures you could ever imagine, the matronly profile, her expression of bland indifference.

He went over to the only chair, book in hand, and sat down with the picture in his lap. The strange thing was that the woman in the painting looked like the woman he had met before Christmas at a sales conference. He had only been involved peripherally, had only attended because one of the firm's clients had asked him. As their auditor, he had overheard the plans for the party, and been invited. It had been the last day of the conference, in some dirty-looking hotel in Bloomsbury that turned out to be marginally better inside than out.

It was well into the evening; he had probably had a drink too many. He had found himself sitting next to her in a booth of the hotel restaurant. He didn't know who she was; he had never seen her before. She wore a grey, rather sacklike dress that showed brown shoulders. He would have passed her in the street without noticing her. He supposed she was older than the usual office girls; maybe thirty-five. Perhaps older than him, as much as forty.

'You've got a tan,' he had said.

'I've been on holiday,' she told him. 'Morocco.'

They talked about that for a while. And, if he remembered rightly, about Italy, and that she was learning Italian.

'You never know when you'll go somewhere,' she'd said.

He had heard the first slurring of her words. 'You're planning to vanish?' he'd asked.

'Maybe,' she'd said.

Later, much later, they were alone in the booth.

'Robert,' she had said, 'what do you want out of life?'

He had tried to look past her; he had thought someone was ordering a taxi. He had wanted to leave, having some vague idea that he could still catch the last train. 'Ordinary things,' he had told her, partially distracted. 'What does anyone want? Security, health.'

'Security,' she had repeated, and laughed. 'Is that all you want?'

'Is it such a bad thing?'

She'd put her hand on his thigh. Outside, in the rain, he hailed a taxi, intending to leave her on the pavement. Yet when it came she stepped straight into it, and he found himself saying the name of his hotel.

It had probably been one of the worst events of his life. And yet it had had such consequences.

When they got to the hotel, he already knew that he didn't want her. He particularly didn't want her in his room all night. So, as the cab drove away, he took her by the elbow and led her to the side of the building. There was an alley, a walkway through to a rusty little garden beyond. The wine bar down here was closed. They stood in the unlit doorway.

'I'm sorry,' he told her. 'Very sorry.'

It was then that she had stood with her back to the locked door, and told him exactly what they were going to do. He found himself both hungry for and numb to her touch. 'Not here,' he had said. 'Not in the street.'

But it was exactly there. The pleasure of it was overwhelming, the sense of thieved satisfaction. She was not even pretty, yet his desire had been fierce, a kind of desire to be robbed of himself, to be obliterated, out

113

there in the dark, to the rattle of the door frame and the sound of the rain.

Insanity.

And then, at the last moment, he found that he couldn't do what she wanted. She had pushed him away in frustrated astonishment. He had been more humiliated by her silence than if she had laughed at him.

Thank God, he had never seen her again. No one had remarked on their leaving together; probably no one knew.

He began to think about her, and what she had said in the booth. 'Is that all you want?' she had asked him. 'Just that?'

He realized that it was exactly what he wanted: the security of being alone. He wanted to be freed of the claustrophobia of need, his and Catherine's. In fact, he would prefer to have no needs at all.

With a shake of his head, he came back to the present: to this day, this room. He had gone to see his mother that afternoon. That was another need, another duty. He didn't know why he had bothered.

She lived in an old house in Bedford Square, the last still to be developed and smartened up, a yawning great warren of a place. She had largely abandoned it, preferring to live in the basement kitchen for most of her time. He had rung the bell and she came eventually, greeting him with a cigarette in hand. 'Ah,' she had said, smiling. 'The wanderer returns.'

She stepped back and motioned him in. He kissed her cheek, which she had pointedly offered him. He followed her down the hallway and went into the sitting room. She had been sitting in a vast wing chair, watching television.

'I've come to live in London,' he told her.

She sat down with a sigh. 'With Catherine?'

'No.'

'I thought as much. She's been on the phone to me.'

'Has she?'

'Asking where you were.'

He remained standing. His gaze edged round the room at the sofas covered with plastic, and the Oriental pieces dulled under a layer of dust.

His parents had worked for a tobacco company in the Far East. The good old days, his mother called them. Gin and orange at four; cocktails at six; dinner at eight. Endless rounds of entertaining and being entertained. Upstairs, in her bedroom, the wardrobes were still stuffed with fifties frocks, all flowered crêpe-de-Chine in tissue paper. And she still had all the Hong Kong twenty-four-hour tailored dinner suits made for his father; vintage suits with ribbed silk lapels, satin-covered black buttons and cream satin linings.

On the floor above that was his old room: a stripped bed frame and striped pillowcases, his old bookcase with copies of the *Royal Encyclopedia For Boys*. Once, when he was just out of college, before he had met Catherine, he had made the mistake of bringing a girlfriend home, and his mother had mortified him by giving her the grand tour of the house, from the cob-webbed rafters to the basement. The girl had picked up one of his encyclopedias and read aloud from the first paragraph she had turned to. He could still hear her. 'E is for the Eastern Question.' She had laughed. 'How very colonial! And *East Lynne*, Eddystone Lighthouse, and Edward the Confessor.'

'He always was a bookworm,' his mother had said. 'I never saw such a stultifyingly silent child.'

'You never saw any children at all,' Robert had commented, causing his girlfriend to laugh all the more, even though it was the truth. His mother had not wanted his friends in the house, for which he had been secretly glad since she and the house smelt of smoke and damp, and she had taken to stacking newspapers in the halls and on the stairs, and leaving clothes where they dropped; the sight of her had revolted him.

'Where are you living?' she asked him now.

'Hotels,' he lied. 'I'm not in any place very long. Auditing abroad, mostly.' He didn't want to be expected to live there.

'What about your house?'

'We'll sell it.'

'Better tell your wife,' she said.

And even though he had left Catherine he hated that. She wasn't to be laughed at. She was, he supposed, to be pitied.

That night he got into bed early. He felt that he needed to sleep for a very long time. He was not tired, just irritated with a world of emotional desire and absorption pressing in on him. He lay on his back and looked at the rectangle of reflected light that lay across his bed from the window.

All he wanted was to lie in the dark, with the skewed square of light coming in at the window, the residue of reflected light from the street below.

Eleven

Since John had come back, if he dreamed about anything it was the house near Alora. He was walking along the dusty road towards it now, a *finca* of olive trees on a hillside. The grit got into his shoes; he stooped and took them off, and carried on walking with them in his hand. The sun was beating on his back, and the house was exactly as he had first seen it.

It sat just below the brow of the hill, a bare block on a cement stand. No roof, no glass at the windows, just a half-finished project that someone else had abandoned. There was no driveway, just a rutted track turning off the lane that led to the farm on the other side of the hill.

He was thirsty. He could taste the thirst now, in his dream: the dry mouth, the sandy dust. He could hear the rustling of the leaves of the olive trees as they swayed in the midday heat. He walked up to the house and put his hand on the rough surface of the brick, just as he had years ago. He felt its texture under his fingers. Over his head plain black iron poles ran from the top of the wall to the edge of the cement block, forming a framework around the front of the property. Someone had thought of planting vines there before they had considered roof tiles. Now the vines were racing up the supports and out across the makeshift terrace. He knew there would be fruit the following year.

He turned, and gazed back down the hill.

He wasn't a visionary. He had never considered himself to be one, even when he had the art of concept. He could tell a client about his plans for their house, and see it in technical shape. But he had no visions, no emotion. Except, of course, with Claire. From time to time in Rotherhithe he had experienced a flash into the future with all the detail and warmth of life. But it had been rare.

Yet now, as he stood in front of the abandoned house, the roofless block, he had a vision, a sensation of himself as the man who could live there. He saw himself sitting there at night. He saw the pool he would build at the back, not a clean architectural device but a deep, green-walled bath, not pretty, not tiled, not terraced, and with no steps, but a shaded dark-watered tank under a ceiling of bougainvillea, with no formal garden, but the tamarisk trees growing wild around him.

And he saw the rooms, cool and plain. A kitchen, a bedroom, a studio at the back where the sun only came late in the day. A wood-burning stove. A desk.

A year later, when the restoration in Alora was half completed, he left the house in Rotherhithe. It was so much easier to leave Claire behind. It had been four years, and he thought that he had her death in proportion.

He made the mistake of taking with him the china they had bought together. A fortnight later, unpacking it in the Alora house, he had wept over the pattern of ribbons and oranges, a sentimental pattern that he found he couldn't bear. He had gone down to the local market in Alora on the second weekend and bought plates and cups; red clay undersides and glazed brown tops. He found it hard to eat when he was first there: the loneliness was almost tactile, alive, like a snake coiled behind every door. But there was time, empty time he had never allowed himself before. And he forced himself to stare it down, then fill it, even though the ache of loss was more acute in a strange place. He would stare for minutes at a time at combinations of colours. It was not getting himself used to the broader, blanker silences on the hillside that saved him, or the building work on the farmhouse. It was the colours. Different shades of green as the light came across the valley in the morning. Food on his plate in the primaries of peppers, tomatoes and lemons. The skin of aubergines and plums. The olives, when they came into season. Deep lilac shade that crossed his bedroom at night in summer. He just looked at colours.

And he saw himself there now, dreamed himself there, one summer afternoon in the third or fourth year, when his own work was finished on the house, and he had, grudgingly, taken up the design of a villa in Ahaurin el Grande. He saw himself alone in the dark pool behind the house, the temperature over a hundred degrees, the country asleep in the dry heat that drugged the air, a sky of violent blue blazing above him through the trees. He had hauled himself out on to the side and lain on the baking stone, and he had seen Claire's wet footprints, as if she had climbed out of the pool alongside him.

And he saw now what he had not seen then. A body materialized next to him. In his dream he saw the shape of the naked woman's shoulder, her skin reddened slightly by the sun, water running down her back. He pressed his mouth to the drops, and felt the heat under the slippery surface.

In his dream, he ran his hands down her back. She turned to him, laughing, lying back, her hands touching his face, whispering something as she pulled his face to hers, took his hand and guided him to her, now wriggling upright, her hair falling over her face, to sit astride him, the sunlight flickering across her, the stone under him hot to the touch, the body warm and silky in his grasp. He put his hands on her waist; she threw back her head. In the arch of her neck he saw the artery pulse; he closed his eyes in the dream and he felt her enclosing him, burning in his breath.

He took her greedily, urgently, altering both his body and hers so that eventually she was on her back and he was above her on the edge of the pool. She kept his gaze; her arms were spread out at her sides; she wrapped her legs round him. Nothing had ever felt so good, so right, as to be lost with her.

He looked into her eyes, closed his mouth on hers.

And, in the same second, he knew that the woman wasn't Claire but Catherine Sergeant.

He woke, with a jolt, to the cold darkness of his own bed.

Twelve

The van from Pearsons arrived at Bridle Lodge at nine. From the kitchen window John had watched it coming up the drive, and seen Catherine's car directly behind it. He walked out now on to the doorstep as she got out. She crunched across the gravel, smiling at Frith, who ran in circles around her.

'I didn't expect you,' John said.

'I didn't plan to come, until last night,' she told him. He was surprised to see her flush. She put a hand to her hair and smoothed it, as if she was embarrassed, then stepped ahead of him, following his gesture, into the house.

He showed the porters through to the kitchen, where everything that had been in the dresser was now laid haphazardly on the table. Without a word, they began to release the backboard. John switched on the kettle for tea.

'Do you want the doors removed, or taped?' Catherine asked.

'Taped,' he said.

She looked at the table.

There was plenty of mundane stuff from the drawers: receipts, maps, the usual stack of bills. She picked up a paperback, read the back cover, replaced it. He tried not to look directly at her. Every time he did so, he saw drops of water on skin, and felt her fingers laced urgently over his.

They exchanged small-talk, watching the dresser on to the van. After ten minutes or so, Catherine let the men go without making any effort to follow them. Instead, she came back to the kitchen with John and sat down.

'Do you have any paintings?' she asked.

The question, out of the blue, startled him. Automatically he glanced at the door to the hall, to the alarm outside the drawing room.

'Yes,' he told her. 'I have some.'

'Any particular period?' she asked.

'Victorian,' he said.

'Figurative?'

He sat down alongside her, putting the items from the dresser into piles, not replying.

'When I worked in London,' she said, carefully, 'we sold an estate once in Ireland. I went all the way to Limerick. It was a huge house, quite an experience. A tabloid newspaperman had owned it, and he had got bored of fishing in his bloody great river so he was selling up and going to Florida.' She smiled. 'He had made quite a feature of his little *pied-à-terre* in the country, though.' She was watching him closely, speculatively. 'There was a swimming-pool in the cellar, and a bowling alley in the Long Gallery,' she said quietly, 'music videos playing on a twenty-four-hour loop in the bathrooms. He had a full-sized billiard table in the library, and a statue he'd commissioned of a page-three girl. She stood in all her glory, shamelessly holding out a bunch of grapes to an Erskine Nicoll, a Deverell, a Mulready, and six Leech cartoons.'

There was a beat.

He nodded slowly. 'You saw the miniature,' he said.

She took a deep breath. 'Yes, I did,' she said. '*The Child's Problem*. Is it a copy?'

'No. That is, it's not copied by someone else. It's his own copy.'

She put a hand to her throat. 'Original? Genuine?'

'Yes.'

She looked up at the ceiling, closed her eyes, opened them again with a smile. 'Oh, my God,' she said. 'My God.'

He got up, and went out of the room. When he returned, she was still sitting in the same position at the table. He put a small box in front of her, took off the lid, folded back the tissue paper.

She leaned forward, took out the disc slowly, then rested it in the palm of her hand. She said nothing for a long time.

'You know this picture,' he said.

'Yes,' she said. 'I've seen it in the Tate.'

'It's not on public display.'

'That's right.' She turned the miniature this way and that in the light. 'It's extraordinary,' she said. 'It's exactly the same. Exactly the same as the watercolour in the Tate. The scale is perfect.'

He watched her face, seeing her appreciation. 'Claire always thought it was disturbing,' he said.

'It is,' Catherine agreed. 'It really is. It's the most peculiar and frightening painting I think I've ever seen. I've always thought so.'

He drew his chair closer to her, and she tilted the picture towards him. 'It's the child's expression,' she said. 'You think at first that he must have seen something terrible on the chessboard. You see the way he's reaching out his hand, as if he's going to move a piece, the castle?'

'Yes,' John said. 'White to play, and mate in two.'

'Except for the contortion, the way the wrist goes . . . He isn't even looking at the castle. In fact, he's not looking at the board. He's looking beyond it, to something outside the picture. Recoiling from something horrible, terrifying.' She sat back in her chair. 'I always wondered what the problem was, the problem in the title. *The Child's Problem.* What was Dadd thinking of?' she said. 'The problem isn't the chess move. I don't think it's even the knife beyond the chessboard, or the grotesque old man asleep in the chair alongside him. It's something else, beyond the board.'

'Something that only Dadd could see,' John said.

'There's another painting of his,' she said, 'of a woman and two satyrs. The same eyes as these look out at you through leaves. The faces are pulled upwards, as if something has hold of the hair. The brows go up and the eyes slant. All Dadd's eyes were like that eventually. Wide open, showing the whites. Mothers, children. Even the babies.'

John seemed about to say something, but had stopped himself.

Catherine glanced up again from the miniature. 'Where on earth did you get it?' she asked.

'I found it,' he said.

'Found it?' she echoed. 'Where?'

He glanced downwards. 'In a flea-market.'

'No!'

She was gazing at him, a broad, delighted smile on her face.

He felt so guilty for the lie.

'You *found* a Dadd original?' she repeated, and laughed in astonishment. 'But it must be worth a fortune!'

'It is,' he said.

'How did you know it was real?'

'There's a signature.'

She had put the miniature on the table between them, but now picked it up again.

'Turn it over,' he said. 'Look inside.'

'I can't,' she said. 'I may damage it.'

He smiled at her. 'You can resist looking at Dadd's signature?'

She gave a quirky grimace. 'Oh, Jesus,' she breathed. With a slow, gentle movement, she prised apart the fastening. 'You didn't take it to an expert?' she asked.

'No,' he said.

She opened the back. Inside, the fabric was folded tight, with a tiny piece of canvas backing held in place with a brass pin. 'I can't do it,' she said. 'This is a job for a restorer, a specialist. I shouldn't touch it.' She stared down at the canvas and the pin, running the edge of her thumb along the rim of the metal. He looked at her with deeper interest, recognizing that look, the longing.

'It's painted on a little piece of stiff cotton, quite dirty,' he told her. 'Like a corner of a handkerchief, perhaps even of a bedsheet. And there's a scrap of paper in there about two inches square. Dadd's handwriting is on it.'

'Dadd's handwriting is under this canvas?'

'Yes.'

She replaced the miniature on the table. 'You know that he'd killed his father? That he was in lunatic asylums, Bedlam and Broadmoor, for most of his life?'

'Yes,' John said. 'And to think he painted something like this in prison . . .' His eyes went back to Catherine's.

'*The Child's Problem* in the Tate has his inscription on the front top left,' Catherine said, 'in tiny script. You almost need a magnifying-glass.'

'That's right,' John said. 'Only the date and address are different on this.'

Catherine's eyes were fixed on his. 'December 1857,' she said. 'Bethlehem Hospital, London, St George's in the Fields.'

'And this one,' John gestured at the miniature, 'says the fourteenth of November 1885.'

'A month before he died?' Catherine murmured.

'Yes.'

'The last thing he ever did.'

He nodded. 'Probably.'

'Even to the eyes,' she said.

'Even to the empty eyes,' he said, 'looking at empty spaces.'

She sat back in her chair, regarding him. There was

silence for a second or two. 'What did Claire think of it?' she asked.

'She thought I should get it insured.'

'And did you?'

'No,' he said.

'Why not?'

'I don't know,' he said. 'It would have meant telling people I had it.'

She looked at him questioningly. 'Art galleries would be very interested in it. There are so few Dadds anywhere. Most of his paintings have vanished.'

'I know.'

'And to find a new one . . .'

'I know,' he said, cutting short the conversation. He picked up the miniature, put it into the box and replaced the lid. He felt her gaze linger on him, not just the miniature.

'Which is your favourite?' she asked, at last.

'My favourite Dadd painting?'

'No,' she said. 'I meant which is your favourite from the others. You said you had other paintings.'

John passed the miniature from hand to hand. 'I've never had them valued,' he said.

'I didn't mean value. I meant which one has the most meaning for you? Which one do you like best?' She saw his mixed expression. 'You don't think I'm asking so that I can assess them?' she asked.

He didn't reply.

'You think I'm showing an interest because I've got half an eye on commission?' she said. 'Just in case you ever want to sell?'

'No,' he said. 'Of course not.'

'I wasn't asking for that reason,' she said, offended. 'I was asking out of interest. That was all.'

'Don't go,' he said.

'I must,' she replied. 'I'm late already.'

'I'm sorry,' he said. 'I'm defensive about them.'

'It's your prerogative,' she said.

He stepped in front of her as she turned for the door. 'I've collected since Claire died,' he said.

'They're personal,' she said. 'I understand.'

'No. You don't.'

'But I do,' she replied calmly. 'I've lost count of the number of clients who don't want to show me. Or who show me by degrees. I understand very well. But I wasn't asking you as a potential client.'

'Look,' he said. 'Please . . .' And he took her arm. She looked down at his hand; he released her almost immediately.

'I worked in London after Claire died,' he said. 'I wanted nothing in my life. I didn't even want the furniture we had owned together. And then, after a while, when I'd gone to Spain, I bought a painting. It wasn't expensive. It wasn't a Dadd, or anything like him. It was a surrealist picture. Nobody famous. I hung it on the wall.' He moved his eyes away from her face. 'I built my house, and that was all I did, except walk Frith. I walked for miles that first summer. I walked at night. I'd moved out there for the landscape, the difference, but I never looked at the landscape. I couldn't.'

She was still, listening.

'And then, one day, I bought the picture,' he said. His tone had dropped. 'And I thought . . . I can't say what

I thought, exactly . . . that there was something here . . .'

'To fill the empty spaces,' Catherine said.

At last, he raised his eyes.

'Tell me your favourite,' she said softly.

He knew which it was, but there was no way he could tell her. She would know right away. If he told her the title, she would realize what he was talking about. See the weight that his life had become.

He tried to think of something inconsequential.

All he could think of was drops of water. The water in the river below the house as it fell from the weir. The drops of his dream, cool on warm skin. And the way he was drowning now.

'There must be something,' Catherine said.

'There's someone called Sorolla y Bastida,' he said. 'Spanish. There's a wonderful painting . . . it has two women . . . the blue behind the women is beautiful. The sea, beautiful . . .'

He couldn't continue. He took her hand. This time she let it lie within his. He put the miniature on the table.

'What do you think Richard Dadd saw beyond the picture,' he asked, 'that was so terrible?'

She didn't hesitate. 'The past,' she told him.

He walked out into the hallway, taking her with him, stopped outside the drawing room and keyed the alarm.

When it was released, he looked at her only briefly before he opened the door and took her inside.

It was a large room with a huge window that must

have looked out on to the lawn, but the curtains were drawn. In the gloom, Catherine saw only shapes: frames on the wall; what seemed to be a sculpture by an opposite door. The panelling close by them was the same as that which ran up the stairs.

'Have you been in here before?' John asked.

'Yes,' she said. 'Mrs Aston used to see me in here.'

They had tea in here, she remembered. The frail old lady had held that tradition, taking an age to bring a little trolley to the window. She had boiled a silver kettle on a spirit hob. All around them the furniture had been mahogany, the larger pieces coated with dust. An enormous French mirror had been on the left-hand wall, six feet tall and four feet wide, with a grey panel above the bevelled glass. It had all been sold: sold, Catherine understood now, to accommodate the new owner, and whatever he wanted to put in its place.

John switched on the light. He walked into the centre of the room, but she stayed where she was. Shock rolled over her.

Three vast sideboards occupied the back and side walls, all matching, eight or nine feet long. They were Jacobean, old oak, very dark. Dozens of items lay on their broad tops. Bow and Chelsea porcelain, vases, dishes, salt cellars, scent flasks, figurines, plates, tea canisters. There was silver, but more porcelain. The nearest sideboard was a flood of ornate gilded blue; towards the back a line of plates echoed the same shade.

She recognized the soft-paste porcelain of Bow from the mid-1700s. The two salt cellars before them were the most complicated design of crayfish and shell, modelled in detail so that they looked almost alive. At one end there was a small service, again from Bow, transfer-printed in brown and painted with enamels of some Chinese design. On one sideboard there was perhaps a hundred thousand pounds' worth of infinitely fragile craftsmanship.

She took a step forward. The other sideboards displayed much more of a mixture. On one there was an 1860s plaster bust of Marianne, of the kind you sometimes saw over town-hall doors in rural France; it stood on a small, battered gilded box. A nineteenth-century Baltic bedroom cabinet dominated the third – a confection of white paint and crown-topped columns, with a white marble figure, barely forty centimetres high. 'This is by Henri Laurens,' she said. She ran her finger slowly along the lines of the female nude, roundly misshapen, with a rigid back, heavy breasts, arms raised over the head, which was twisted on an impossibly long neck.

John had still said nothing, but Catherine was aware that he was standing behind her. She turned to say something to him, and saw the Sargent portrait.

She was on the far wall, behind where John was standing. She was half sitting, half lying on a seat by a window, her head tilted, her arm extended along the back-rest. Summer light flooded her face, her dark coiled hair, the diamonds that glittered at her throat, the bare shoulder above the cream-coloured gown. Her face reflected removed, even bored, calm. Beyond the open window were a bank of roses and distant parkland, shimmering in the haze of an August day. Her dress cascaded to the floor in deep folds of cream satin.

As the fabric fell further from the light from the window, the painter had picked up its drop in swiftly executed single lines of colour, shining in the shadows. A shawl, patterned with red and gold, had dropped to the floor.

Catherine walked forward.

John Singer Sargent's style was unmistakable. The work of the greatest Victorian portrait artist shone out in the subdued light, spilling a summer day into the north-facing drawing room that, even with the curtains open, would be dark. Voluptuous, light, fresh and lovely: the woman's flawless skin gleamed above the dress. One of Sargent's heiresses. One of the endless procession of American and French women who had sat for him in the 1880s and 1890s and, with the English aristocracy, had bored him beyond endurance.

John was watching Catherine's face. 'Her name was Amy Clanville-Wright,' he said. 'She was sixteen.'

Catherine said nothing. She couldn't. She walked to his side.

'I was given her by a client to settle a debt,' he said.

Catherine stared at him. 'A debt?'

'I built him a house in Guadalhorce, and he couldn't pay,' he explained, and smiled. 'I think he was a crook. One of those East End boys living in Spain to escape the long arm of the law. I never dared ask how he made his cash. And I never dared ask where he'd got Amy Clanville-Wright. I dread to think.'

'John,' Catherine said, 'this is serious money. Are you crazy, keeping it here? My God!' She turned. 'And this . . .' she said, waving at the porcelain.

'I've bought it over the last eight years.'

'All this? Everything?'

'All of it,' he said.

'The Laurens . . .'

'I had to have her,' he said.

She met his eye. Then, she looked about herself again, trying to take it in. 'I don't know what to say to you,' she said.

'It isn't about money,' he said.

'Not about money!'

'No,' he said. 'You know that, of all people.'

And she did. She knew the fixations and passions. Above all, she knew what came out of loneliness. She glanced back at John, with sadness.

'Don't pity me,' he said.

'I don't,' she said.

'I didn't buy them to collect,' he said, 'although I *did* collect. I bought them because they reminded me of what the world was like.'

She waited.

He went to the Laurens and rested his hand on the figure's neck, on the cool and perfectly smooth texture. 'It was made for love,' he said, 'not money or status, but because it had to be made. A compulsion.'

He looked across at the porcelain. 'A compulsion to make something wonderful,' he said, 'to be alive in the world.'

She put her hands over her face.

'What's the matter?' he asked.

'It's nothing.'

But it was something. She had begun to cry. 'Catherine,' he said. 'Catherine.'

She was overcome with memories. Herself, alone,

while she studied. Herself as a little girl, alone in a house, sitting at a window, very like the window in Sargent's painting, looking out on to an empty garden. Playing with the flaking paint of the sill, making it into patterns, drawing with a pencil around them, while the day drifted away. She saw herself with Robert, making do with less than she needed, for an idea of what he was, instead of what he was in reality, a private person who would never bend.

She saw herself in the empty spaces. And John Brigham too, scribbling in time, filling it with colours and shapes. Living in paintings.

That's all they did, she thought. They lived in paintings.

He held out his hand: a hand that had sent a rush of feeling through her, a telegraphed impression of longing, just yesterday.

'Catherine,' John said. He took her in his arms. 'Catherine.'

It was nothing more than a whisper, in a room crowded with desire.

Contradiction: Oberon and Titania, 1854–8

There were new rooms. He had been told that the better class of criminal patients would be moved from the ordinary wards, and that the new rooms were large and airy, with pictures and statues. He thought of them while he was on the ward, keeping silence while others ranted in the dormitory cells. In his silence, that leafless forest, branches locked over his head, footfall soaked into the earth, smothered by sandy ground, he waited.

Seeing airy rooms, airy rooms.

On the day he was moved, he was shown a book of his confinement. He had been quiet and amenable, footfall lost in smothering sand, head bowed under the ceiling of branches, so that, when they came to take him, he was calm.

He looked at the book, laid out on the great oak table. In it was written the date of his admission, his trial, and his transfer from Maidstone prison.

He had leaned over the page, tracing the copperplate, fixated on the curvature of the lettering and the neatness of the figures. He put his hand on the page to *absorb its contours, its ridges and rises, its mountains and valleys. Inside the scroll of the downward strokes were rivers, their moisture coiling in warming drops on the fine tipping slant of the R, the expansive curve of the D.*

These things were in his name: rivers and drops of oil and drops of paint and drops of blood. In his name and the dates of his life were continents and countries. He had come here on 22 August 1844 – he pressed his fingertips to the line – in a strait-waistcoat and his blue cloak, his hands shackled, a dark beard and combed hair, a Christ in chains, driven by the Devil.

It was May. In the new rooms he found a calendar. It was the first thing he saw. He didn't care to view the country from the windows: the lost city, the distant grey edge of the Thames. He cared only to walk up and down beside the wall with the door that had admitted him. He asked who bore the expenses of the rooms, who paid the salaries of the doctors. He asked in which direction was the Keeper's Room, the sink and water closet, the staircase. He asked where were the iron rods that made the cages that communicated with sleeping rooms, like the one he had inhabited for several months in the past.

For some time after he was taken to the new rooms, he could not get the thought out of his head: who owned the rooms, who had built them, who paid for them – where he was in the building as he stood in the different places, where the corridors ran. The voice of the minor demon, who sat with him in the long hours, told him that he had been cut adrift. He turned his head and leaned on the wall of the airy room, and tried to hear, through his temple, the voice of the building, its roots growing down through the clay and gravel beneath.

He took a place in the corner, with his back to the light.

Edward Brigham, his new attendant, brought him his easel. Dadd drew a line on the floor to keep the other patients away. Behind the line, the Devil whispered and writhed, subdued by the changes, muttering in sleep.

He had begun this painting three years before. He thought that perhaps it would take him still another year. He had marked it out in a grid, and worked from the bottom right-hand corner upwards. It would have been easier to work in the opposite direction, downwards from the left: that way he would not have had to hold his arm and hand at such an impossible angle. But, as his elbow and shoulder took the strain of the painting, they carried it, and he could feel himself crawling upwards, inch by inch, slowly towards completion, like the snails and insects that inhabited his pictures, and took week upon week, month upon month, to illustrate.

Last year, in addition to Contradiction, he had painted the last of the Passions. Sketches for each torment: for duplicity and disappointment, grief and anger. In 1853, he had painted poverty and splendour, wealth, idleness and treachery. All watercolours. Jealousy and hatred were taken from Shakespeare. He remembered Othello, and had taken Jealousy from there. Ancient days, it seemed, since he was ever in a theatre, but he remembered Othello and the blacking of the actor's face.

In Hatred *he could not help himself. He painted the Duke of Gloucester – 'see how my sword weeps the poor King's death' – but he didn't paint Gloucester's face above the body: he painted his own, staring at the long blade.*

Jealousy *and* Hatred *had been painted within days of each other. He couldn't separate them: they were woven, knotted in his head.* Murder *was easy: his brush flowed. Cain standing above Abel, a club in his hand, the bodies almost indistinguishable from each other. This was what he could never tell others, not even Mr Hood, who had been so understanding of his work. That he and his father were conjoined in the same way as the Biblical brothers, sealed for ever in the same terrible moment. He had stood above his father, connected to him by ties of blood in more than one sense. He would think about this often: the hand to the weapon, the weapon to the throat. Such were family ties: the constriction, the conjunction, the dispatch.*

After it, his hand was shuddering. Brigham, with kindness in his touch, took away the paints.

In the bottom of Contradiction, *he had painted an archer. Grotesque, with his arm drawn back, he is aiming at the fairy queen. Sprites struggle to save her life, but she remains unaware. So unaware, in fact, that she has crushed another tiny winged figure under the ball of her foot. She is cruel. Bulky, unappealing and cruel, dominating the painting, while scenes of frantic defence unravel around her.*

He couldn't bring himself to love her. His Titania was rigid, static, swollen with greed, sated with bodily lust. She had changed since he last drew her twelve years earlier, grown huge, self-satisfied, bored, unflinching.

She was the embodiment of anger, the central core of the quarrel between fairy king and queen. He disliked her with an increasing passion, an increasing need to be free of her. And yet she grew there in the centre of his mind, taking on a bright yellow gown and a robe that hung from her hand and trailed below her feet, representing all the distortions, details and objects that had come to possess him. He longed to be free of her. He longed to rush out into the daylight and breathe fresh air.

He longed for that air to blow through him, and make him clean.

He painted obsessively in the new rooms, filling the days with centaurs, wings, sprites, fauns and fantastical creatures. By the end, it was agony to fill the last quarter of the picture, the upper left-hand side. His neck and shoulders groaned; his eyes hurt.

The creatures crept into the paint and blossomed there, wriggled out of the brush, spilled themselves across the canvas. At night, when he went to bed, but only occasionally to sleep, he could see them, the dew dripping from their clothes and running down every surface, trickling from the leaves, soaking the grasses.

He finished the painting at the end of the month.

When he stood up at last, and looked out, the year had turned miraculously to summer.

Thirteen

Friday morning, in the early hours, he heard a bird singing loudly. John had no idea what species it was, only that the song was extraordinary, and seemed much louder because of the silence of the dark. It was in a tree somewhere close to the house, and the song was a true melody. Lying flat on his back, he had been awake for more than an hour.

He had met Catherine the previous evening in a local pub, a small place in the next village. Over the meal, the conversation, predictably, had turned to Richard Dadd.

'I wrote a book about him,' Catherine said.

'Did you? I'm sorry, I should have known that.'

She shrugged. 'I don't see why. It wasn't a bestseller. It sold about three copies.'

'You're being modest.'

'I'm not,' she retorted. 'I produced it when there was a retrospective for him. OK, it sold a few while the exhibition was on, but not many after that.'

'I'd like to read it.'

'It's more about the paintings than Bedlam or Broadmoor.'

'So much the better.'

'I rarely meet anyone who's even heard of him.'

'Do you have a copy I can borrow?'

'Yes, I . . .' She frowned.

'What is it?' he asked.

'I have several,' she said, 'but I think Robert took one.'

'He did?'

'There's a gap in the bookshelf. I'm sure it was my book.'

'Is it so surprising that he should take a copy?' John asked.

'Yes,' she said. 'He thought Dadd was grotesque.'

'Well, so he could be.'

'Yes, but . . .' She lifted a hand to her face. 'Robert thought it was all pretty much a waste of time.'

'Just Dadd?'

'Art generally.'

John frowned. 'That's a lot of your life not to have in common.'

'He wasn't obstructive about it,' Catherine said.

'Nevertheless.'

She had finished her food. She put down her knife and fork slowly. 'I met Robert when I first moved to London, straight out of college,' she said. 'I was waiting for a train, actually.'

'You were working there?'

'Yes. For an auction house.' She smiled. 'A little bigger than Pearsons.'

'And Robert worked in the City?'

'Yes. He had just finished his articles for an accountancy firm.'

'So you would have been twenty-one, twenty-two?'

'Twenty-one,' she replied.

'I was in London fifteen to twenty years ago,' John said. 'Took my degree there. Lived in Hammersmith.'

'Earls Court,' she responded, pointing at herself.

'Glamour.'

'Yes.' She giggled at his exaggeration. 'I had a rotten little bedsit. No view, and hot water every other day. Oh, and a nice verdigris collage on one wall.'

'I can beat that,' he replied. 'When I was a student, I lived in a kitchen.'

'What?'

'Really. I had a job in a kitchen, and I got thrown out of my flat – well, it was a squat, to tell the truth – so I used to sleep in the kitchen. About three months in all.'

'Bed and breakfast, then?'

He pulled a wry face. 'I won't go into details.'

She smiled, then glanced away. 'Though it wasn't a very nice time overall,' she added.

'Any particular reason?' he asked. 'Besides the allure of the verdigris.'

'Well . . . my parents had died a couple of years before,' she said, 'in a car accident.'

'Oh, I'm sorry,' he said. He waited for some other detail, but none came. 'In London?' he prompted eventually.

'No,' she said. 'They worked abroad. They were in Africa.'

'Permanently?'

'They worked all over the place,' she said. He

watched her hand describe slow circles on the tabletop, pursuing the grain of the oak. 'They were on a dirt track and another car was following them. The driver behind – they were in a convoy of three – said that the car flipped so slowly and landed so gently he was sure they would both be OK. But they weren't. My father was killed instantly.'

He waited, trying to read her face. 'What kind of work did they do?' he asked.

'They were with an aid agency. They weren't home very often. Never had been.'

'Still, you were close?'

'Yes,' she said.

'And this happened in your final year at school, would that be? Or your first year at college?'

'At school.'

'Very tough,' he commented. 'Are you an only child?'

'Yes,' she said. 'Are you?'

'No,' he replied. 'I have a sister, Helen.'

She smiled. 'Older or younger?'

'Younger. She lives in London.'

'Do you see much of her?'

He shook his head. 'I haven't seen her for some time,' he said. 'She . . . she's very busy.'

'Doing what?'

He glanced up at her. 'Sorry?'

'Doing what?' Catherine repeated. 'Working?'

'Yes,' he said. 'She's in television.'

'Oh,' Catherine said. 'As an actress?'

'No. She's a designer. I think the last thing she worked on was *Byzantium*.'

It was a well-known historical series that had come

high in the year's ratings. Catherine looked impressed. 'And she would . . . do what on that?'

'Come up with the concept of how it should look, the locations, the overall tone, working with the director.'

'But that's an amazing job,' Catherine said. 'She must be an interesting person.'

'Yes,' he said. He did not want to talk about Helen, or what she represented to him. 'She *is* quite interesting.' He hoped she could not hear the irony in his voice.

The waitress came; they looked at the pudding menu, then ordered coffee.

Catherine glanced around the room, and back at him; then she ran her hand over her face, and rested her head on it.

He gazed at her. It was strange how the head resting on the hand affected him. He had been drawn to her earlier in the day, felt bound by the kiss, even overwhelmed by the sensation of her in his arms, but something far more powerful and basic took hold of him now. He looked at her hand, its shape, the smooth texture of her skin, the shape of the fingers and the angle of the wrist, and suddenly wanted her. It took the strength out of him. He wanted to feel her skin; he wanted his mouth on her. He crossed his arms over his chest as if to hold the feeling in.

She was not looking at him now but at the people at another table. Then she turned back. 'How long were you and Claire married?' she asked.

'Four years.'

'And was there someone in Spain?'

'No.'

'That's a long time to be on your own.'

144

He didn't reply. He felt Claire somewhere at the back of his mind, where she had been for the last two or three years. She had finally retreated from his daily consciousness; on first realizing it, he had felt guilty, then saddened and relieved. She lived there, half-way to being forgotten, an icon of what it was to be loved rather than a woman of flesh and blood. From time to time he would concentrate on her, with a kind of two-dimensional longing. She was no longer living in his mind but, rather, reproduced there.

He noticed that Catherine was watching him. There was a curious expression on her face. 'I saw them afterwards,' she said.

'I'm sorry – saw who?'

She blushed, made a face, as if she had said something out of place. 'It doesn't matter.'

'Saw who?' he repeated.

She bit her lip. 'Did you ever see Claire?' she asked.

He thought of the dream, the footprints. 'I saw where she had walked,' he said quietly. 'The imprint.'

There was a perfect silence. She did not say, as he had half expected, something placatory, that it had perhaps been an hallucination, some false memory. She accepted it; she nodded.

'They were in my room,' she explained simply. 'About a week after the funeral.' She sat back in her chair, her hands clasped in her lap. Her face was calm; thoughtful rather than unhappy. 'I came upstairs,' she continued. 'It was early in the year. It was dark and I hadn't put on the light when I walked into my bedroom. I saw them standing . . .' She stopped.

'In the room?'

She frowned. 'It was very odd,' she said. 'I don't mean just seeing them. But they were standing on either side of my bed, very straight, very still. And at the time I didn't think, How peculiar that you're here. That was the strangest part. I didn't think that at all, or anything like it. I just wondered why they said nothing. They were like sentries on either side of the bed.' She crossed her arms. 'I put on the light,' she said, 'and they stayed for three or four seconds. I saw the light on their clothes, the colours come up after the shadows. I saw the colour of my mother's hair. I saw the ring she always had on her thumb, an African ring.'

John thought of the distinctness of Claire's footsteps in his recurring dream in Alora, and how they had lived with him, how he sometimes thought that he saw them when he was awake, and how he accepted their presence unreservedly. 'Did it frighten you?' he asked.

'No,' she said. 'But I kept seeing the amber in the ring. It was in a thick silver setting, with a kind of hatched pattern in the silver.' She smiled at him hesitantly now. 'Do you know a painting called *The Last Chapter* by Martineau?'

'No,' he said.

'Oh, well, it doesn't really matter. But I had a print of it. It's a wonderful painting for the firelight. A girl is reading a book with only the light of the fire and . . .' her voice trailed off '. . . she's wearing a sash, with a hatched, criss-cross pattern . . . the two stuck together, the colours of the clothes, the painting, the patterns. And sometimes Dadd did that kind of shading. I would glimpse that design, a sort of echo, when I was doing

146

other things. Working, or sitting on a bus, or . . . I was crazy, I suppose.'

'No,' he told her. 'That kind of crazy is sane. A repeating pattern, running through, everywhere you look.' And he thought of particular designs he had done after Claire's death in which he had inadvertently used drawings she had made for costume, the cut or angle of a shape. How it came out in everything. How everything was linked. Paintings, shade, shape, memory, feelings: longing or desire or preoccupation. How satisfying it was to draw the line and find it linked two disparate objects in your mind.

Catherine was giving him a bright smile of gratitude. They lapsed into silence; he paid the bill. After another couple of minutes, they went out of the pub together. They crossed the car park and paused by his car.

'Thank you for the meal,' she said. She was holding her own keys.

'You're very welcome.'

'Have you finished the work on the river?' she asked.

'For now,' he said. He looked at the keys in her hand. 'Would you like to walk down to the bridge?' he asked her.

'Yes,' she said, and put the keys into her pocket.

The village street was quiet. Only one car passed them as they went down the long, gentle slope to the eighteenth-century bridge that John had seen almost swamped by floodwaters earlier in the year. It was a narrow bridge, with two small niches on both sides half-way across, so that pedestrians might avoid the traffic.

They stood there now, looking at the water-meadows

on one side and the river on the other. Two or three hundred yards out in the meadows there were blurred white shapes.

'Can you see them?' Catherine asked. 'The swans?'

And so they were: three pairs, heads dipped into the short grass, so that they presented curious shallow figures, almost horizontal. Six white ghostlike boats moving across the dark canvas of the fields. They might have been invisible if it hadn't been for the moon.

'Did you see the swans in the fields near Dorchester last week?' Catherine was asking him. 'I counted at least twenty.'

He looked at the meadows, the water pouring out from under the bridge arches and swirling into the wider downstream reaches. He took Catherine's hand and crossed the little road, stepped down beside the river on to the narrow chalk path under the trees.

It was impossible to walk alongside each other so he went ahead, still clasping her hand behind him, not looking back at her, until they had been walking for more than a minute, and the path broadened where the river widened and two tributaries joined: there was a wide, rushy gap of water and a few feet of gravelly shore. On each bank, trees dipped down to the river. He knew that, behind him, the land stretched away to the foot of Derry Woods, though nothing could be seen of the woods now. In fact, he could see nothing but the shadows of the trees on the bank, and the lazy movement of the river, a slow dance where the waters merged, breaking up the reflection of the moonlight.

He realized that Catherine had stopped, and was staring at the water.

'What is it?' he asked.

'I've been waiting for them to come back,' she said. 'I've been waiting for my mother's hand.'

He drew her arm so that it locked behind his back. She said nothing, but turned towards him. He could barely discern her face, although he saw the lightness of her skin, the fall of her hair on her shoulders.

'They won't need to,' he whispered. 'I'll stand with you now.'

She remained stock still for a second, then put her head into the crook of his shoulder. There was nothing but the whispering of the river, the black and white photographic print of water and trees, so distinct in its contrasts that it was almost abstract.

They were part of a pattern, a ribbon of light and dark. He felt the world fragment, move and alter. He felt a rush, a disorientation. He shifted his balance to hold her closer, pressing his mouth to her neck, her face. She tilted her head, returned the pressure of his touch. He lifted her free hand and pressed it to his mouth, then turned up the palm and ran his lips from fingertip to wrist.

He heard her intake of breath. She put an arm round his neck, tightened the embrace in the small of his back. And the only picture in his mind then and afterwards was the light on the water: the cold moonlight breaking and rejoining, breaking and rejoining, as the water rolled past them, under the wide span of the arches, and beyond the bridge.

Now John turned on his side in the bed, and felt the

faint trickle of cold air from the open window. The bird had stopped singing; the silence it left was almost tangible. He listened for a while, hoping it would continue, then turned back.

Catherine was lying at his side, asleep, her head turned down into the pillow so that he could not see her face.

Tentatively, he reached out and touched her; felt her warmth.

And, for the first time in years, certainly for the first time without grief, he cried, quietly and steadily, in the dark, with his hand in hers.

Fourteen

The knock on the dressing-room door of the London theatre came as Nathan Fitzgerald was leaving.

'There's a woman to see you.' It was one of the front-of-house girls, still in her black uniform, with a coat thrown over it.

'I've seen them all,' he said.

She grinned at him. He shut the door after him and slung the rucksack over his back. He was always the last of the cast to leave, and tonight had been no different: he had had an interview with the *Evening Standard*, given while he lay on his back with his feet propped on the dressing-room wall, the only comfortable position for a back that arched fiercely after every performance. He winced now, and the girl glanced at him. 'Still a problem?'

'Bloody chiropractor's no good,' he complained.

'You shouldn't throw yourself around the stage, maybe,' she suggested. 'Or anywhere else.' They came out on to the stairs. She started down them, but pointed to the entrance to the stalls. 'She's in there, and won't leave,' she said. 'You'd better hurry up – Webster's wanting to shut up shop.'

Price sighed. 'Who is it, anyway?' he asked. 'Has she got a name?'

'Brigham,' the girl said, over her shoulder. 'Helen Brigham.'

He tried to remember, as he walked towards her, how long it had been since he had seen her. Maybe three weeks. Maybe four.

She was sitting near the front, her knees drawn up on to the seat, her large black velvet coat wrapped round her. She looked fragile. A small, thin body and a child-like face. She had cut her hair: it was cropped and spiky, and only added to her air of edgy vulnerability.

Deliberately he didn't sit beside her. Instead, he walked along the row in front and took the seat slightly to one side.

'I'm here,' she said. 'You told me not to come, but I did anyway.'

'It's OK,' he said. 'I didn't mean you to keep away for ever.'

'Didn't you?'

He avoided the question. 'How are you?'

'I'm fine,' she said. It was her standard response. She was always fine, even in the throes of one of her moods.

He studied her now, trying to gauge her state of mind. 'Did you see the show?' he asked.

'No,' she said. 'I've seen it often enough.'

When they had been together she had come frequently, sometimes seeing the whole show or just part of it. Sometimes she stood in the wings, which he had tried to discourage as he could feel her gaze.

'We've got another Daniel,' he said, naming a character.

'So I hear. Is he any good?'

'Yes.'

'He'll be taking the shine from you,' she said.

'Nothing can do that.'

She smiled. 'Oh,' she said. 'That's right. I forgot. You're an actor.'

There was a silence.

'How are you really?' he asked.

She looked to the stage. 'I got fired,' she said.

'What? When?'

'Today.'

'Oh, shit. How did that happen?'

She pulled the coat tighter across her. 'I'm not allowed to have any opinion at all,' she said. 'And this . . . this Price . . .'

'Price is directing?'

'Yes.'

He had seen her tears many times; he almost could grade them according to authenticity. But this seemed sudden and real: she put one hand over her mouth, then both over her face.

He reached out and touched her knee. 'It's a misunderstanding, surely.'

'No,' she said, from behind her hands. 'No.'

Out of the corner of his eye, he saw the manager, Webster, come to the door, and signal him that he was switching off the lights.

'Listen,' Nathan said, 'come outside with me.'

She carried on sobbing; childlike snuffles that now,

he guessed, were probably intentionally prolonged. He patted her knee. 'Up you get,' he said. 'Webster wants to go home to his cocoa, and so do I.'

She appeared from behind her hands. 'You don't like cocoa,' she muttered, with a comic sad smile.

'Then we'll go to the Metro,' he said.

She stood up almost immediately, the smile widening. She followed him to the edge of the row, and linked his arm. 'I've missed you,' she said.

His heart fell about a hundred feet into an abyss.

The Metro was crowded.

Several people smiled when they saw him. Then their gaze went to Helen, and back to his face. They were given a table facing into the body of the restaurant. Helen shuffled along the bench seat, and wriggled out of the coat. She seemed pleased to be noticed with him, he thought.

'I'm not going to eat,' he said.

'Oh,' she remonstrated. 'Just something.'

'I'm not hungry,' he said. 'I'm very tired, Helen. I really do have to go home in a little while.'

She dropped the menu onto the table. 'We've only just walked through the door, and already you're telling me you have to go,' she said.

'OK,' he said. 'I'm sorry. But I'm not hungry. You have something.'

She did. She ordered a glass of wine and the Italian plate. He hid his frown. He knew it was a code – he knew her. They had been to Italy at Christmas, to Florence. He had hated it. He didn't like galleries. He didn't like churches. But she had insisted; she had even taken a little notebook and camera. *Research*. She had been there before, as a student. She kept talking about paintings, and how much, how intimately, she understood them. It was in Florence that he had known for sure that he could not bear to be with her any more, and it had been sad, very sad, to be with her, with all her enthusiasm, taking the notes and the photographs, and to know that he would soon tell her he was leaving her.

It had been her idea that they lived together. He had always resisted it. She had talked about it almost from the first moment they met, and she could be persuasive. My God, persuasive wasn't in it. She could be exhausting, monopolizing him. Very sexy at first. Very wearing, very boring after the first two months. And the moods.

Then he had lost his shared apartment. He took advantage of her, he could see that. That he had used her to avoid looking for anywhere else was not an appealing character trait, so he had tried to ignore it. But in Florence he had known he could not spend any more time with her.

She had made plans. She was good at that – good at organizing. It was her job, she would point out to him, laughing.

So she had organized everything: the holidays they had together, and the weekends. She was alarmingly generous, and he had thought she must have private money. They went to Paris, to Crete and Sardinia. She booked them a long weekend at a place in Cornwall, and tried to teach him to sail. She had been adamant about it. 'You'll sail, and look like those thirties film stars,' she had told him. 'It's amazingly good for the image, Nathan. Think about it. Outdoor guy, blue sea.'

But he wasn't a sailor. He wasn't anything, it seemed to him, that she wanted him to be. He was an actor, but he wasn't literary, and he didn't like art, and he wanted to be down the pub, and perhaps go running with the two mates he had shared the flat with.

'I'm an ordinary person,' he would tell her.

'You're an extraordinary person,' she would correct him. And she would wave a newspaper at him. 'It says so here in the reviews.'

'I'm an "extraordinary actor",' he quoted. 'Otherwise I'm just a bloke. Don't make me something I'm not.'

'You won't make a name for yourself propping up a bar in the Mile End Road.'

'I don't want to make a name for myself,' he had told her. 'I'm not some superannuated grandee of the bloody theatre. I'm twenty-six.'

'You're lying,' she had retorted. 'All actors are egotists.'

Perhaps she was right, and the man-of-the-people was a nametag he wore, but he didn't want to go to showbiz parties, or stand around the Royal Academy at the summer show pretending he knew his arse from his elbow.

'Look,' he said, one day as they lay in bed, 'you've got to understand this. I'm a boy from Salford. That's what I am.'

'And that's what you want to be all your life?' she had replied, taunting.

'Yes,' he had told her, as he got out of bed.

He looked at her now. 'What have you been doing with yourself these last few weeks?' he asked.

'Working.'

'With Price.'

'For him. Much good it's done me.'

'There'll be another job.'

To his horror, she began to cry again. 'There won't be another job,' she said. 'No one will take me.'

'You're exaggerating.'

'I'm not.'

'You're just depressed over . . .' He realized what he'd said as soon as it was out of his mouth, but it was too late.

'I've got a good reason to be depressed, haven't I?' she demanded. 'You walk out on me . . .'

He couldn't deny it. He had told her the moment they got back from Florence. In fact, to lessen the tension for himself – selfishness, selfishness – they had barely put their bags on the floor of her flat before he told her he was going. He couldn't see the logic in unpacking his case only to repack it in the same week.

'Going?' she had echoed. 'Going where?'

Of course he was sorry. But it had never been a long-term relationship, as far as he was concerned. He was stupid enough, cruel enough, to tell her so.

'Why?' she had said, sinking into a chair. 'Why?'

Because she was so helplessly clinging. Because she never woke up in the same mood. Because he was forever guessing what he had done that day to upset her. Because she would sometimes sing all day, or cry all day. Because she wanted, planned, visualized a future with the full entourage – the children, the admiring friends, the fawning fans, the full celebrity-couple status. Because other people, who had known her longer than he had, told him she was crazy. And they were right. Because she wanted to suck out his bloody soul with her questions. Because he wanted to breathe again, and not be looking over his shoulder, afraid she was at his back, watching him.

But he didn't tell her that. 'I'm not ready,' he had said, eventually, 'for everything you want.'

'I'll change,' she had offered.

She had held his hand tightly as he tried to get out of the door.

'I'll ring you tonight,' he lied.

'Meet me tomorrow.' She was clutching at his arm.

'I will,' he said.

But he didn't. For two weeks, he ignored all her calls, emails and text messages. Then he saw her, by accident, at the Royal Festival Hall. He had gone to meet someone, a woman. Helen was just coming out of the bookstore. She stared at him, then made a little waving motion with one hand. He had turned away.

Now the food was delivered to the table. She didn't touch it; just sat looking at it.

'I'm leaving the show in three weeks,' he told her.

She glanced up at him. 'You are?'

'I've got an offer in New York.'

There was a second's pause. 'Doing?'

'The same play.'

'On Broadway?'

'Yes.'

It was hard to hide his excitement. He didn't mean to hurt her. As she looked at him, he knew in that instant that she had come back to him to try again. He saw a flash of some complicated, strange emotion pass over her face.

'Perhaps I should come to New York too,' she said brightly. 'A new start. Perhaps they would like me over there.'

He waited a beat. 'Helen,' he said.

She stood up. Her eyes were full of tears; one hand lay across her stomach. Then she leaned down, kissed his cheek, and snatched up her coat.

He had a horrible misgiving, a premonition. 'Why did you come tonight?' he asked. 'Specifically tonight?'

'It doesn't matter,' she replied.

'But where are you going?'

She put on her coat. A girl at the next table glanced at them both, and smiled behind her hand. Helen froze for a second, then continued, eyes downcast, movements fumbled. 'I will have a holiday for a while,' she said. 'I think I will go and see my brother.'

She nodded to herself, and went out of the door without looking back at him.

Sketch to illustrate the passions: Treachery, 1853

A new physician came to Bedlam in 1853. Brigham took Dadd to see him: a walk along the galleries and down a staircase, past the pump room, where a vast cast-iron boiler was rattling behind the doors. He would have liked to stop and listen to the sound, the choke of steam echoing along the steps and tiled walls. But he was not allowed to linger. They carried on – small, high, square windows cast smaller squares of ochre on the red floor edged with blue tile, as if streams ran along the edges – until they reached Dr Hood's room.

Dadd painted him soon after. The physician was sitting on a chair without a desk before him, facing the door, very composed, hands laced in his lap. He had a solid gaze. He wore a dress coat of black, a black waist-coat and trousers, a starched shirt and black stock. Remembering him, Dadd painted him in a garden, for Hood's demeanour and office were garden-like, he thought, with none of the airlessness and suspicion of other men. He painted him sitting on a blue bench with a back made of entwined branches, ivy curling between his feet and a puzzle of a leaf lying on his shoulder.

Whenever he thought of it, Dadd smiled to himself. No one had noticed that the leaf – a large, thick sunflower leaf – looked as if it might be both behind and in front of Dr Hood. The perspective was twisted. If you studied the head and shoulder it looked as if it might be behind the man's figure; but the tip actually lay over the nearest branch that formed the back-rest of the seat. Dr Hood carried the upsurging plant on his shoulders; it hung over him like a green umbrella. Pure foolishness, worthy of a lunatic left to his own dreams and devices for ten years.

In the background, the mountains and cedars of Lebanon; in the foreground, the iron lawn-roller of an English garden. On the seat beside Hood, a Turkish fez, and the all-obscuring piece of cloth that hung over the face of the man in The Child's Problem. Cloth had properties, he told Hood that first day, of substance and flexibility. It could ripple and fall. It could be starched into ruffs that enclosed necks. Over and over again he painted great folds of shawls, pleats in skirts, sculptural drapes that almost – but not quite – covered feet, faces or hands. Inside the folds, what was hidden? Merely the cloth itself, perhaps. Or perhaps the depths of other things; the cloth was merely the wrappings of sleeping vices.

He painted Cupid and Psyche this year. Cupid had fallen in love with the King's daughter, but left her when she stole a look at him. The two are caught in a kiss, but Dadd could not get the woman's face. The finished portrait was strange: her hair would not fall past her throat. The breasts, the curve of the shoulder *and stomach belonged to some other, larger woman. And under the folds of the material, above which her own feet were balanced, came another foot, the foot of the chair: a griffin's claw, scales and bone.*

You never knew what was hidden in commonplace objects or commonplace minds.

'Mr Dadd,' *Hood had said, standing up and holding out his hand.* 'I'm honoured to meet you.'

It was probably five years since anyone had shaken his hand formally.

Dadd received it with interest, this touch of another's flesh. The hand was cool, without much pressure. It was a disappointment to him. He resisted the urge to inspect it, as he often inspected his own fingers, which had been responsible for etching his commands on other skin, on canvas and paper.

'Tell me,' *Dr Hood asked, when they were both seated,* 'what have you been painting this year?'

It was difficult. Dadd recalled Dymphna Martyr, *but he didn't wish to tell Dr Hood of that watercolour. St Dymphna, said to be efficacious in cases of insanity, had her pilgrimage place in Gheel; Dadd had seen it in 1842 when he had passed through Belgium with Thomas Phillips. Dymphna had been the daughter of an Irish pagan king and a Christian mother. After her mother's death, her father had wanted to marry her, his own flesh and blood. She fled to Gheel, where the King caught up with her and beheaded her, spilling on the ground what had sprung from him.*

No, he would not tell that. And he would not tell of The Death of Richard II: *four figures wrestling on the edge of eternity. Or of* Hatred.

'I have painted a watercolour,' he said quietly, 'It is called A Hermit. It is peaceful. There is an hourglass and a book.'

'Do you have anything to read?' he asked.

'Mr Brigham brought me a Bible.'

Hood nodded approvingly at the attendant. 'Would you like something else?'

Dadd considered. 'Shakespeare,' he said. 'Poetry.'

In his casenotes that year, Hood would write: '... a very sensible and agreeable companion, a mind once well educated and thoroughly informed ...'

The interview was soon over. Dr Hood was very busy, Dadd was told.

He was busy, it transpired, with all kinds of improvements. Every single window in the hospital was enlarged that year, flooding Dadd's sleeping cell with an unexpected brightness late in the morning, when the sun was at a particular angle. Busy with other changes, too: unheard-of things. Every ward had an aviary of singing birds.

Men crowded to them. Some tried to take the birds, but were defeated by the height of the cages and the welded doors. Others, like Dadd, could not bear their voices. The birds sang at twilight and at first light. It seemed to him unbearably mournful. They had been imprisoned for no crime, and all they could do was call, and call, and call.

He struggled with his rages. He swore rambling oaths at Brigham. He spat his food on to the floor.

When Dr Hood next visited, he found that Dadd had begun a great raft of sketches of the passions: poverty, splendour and wealth, idleness, gaming and treachery.

Hood examined the last watercolour closely. 'It is three Chinese,' he said.

Dadd hardly took his eyes from the paper. 'We are at war with China,' he said. 'That is why they are treacherous.'

'We were at war with China until twelve years ago,' Hood murmured.

Dadd did not pause. 'All wars and trickery have the same root,' he said.

Hood looked at the painting: a flight of steps, an open door. A man on the steps relays some secret to another, hiding below. The long curved blade in the man's right hand waits for the unsuspecting figure stepping out of the house. 'The Chinese dress is very well drawn,' Hood told him.

'It is not correct,' Dadd told him. 'It hangs wrongly from the waist.'

'I can see no fault,' Hood told him, truthfully.

And Dadd finished it in that moment, writing his name and the date along the bottom step in the picture. 'Not all faults are visible,' he murmured. He thought of his father, retching in the evening darkness on a public path, unable, even then, to let go of his trust. Falling, one hand clutched to his collar, looking about him for the murderer who could not be his own son, and his eyes finally resting on Richard in disbelief. That had been his last expression: blank disbelief.

'Treachery in those who pretend to love us,' Dadd said, wiping the paintbrush on the corner of the paper.

Fifteen

When Catherine woke, first light was showing.

She and John had been together for two months, and it was the warmest May for years. The copper beech on the lawn was coming into leaf. She could see the crown of the tree now, through the open curtains. It was a glorious tawny red, made more distinct by the oak and tulip trees behind it.

'What's the matter?' John asked.

She looked across at him. 'Nothing,' she said. 'It's OK. Go back to sleep.'

He held out his arms; she eased herself into them, and lay with her head on his shoulder. She savoured the moment: the warm length of his body, the way he immediately responded to her touch. He caught her hand in his, raised it to his lips, then wordlessly held it against his chest. 'Do you want me to go to the house with you today?' he asked.

She considered. 'No,' she said finally.

Robert had sent her a letter, asking her to meet him at their home, giving today's date. It was now three months, perhaps a little more, since she had seen him. When she had gone yesterday to check the house, she had found the letter among a pile of mail. It was post-marked London, and dated the week before. When she had come back to Bridle Lodge, she had held it out to John.

'It had to happen sooner or later,' he said.

'He will want to sell,' she said. 'That's all it can be.'

'You don't have to do anything you don't want to,' John had said.

They had been standing in the hallway. She had been living there for just over six weeks; since that first night, she had never had any inclination to go home. Sometimes she wondered what life had been like with Robert. It seemed pallid, when she looked back at it. A world she had stepped out of, like Alice passing through the looking-glass. Or a character out of a canvas. Except she felt that she had come from a dream into life, and not the other way round.

John gave her back the letter. He stepped down from the tread he had been working on: he was restoring the panels under the balustrade, tracing the twisting vines back where they had been painted out. It was meticulous work, and it seemed to Catherine that he had dedicated himself to it as if it were a religious mission. 'Can you see the resemblance?' he had asked her, that first morning they had been together.

'In the window?' she asked. 'You mean the girl?'

'She's just like you,' he said.

She had regarded it critically.

'And like the girl in the green-glass mirror,' he added.

She'd turned to look at him. 'I don't understand.'

He'd simply smiled and kissed her. She had left to go to work. When she had come back to him that evening, he had a poster of *The Fairy Feller's Master Stroke* on the table, weighed down at each corner with books.

'Oh, my God,' she said, laughing, as she came in at the door, 'for a second, I thought we had another copy of an original.' She had shaken her head, holding her hand over her heart in mock-fright.

He took her hand. 'Look at the girl with the mirror,' he said. He had pointed to the left-hand side of the picture. There in the centre stood two women, directly to the left of the magician, whose open arms and wide-brimmed hat commanded the middle of the painting.

Catherine bent down to look closely. 'She doesn't look like me at all,' she murmured.

'She does,' John countered. 'The way she holds her head, the turn of her body. She's got your colouring too.'

Catherine smiled. The two women were famous for their eroticism, particularly the mirror girl's companion, dressed all in white, a hawk moth on one hand, a broom in the other – a lady's maid straight out of a Victorian gentleman's fantasy, the kind of woman that every repressed schoolboy must have hoped would be hired for the house. Her calves bulged above tiny feet; her waist was nipped in to nothing; above it, her breasts strained at her bodice. The girl with the mirror looked towards her, but not directly at her: her eyes were downcast. She looked like a nymph ballerina, with translucent wings fanning out from her shoulders.

'I always thought she looked Spanish,' Catherine said, thoughtfully.

'Spanish?' he echoed.

'Yes,' she said. 'Look at her dark hair. She's got such a secret smile. She reminds me of those Spanish dancers. Their expressions. And her hands are almost clapping.'

'Except for the mirror.' He took the books from the corners of the poster and held it up. 'Look what's in the mirror,' he said. 'Look at the reflection.'

She stared at it, frowning. 'I can't see. It's just a plain green disc.'

'Look closer.'

She did. She could still see nothing.

'I always thought you could see the edge of her face,' John said, 'and it's different from her real face. Warmer.'

'Another girl living in the glass?' she asked.

He had put down the poster, laid his hands on her shoulders. Then, with his right hand, he traced the line of her neck, the curve of her cheek. Electricity ran through her, a visceral, nearly desperate desire to touch him. 'You stepped out of the reflection,' he murmured.

She took his hand. 'What do you feel when you draw?' she asked.

'I don't draw.'

'I meant your technical drawings.'

'That isn't like this,' he said, nodding in the direction of the picture.

'Why not?' she said. 'You make something that didn't exist before. You imagine it in your head and transfer it to paper.'

'You're comparing me with Dadd?' he said.

'I'm comparing the process.'

'I never thought of it in the same way.'

'You are creating something.'

He frowned a little. 'I'm not a painter.'

'Any more than I'm a painter's subject,' she said.

'You're very like her,' he repeated.

'Perhaps the two of us are the modern equivalents.'

'You have something,' he said. 'I could paint you. Will you dress up as a ballerina, with wings on your back?'

She had taken his hand again, the one with which he had caressed her face and shoulders. She ran her finger down the centre of the palm. 'I'm not a girl in a painting,' she said. 'I'm real.'

An expression almost like pain crossed his face. He pulled her close to him. 'You think I don't know that?' he said.

'You didn't answer my question,' she said.

'Which one?'

'What do you feel when you draw?'

'Contact,' he said. 'Understanding.'

'You feel an understanding . . . of what?'

'Of whatever it is I'm trying to see in my head. And then it's a matter of transferring it.'

'The point of contact.'

'The touch,' he said. 'Where it meets.'

She moved under his hand. 'You're making fun of me,' he said.

'Like this?' she said. She lowered her eyes, and turned her head, so that he was presented with the profile of the fairy dancer, springing into life. He grinned. 'Real and unreal,' he said. 'That's what you are. Real, and . . .'

She put her fingers over his mouth.

He never finished the sentence.

Now she lifted her head, in the half-light of the day. 'John, I can't sleep. I'm going to get up.'

He moved, as if to get out of bed with her, but she restrained him with a shake of her head. He watched her as she pulled on a pair of jeans and a sweater; at the door, she turned to say that she would call him when she had made breakfast, but he had already closed his eyes.

She went downstairs, looking up at the stained-glass window as she passed it. In the dawn light, the figure was filmy, picked out only in shades of bluish grey. She sat on the bottom step, wriggling her feet into her shoes. Frith eased himself grudgingly from his basket, looking up at her questioningly. She took the key from the hallstand, unlocked the front door and went out into the garden.

Everything was perfectly still. The full moon that they had commented on last night – a swimming blur in the clouds – now sat low in the sky, almost invisible. The clouds had gone: the last stars showed in the sky. She tilted back her head, drank in the cool air. She walked through the heavy dew of the lawn, leaving a darker trail of footprints.

Most of the trees on the lawn had been planted, like the rest of the garden, in the year that the Lodge was built. Now a hundred and thirty years old, they stood like a small army of green ghosts, towering above her. A week or two ago, John had taken her on a guided tour, naming the ones he knew, guessing in a comical fashion at those he didn't. Closest to the house was the magnificent chestnut-leaved oak, at home in the mountains of Iran from where its seeds had been brought. Beyond that, the tulip tree, graceful, soaring, with its palm-shaped leaves just opening out. And then came the maples: slender, with curving trunks, like bodies wound round each other. Today, as she passed, she noticed the bundles that would become leaves, opening in pale, shrimp-coloured fans.

Frith was way ahead of her. She could hear him skittering down the damp path towards the ponds and the stream.

'I want you to live here,' John had said, that first night. 'I want you to stay.'

'It's too soon,' she'd replied. She had lain back on the bed. He sat next to her, looking not at her body but at her face. 'It's too complicated,' she added. 'With Robert, and everything.'

'You would rather be with Robert?'

'No,' she said. 'Of course not.'

'You would rather wait for him.'

'No!'

'I don't understand,' he said. 'You want to stay in that empty house and for me to live here without you?' He had pressed his lips to her stomach, her breasts, her shoulders. His voice was soft, not insistent.

'John,' she said, trying to lift him so that she could see into his eyes, 'aren't you afraid of rushing into something?'

He considered a moment. 'No,' he replied.

'But you hardly know me.'

He sat back, holding her hand. 'Tell me how long you knew Robert before you married him.'

'Eighteen months.'

'And did you really know everything about him then?'

She thought about her husband: the man who had made her feel safe because he was so sure of himself. A man who rarely told her what he was thinking, who didn't seem to have dreams.

'I don't imagine he thought it was necessary to know everything,' she said.

'Did you?'

'Oh, yes. I wanted to be part of him. I believed in that.' And she wondered again how she had come to be so connected to someone who was not connected to her in his heart.

'You loved him.'

'Yes.' She remembered how driven she had been to make things right between them. 'It's peculiar,' she murmured. 'I always had this sensation that I was trying to knot us together, and all the time he was turning away. Not pulling away. Just – if anyone had painted us – I imagined him in the act of half turning away, as if he'd been distracted.'

'Did he have affairs?'

'No,' she said. 'Not until this one.' And she tried to get her head round it: that she had always been trying to turn Robert towards her. 'I don't know why I did it,' she told John now. 'I just felt that that was how it ought to be. All or nothing.'

'Swept away,' John suggested.

'No,' she replied, 'because that sounds like losing touch. I wanted to be in touch, inside his heart. But I don't think he ever gave it away,' she concluded quietly, as if confirming what she had said. 'That's what it was,' she said. 'He kept something back.'

She saw that John looked regretful, but also horrified. 'You can't be in love,' he said, 'and hold anything back.'

'People do,' she said.

'Is that what you do?'

She pulled his arms round her, laced his fingers behind her back, put hers round his neck. 'No, John,' she told him.

She followed the path that Frith had taken, down through the camellias and rhododendrons. There was one rhododendron, just where the path took a dog-leg turn before it descended steeply to the water, that was astonishingly beautiful. It must have been eighty feet tall, and was covered with startling pink flowers, almost too gaudy to be real; hundreds of miniature bouquets of densely packed cerise hung over the path. She stopped now, and looked up through the branches at tier upon tier of colour sandwiched between the glossy dark leaves. The pink had a blue tone, close to lilac, in that light.

She turned to gaze across the fields below the weirs. The wild garlic was in rank profusion by the water's edge; beyond it, the grass grew higher than it did in the nearest meadow. She spotted Frith running across the field, bouncing like a jack-in-the-box towards the woodland.

'Frith,' she called. But he didn't hear her.

She went on down the slope to the water.

John had finished his work with Peter Luckham a month before. All the irrigation ditches and gates were now clear; Catherine stood on the little bridge and looked down the line of five gates, showing as dark bands against the lightening grey of the river and ponds. John had planted the edges of each of the four circular ponds with a long line of whitebeam saplings. Their leaf buds curved in semi-circular arches almost to the water's surface; on the banks he had planted wild species – cuckoo flowers, dame's violet, wintercress. And despite Luckham's disapproval – because he thought John would be overrun by it within three years – in the water he had put watercress.

'Fast-flowing water over chalk beds,' John had said. 'Perfect.'

'Choke the stream,' Luckham had muttered darkly.

John had only smiled. 'I don't care,' he had replied. 'I'll clear it out.'

She could see the cress beginning now, dark, fertile clumps where the gravel could be glimpsed in the shallows. She walked round to the far side, across the bridge, and sat down on the edge of the path. She looked past the shallows to where the stream widened out into the nearest pool. In its undisturbed surface she could see the faint reflection of the pink rhododendron, and the fainter apricot and pink of the first light of day. The house was invisible behind its wall of trees. Nothing moved either there or in the fields behind. It was magical, a fairytale place.

Frith had disappeared on his private mission across the valley. The sun was just touching the trees over there, turning the darkness to the acid lime of spring.

She reached down and felt the temperature of the water. It was cold, but not icy. She took off her shoes, and stood on the prickling gravel bed. Then, a secret smile came over her face. She had been eight or nine when she last stood barefoot in a river. There had been a stream at the bottom of their road. The house they had at weekends was ringed with oak trees, and the stream ran there, between the garden and the farmland beyond. As a child, she had always wished it was bigger, entertained fantasies of sailing away, through the countryside, to the sea, past all the sleeping churches and farms, plunging into the ocean, carried out on a blue-black tide.

She jumped out on to the bank, glanced around, then eased herself out of her jeans and sweater, then wriggled out of the remainder of her clothes.

She stepped back into the water, made her way slowly across the stream, and on into the deeper pool. Soon the ground dipped away under her feet, and she launched herself forward, gasping at the cold. Swirls of mud appeared in the pool, disturbed by her feet, twists of liquorice curling in the green.

She swam for a few hurried strokes, until the water felt warmer; laughing, caught up in the secretive pleasure. She swam through the muddied picture of the rhododendrons, a brightening haze striped with ripples. Her hands brushed the stems of the waterlilies, their first leaves forcing upwards to the light, scrolls of purple and pale roots extending sideways, catching her skin, touching her with blind fingertips. Then she lay on her back and stared up at the sky.

'Catherine!' a voice cried.

She heard the vibration vaguely, as if she had dreamed it.

'Catherine!'

She turned on to her stomach. John was at the edge of the water, near the bridge. She laughed, and held out her hands.

'What are you doing?' he shouted.

'Come in,' she said. 'It's amazing. It's warm.'

'Oh, Christ,' she heard him say.

He sat down suddenly on the bridge, his head bowed.

'John?' she called.

He didn't respond.

She waded towards him and got out. He stood up, and she ran to him along the herringbone brick border, naked, dripping. 'What's the matter?' she asked. 'What is it?'

He shook his head.

'Did I scare you?'

He smiled. 'Don't do that again,' he said.

'But I was only swimming.'

He took an enormous breath. He was very pale. 'What did you think?' she asked. 'I was just swimming. Look, I'm fine.'

'In this,' he said, not a question. He looked her up and down. 'My God.'

She pressed herself to him. 'I'm all right,' she told him.

'I took Frith out of there four months ago,' he said. 'He nearly drowned us both.'

'I'm not drowned,' she said. 'I'm warm.' And she pressed his hand to her stomach. He let it rest there. 'I'm here,' she said.

She took his hand and held it against her heart. Then, holding his gaze, she lowered his hand down the length of her body.

The water drops danced in his head, on his tongue, in his throat. It was like relieving a lifelong thirst, the cold green rush of her, the water drops of the dream, the skin almost hot to the touch underneath.

He knelt down, brought her with him, laid her on the ground, all the while thinking of the racing flood of needing her since that very first second that he had seen her at the door to the house.

He closed his eyes, and the storm when he entered her was like nothing he had ever known, would ever want to know; it flung him out of the day, the newly sunlit garden, away from the sound of her cries. He felt nothing: not the wet ground, or the water, or the morning air on his back, or even her hands on him. He had the curious and frightening sensation of travelling at ungovernable speed.

When he came back to her, he looked down at her closed eyes and parted mouth. He peeled a strand of wet hair from her neck; he listened as the pace of his heart slowed, and the familiar dull ache returned in his chest.

'I want to live for ever,' he whispered.

She opened her eyes, and smiled.

Sixteen

It was one o'clock when she got to the house. As she turned the key in the lock, a small rush of warm air came out of the hall, the staleness of unlived-in rooms. Catherine put down her briefcase, took off her jacket and went through all the downstairs rooms, opening windows. She got to the back door and went out into the courtyard garden. She hadn't looked at it in weeks. Weeds were growing in the pots and containers; she picked off the dead heads of some daffodils.

In the house, the doorbell rang.

She checked her watch. One ten. Robert was early.

She opened the front door without a thought, or even a tremor of nervousness. Yet when she saw him, she felt sick. Like a small, hard blow to the stomach.

He was thinner, leaner.

'Hello,' she said. 'You're early.'

'I've been waiting round the corner for half an hour,' he said. 'Is it all right?'

She moved back to admit him. 'You've driven down from London?' she asked.

'Yes,' he said, inflecting it like a question.

'Eventually they told me where you were,' she said. 'After I rang your office for the fourth time.'

He coloured.

'They were loyal to you,' she continued. 'The first time I rang, they denied knowing anything about it. They said you were on holiday.'

'I'm sorry,' he said.

'What an effort you took,' she said. 'It must have been complicated.'

'No,' he said. Then, 'I'm sorry,' he repeated.

She sat on the sofa and looked at him, her hands in her lap. He chose a chair, dragged it closer to her. 'You're looking very well,' he said.

'Thanks.'

'Busy at work?'

She shook her head, dismissing the question.

'I'll come to the point,' he said.

'You should,' she replied.

He shifted in his chair; seemed to consider where to start.

From the initial jolt at seeing him, Catherine now felt curiously objective. Robert was an old-fashioned type. If she met him now for the first time, she would think just that. Old-fashioned, a little formal in the way he held himself. Had she ever thought that before? Yes. He had been particular about things, meticulous. With that studied look on his face.

How peculiar, she thought. I'd forgotten him. 'What's her name?' she asked.

'Whose name?'

'Oh, come on, Rob.'

'Does it matter?'

'I suppose not,' she said. 'Where did you meet her?'

'London.'

'Is that why you've gone back there?'

Her voice was calm. It wasn't the reception he had expected. He had steeled himself against a scene: tears, at the very least. He let it pass. 'I want to buy a flat in London,' he said. 'I've seen a place.' She wasn't going to help him, he realized. She was regarding him with something like indifference. 'It's not big,' he continued. 'Nowhere is, even for hundreds of thousands.'

There was still no response. His eyes went back to her face. She had started to smile, which he found unnerving. 'Have I said something funny?' he asked.

'You and money,' she said.

'It might have passed your notice,' he said, 'but that's how the world revolves.'

'Around money?' she said. 'I don't think so.'

It was his turn to smile.

'Say it,' she said. 'Tell me how naïve I am.'

'Look,' he told her, 'you've no doubt worked this out for yourself, but we need to sell this house.'

'Oh, yes?'

'We each put down half of the deposit, and we each paid half of the mortgage,' he said. 'You surely don't dispute that?'

'I'm not disputing anything,' she said.

'Well, then, this is half my property,' he said. 'There are no children, so we have to sell.'

* * *

She was listening to him both now and in the past, to the same measured voice that now came back to her with full recollection. It was strange how much money mattered, she thought. If you had none, or you had plenty, it made no difference. There were still arguments, gulfs. Money had an emotional dimension: the source of control, the link to pleasure. Robert, whose salary had always been high, had married a woman whose wages almost matched his, yet he had been inordinately careful when it came to spending.

She imagined Amanda rolling her eyes. 'Mean,' she would say. 'Why don't you be honest?' In fact, they had laughed about it once over dinner, Robert good-naturedly protesting, Amanda pretending to raid his wallet, and flapping her hands at the imaginary moths that fluttered out of it.

On honeymoon, Catherine and Robert had gone to Rye. It had been Catherine's choice: she wanted to see the antiques and art, to be by the sea. They had married in January when any other couple would have gone abroad. But there was something about the English coast in winter that she loved.

They had seen a bureau in a Saturday antiques market. It wasn't very expensive – Catherine had thought it a bargain. Robert hadn't objected, but neither had he enthused. She had a clear memory of him slowly taking out his chequebook, removing the pen cap, arranging his cheque card just so on the counter.

That first spring together they had gone to Paris. She recalled him standing at the gate of the Métro at Hôtel de Ville, counting centimes carefully into his palm.

'Why don't you share the joke with me?' he asked now.

She blinked. 'Sorry.'

'Are you listening to me?'

'Yes,' she said. 'The house. I know.'

'Well?'

She got up, suddenly short of breath. He winced, as if he had expected her to hit him. She looked at him in astonishment, and walked past him into the kitchen. She picked up the coffeemaker, remembered that it hadn't been used in weeks and put it down again. 'Do you want tea?' she asked.

He had come to the door.

She was about to say something about the house when she was struck by how often they had stood in this pose, she preparing a meal, he at the door, telling her something ordinary. They had been ordinary, not happy, maybe, but not many of the couples she knew were terribly happy. 'Is she older than me?' she asked.

'Catherine,' he said. 'Please.'

'Do I know her?'

He went back the way he had come. She followed him. 'Do I know her?' she repeated.

'No,' he said. He gave a great sigh, and put his hand to his head.

'Why did you do it?' she said. 'I mean, why just leave?' she persisted. 'Just a letter, Robert. How could you do that?'

'Let's not go into this.'

'Why not?' she demanded. 'It's a reasonable question.'

'I don't want an argument.'

'Neither do I. I just want to know.' She struggled to control her temper.

'I didn't want a scene,' he said.

'You deserve one,' she said.

'Maybe.'

'There's no maybe about it,' she retorted. 'I'd never have believed you could be such a coward.'

He said nothing, seeming disappointed, disapproving. As if the subject were distasteful.

'You're not sorry,' she said.

He didn't reply.

She walked towards him. 'You really aren't,' she said. 'Look at you.'

'I'm not sorry to have left,' he told her, 'but I'm sorry for the way I did it.'

She looked hard at his face, and saw nothing but a kind of patience, as if this was the price he had to pay to get what he wanted. He looked like a man waiting in a queue, she decided, in a bank or at a petrol station. A little bored, irritated.

'Oh, my God,' she whispered. 'This is such a pain for you, isn't it?'

'There's no use going into it,' he said. 'Can we please just talk about the house?'

'No use,' she repeated. 'Oh, fine.' She was so close to him now. She wanted, more than anything, to hit him, to wipe the indifference off his face. 'Did you ever love me?' she asked. '*Really* love me?'

'Catherine,' he said, in a warning tone.

'I don't think you did,' she said.

'This is ridiculous,' he snapped.

'You didn't love me.'

'Maybe not.'

They were silent; then she repeated his last few words under her breath.

'Look,' he said, 'this will get us nowhere. When all's said and done – love or not, or whatever you want to call it – I was a bloody good husband to you. I was the perfect husband.'

'Robert,' she said, 'you should hear what you just said.'

'I never cheated on you, or laid a hand on you, or kept you short of money,' he said. 'I never stayed out late, or humiliated you, or let you down.'

'And that makes a perfect husband?' she said.

'It makes a far more decent partner than thousands upon thousands of other people are.'

'I don't live with thousands upon thousands of other people,' she retorted. 'It's you we're talking about. Us.'

He glared at her. 'You've changed,' he said.

'What?'

'You're different.'

'Like I say,' she retorted angrily, 'you're no different. You're still a smug, frigid bastard.'

He recoiled.

All she could think of was that she had done everything he wanted. If he could describe himself so perversely as the perfect husband, then she had been the perfect wife. She had given up her job in London to come and live where he wanted, given up the prospects of a potentially better career. Left her work colleagues and friends behind.

Yet now it dawned on her that none of it was his fault, tempted as she was to think it was. He had taken what she had offered him; he had never questioned it. He had been loved. She had been faithful. All the things that he ascribed to himself could also be said of her.

Except that she had never thought of it as being the perfect wife. Yet she was thinking of it now, she corrected herself. She was thinking of herself as a martyr who had been so wonderful and supportive. It was comforting to be the victim, she mused. It was to occupy the moral high ground. She was left with this unpleasant idea, and the usual creeping sensation that she was being squeezed out of Robert's life, that she was on the fringe of his interest.

She had been like one of those memos you saw on an office, the one that said, *I called, but you were out.* She had spent a vast amount of time calling him, trying to get his attention, but he had never been there.

Whenever he had gone away on business, he had always dutifully sent her a postcard of the city where he was staying. She used to prop them up on the mantelpiece. Freiburg, Bruges, Munich. When he had come home, the cards would be lined up in a row, and he would be sitting in front of her, but he would be as absent as ever. He had kept himself closed up, shuttered, private. Sometimes her fingers had itched to take a blade, open him up and confirm that he was made of flesh and blood. Shaming thought, stupid thought. But just to know he wasn't the automaton that he was becoming in her imagination . . .

Once or twice she had travelled with him, but it had made no difference: she had spent all her time waiting for him. She would stand in some bar, watching the barges in Innsbruck slip like whales under the Deutzer Bridge. Or she would sit on the wall of the Hofkirk, under the shadow of Maximilian's tomb, and she would think that his smile would be different when he came to meet her in this foreign setting. But it was always the same.

She understood, with a great thrust – like stepping off a cliff into thin air – that she had been waiting all the time she knew him to see the reflection of her own feelings in his face.

She looked away from his enquiring gaze. 'I'm no different,' she said. 'Take the bloody house,' she said. 'Have the lot. It doesn't matter.'

'I shall take half,' he said, 'and you will have half.'

'All right. Whatever you think.'

'It's the law,' he told her. 'It's not what I think.'

She turned fully towards him. The bureau they had bought on their honeymoon was in the corner by the door to the kitchen. She walked to it, and laid her hand flat on the top. 'There's all the furniture,' she said.

'We can meet another time to discuss it, if you like.'

'This bureau . . .' Despite herself, she began to cry.

He tried to get between her and the desk. 'Don't, Catherine.'

'What do you bloody care?' she said.

'But don't cry.'

She pushed his hand off her arm. 'Go away,' she said.

'I'm not leaving while you're upset.'

She wiped her face with her hand. 'You really are fucking astonishing,' she muttered.

He watched her with a critical frown. Eventually she went back into the kitchen and tore off a piece of kitchen roll, then went back to him. 'I'm OK,' she said. 'See? I'm fine. I'm great. You can piss off now with a clear conscience.' She gestured at the bureau. 'You remember where we got it?'

'Of course.'

'Well, do you want it? You paid for it.'

'I never liked it,' he said. 'You can have it.'

Then he walked away, through the hallway, to the front door. He opened it and stopped on the threshold. She had followed him, and was standing a few feet behind him. 'You know, Catherine,' he said, 'before all this, if I ever did anything, said anything, that upset you, I apologize.'

He was waiting for an answer. She didn't give one.

He stepped out of the house. She walked to the open door and watched him go. As he turned the corner, he looked back at her.

She closed the door.

Seventeen

That day, Mark was in the process of preparing the Fine Art sale. The back door to Pearsons had been opened to allow for a delivery. It was an executor's sale: Mark was watching the unloading of an entire married life. He watched as it passed him, noting the details against the record: half a dozen mahogany bar-back armchairs and an oak secretaire, a George III giltwood wall mirror. He glanced up, and noticed a man crossing the car park, heading straight for him. 'Mark Pearson?' the man asked.

'Yes.'

'John Brigham.'

It took a second for the name to register. Mark took the proffered hand. 'Ah,' he said, smiling. 'Catherine isn't here. She's due back any minute.'

'Can I wait?'

'Please do,' Mark said. He stepped back, and ushered the man into the saleroom. They made their way to Mark's office. Brigham stopped on the way to look at his dresser in the far corner.

'We thought it worth the wait,' Mark said. 'It's too good to go in the fortnightly General.'

Brigham said nothing. He glanced around the room at the rest of the lots. 'You have a good selection,' he said.

'A death,' Mark commented drily. 'Always good for business.'

There was a beat, then Brigham walked on. They passed out through the double doors to Reception and Mark and Catherine's offices.

'Come in,' Mark said, opening his door. He called to the receptionists, asking for coffee; when he came in, Brigham had already seated himself in front of the desk.

The catalogue was in the process of final editing; reference books were piled on the rear cabinet.

'Researching something?' Brigham asked.

Mark smiled. 'Medals,' he said. 'There was a stack of them in one of the chests of drawers. Burma Star, Africa Star. A First World War death plaque. Not my field – I had to resort to help.'

'Is there always such a range?'

'Always,' Mark told him. 'Last Fine Art we had a harp. Carved angels, winged beast feet. Then there was the polyphon, and a couple of train sets, and an elastolin set of a British Army band, christening spoons, a trophy celebrating a tennis tournament in 1952 . . .' He grinned. 'Oh,' he added, holding up a finger, 'and the *tazza* with pierced and gadrooned floral border.'

'A *tazza*?'

Mark spread his hands. 'Search me,' he joked. 'Sounds brilliant, though, don't you think?'

The coffee arrived. Mark took the opportunity to

inspect John Brigham in detail for the first time. Catherine had not given much away: all he knew was that she was practically living with the man. What seemed to be the almost total submersion of her previous life into his disturbed him; and yet, at the same time, it gave him some satisfaction to see her smile, which she had not for many months. If this tall, greying, handsome man was responsible for that, he felt he should be grateful to him. But Brigham didn't look too approachable now as he stirred sugar into his coffee.

'How are things at Bridle Lodge?' Mark asked. 'I heard you altered all the waterways, restored them.'

'Yes,' Brigham said.

'Must have been quite a project.'

'It was.'

'Have you anything else planned?'

Brigham glanced up at him. 'No.'

'I gather it's a fine Arts and Crafts house.'

By way of reply, Brigham frowned. OK, Mark thought, so you don't want to talk. 'Would you mind very much if I carried on with the delivery?' he asked. 'It's a busy day.'

'No,' Brigham said. 'Not at all. Please go ahead.'

As Mark came out of his office, he saw Catherine coming in at the front doors. He waited for her; she said something to the girls on the desk, then came over to him.

'You look tired,' he said.

'I've just seen Robert.'

'Where?'

'He came to the house.'

'Are you all right?' he asked.

'Yes.'

'What did Robert want?'

'To sell. To divide everything equally. He's buying a place in London.'

'I see,' Mark said. 'Well, it's nice of him to tell you.' She smiled wanly. 'And will you?'

'I suppose so.'

'You don't have to leap to do his bidding, you know,' Mark said.

'I know.'

'Was the mysterious new woman with him?'

'No.'

Mark put a hand on her arm. 'You've got a visitor,' he said. 'John Brigham's in my office.'

'He is?'

'Cheerful sort of chap, isn't he?' Mark said. 'Never stops talking. Is he checking up on his goods?'

'I shouldn't think so.'

'He looked at the dresser.'

'It shipped all right, didn't it?' she asked.

'Of course. It only had to come ten miles down the road.' Mark pulled a face. 'He looked like something didn't quite meet his standards.' He raised his eyebrows at her, then walked back through the saleroom.

She watched him go, then went into his office. John was already standing. 'I thought I heard your voice,' he said.

She kissed him. 'What's the matter?' she asked.

'Nothing,' he said. 'How did it go with Robert?'

'I don't know,' she said. 'He's getting a place in London.'

'And?'

191

'Nothing, really,' she said.

He regarded her closely. 'Are you busy this afternoon?'

'A bit of paperwork,' she said. 'A few return calls.' She looked at a piece of paper that the receptionists had given her. 'And I have to call in on Mr Williams. He wants to see me. Something urgent.' She flopped into a chair. 'Oh, God,' she murmured.

He sat down again next to her. 'What do you want to do?' he asked.

'You mean now? This afternoon?'

'No,' he said. 'About Robert. Do you want to go back? Do you want to stop . . .'

'Stop what?'

'Us,' he said.

She stared at him. 'Is that what you think?'

'Breathing space. Now that you've seen him.'

She gave a short laugh. 'And that has something to do with us?'

'Of course it does,' he said.

She wondered if he had come here, with a frown on his face, to find an excuse to stop seeing her. It washed over her quickly. *That can't be it*, she thought. *Surely that isn't it*. It couldn't be it, she reasoned, because she was carrying an imprint of him: his hands, his thoughts. She wanted to be away from Robert, from Mark, from the saleroom, the noise of the traffic outside. She sat motionless in her chair and wanted John acutely, a physical necessity: like salt dissolving on the tongue, an acute, dry, heightening texture in her mouth. This peculiar longing, something like impatience: anxious at one moment to be out of his arms to breathe, to walk away; anxious in the next to be with him, to swallow the world in an instant, to obliterate it.

'Do you want the truth?' she asked.

He was holding her hand loosely, almost reflectively.

'I haven't given Robert a thought,' she said, 'for weeks. I should have, wouldn't you say? Don't you think that a newly abandoned wife should give a shit for where her husband is and what he's doing?'

She still couldn't read his face.

'Well, I'll tell you,' she said. 'I don't want to think about Robert, because for one thing he lives in a prison in his head, and for another, I can't think about him because, since you, there isn't room.'

At this, John's expression relaxed.

She leaned forward. 'I've just talked to a man who . . .' She searched for the words. 'I got the same feeling that I was dying on my feet, that I'd become invisible . . .'

'You're not invisible.'

'Walking around inside a maze,' she murmured. 'What was it like with Claire?'

'Claire?'

'Did you ever feel that you were staring at a brick wall? That she didn't understand you – something you'd said, an idea you'd had, what you wanted?'

'No.'

'Did you feel like two people?' she asked. 'Two people with different feelings?'

'No. Never.'

'Did you know that it's a weakness to be like that?' she asked, her voice heavy with irony.

She stood up abruptly, dragging at his hand so that

he got to his feet. 'Let's go,' she said. 'Take me out of here.'

After lunch they drove out to Sandalwood. The journey took them through the river valley as it wound out of town between the shallow hills. When they turned off towards the village, the river widened and the road narrowed. The water spread out into reed beds to the left; to the right, the land rose gradually. Barley had been planted: it was too short to ripple under the wind, and stood in feathery green tracts up to the edge of the woodland. The road curved and twisted through other fields, over bridges. At last they came to the village, and drove up the lane towards the house.

'Did you ever come to this village at the start of the year?' Catherine asked.

'No.'

She slowed down, nosing the car through the entrance, over a cattle grid. Lilac, with its first fists of purple and white, hung untended over the driveway.

'The churchyard is next to the house,' she said. 'In the spring snowdrops come out on the graves. They've been planted on almost every one. They look like featherbeds.' She glanced at him. John was looking out of the window at the grounds. She parked the car, and pulled on the handbrake. 'Why don't you tell me what's wrong?' she asked.

'There's nothing wrong.'

'You've barely said a word to me. And Mark said you hardly spoke to him.'

He pursed his lips. 'I don't think I like him much.'

She was amazed. 'Mark?' she repeated. 'He's the

nicest man you could wish for. What did he say to you? Did he crack some sort of joke?'

'Yes.'

'Look,' she said, 'you don't take him too seriously. He has a black sense of humour. Are you worried about the dresser?' she asked. 'The catalogue description is fine. It's exact. The dresser is unmarked, and insured.'

'It isn't the dresser.'

'What, then?' She was anxious: he had never cut her off like this before.

'Something I want to do.'

She waited. He didn't elaborate. It was evident that he wasn't prepared to tell her what was on his mind. She fought down the feeling that this was just like Robert.

After she had knocked she stood on the step and took in the white wisteria that swamped the front of the house; it had wound itself round the drainpipes and was curling its way on to the roof.

John got out of the car. Above their heads, house-martins were darting, in their easy ballet, and disappearing under the timber eaves.

Catherine knocked again. A window was open on the upper floor; the edge of a curtain fluttered from it. 'He rang me first thing this morning,' she said. 'I was talking on another phone.'

'Perhaps he went back to bed,' John suggested. 'How old is he?'

'Eighty?' she guessed. 'Eighty-five.' She looked doubtfully at the front door and again at the window. 'I'll try the back,' she said.

They went round the side of the house, on a flagstone path, green with moss and lichen, in the shade of heavy conifers. Bindweed grew up through the roots. They passed two huge bay windows, which must have been permanently overshadowed, even when the heavy curtains were not drawn. Catherine noticed whorls of damp on the linings, the encrusted paint on the frames, the rust marks running from the outdoor sills to the ground.

They came to a garden gate, and opened it on to the back of the house. The terrace here was shrouded in a gloomy half-light, so thick were the trees alongside. A garden potting shed stood in the deep shade, covered in a thick, pale green climber with star-shaped white flowers. The padlock hung from the lock, open; the floorboards of the shed were rotted. No one had been in there for years, Catherine thought.

They got to the back door, which was open.

'Mr Williams,' Catherine called. 'Are you there?'

There was no reply, except from a cat that ran down the hallway, mewing loudly. Catherine held out her hand, but it backed away. 'What's the matter?' she asked. 'Hungry?'

It skittered past her, tail up. When it got to the terrace, it turned back and scowled, fixing them both with a yellow stare.

'Mr Williams,' Catherine called, and stepped into the hall.

They looked into the kitchen. It was old-fashioned, with wood cupboards, a wooden draining-board bleached to ivory, and two iron taps over the stone sink, but it was clean and tidy.

'John,' Catherine whispered, 'come and see.' She took him up the hall. This, too, was tidy, almost antiseptically so, with an antler coat rack and umbrella stand, cracked Delftware on the walls, and the plates that Mr Williams had said were not worth selling. She had always been shown into the room on the left of the front door: it was like a waiting room, with a row of hard-backed Edwardian chairs, and a small pine table. She took John into it now; just a tiny space, little more than a cupboard, the original clothes-drying and boot-room of an Edwardian family. Coat hooks lined the wall, with panelled cupboards underneath them. Green brocade cushions, flattened by use, faded by age, ran along the top of the cupboards.

'Oh, my God,' John murmured.

The dim ochre walls were filled with photographs. They were all framed, and all but a handful featured the same woman. Catherine put her hand to the nearest one, a studio portrait of a pretty girl in a soft-collared frock, her hair waved neatly to her cheek. She was smiling modestly, chin dipped. The black-and-white print was so old that it was becoming sepia. The girl looked no more than eighteen, perhaps younger, and held a posy of violets in her lap.

Next was a wedding picture. Small and rather out of focus, it showed a large group of people on a flight of wide-fanning stone steps, the front door of a country house that was not Sandalwood. This was far more opulent: the women were trussed in furs and fancily buttoned shoes, despite the glare of the sun. In the centre of the front line stood the bride and groom: the girl in the previous photograph was now in a dress

197

with a long lace train, holding a bouquet of lilies. The man alongside her was Mr Williams, uncomfortable in a starched collar and dress coat.

Further still along the wall, the photographs and the country changed: inscriptions were written diagonally across each one in black ink. 'Jaipur 1946, Sandy and Denny Marshall, Col & Mrs Powell.' Here, among the wide-brimmed straw hats, the military fatigues and embroidered mess dress, were nameless dusty outposts and hillsides. Camels at a water-hole, knees buckled under them, with naked boys, arms crossed behind their backs, at the edge of the water. An army jeep drawn up at a crossroads in the middle of nowhere; a rocky promontory in a vast empty backdrop, men swathed against the wind with cotton shawls wrapped round their necks and faces.

There was an older version of the pretty eighteen-year-old girl: now obviously in her thirties, she lay full-length beside a pool, in dark sunglasses, holding a cigarette. Playing cards lay on the small table next to her, and a mixing jug for martinis.

'Look at all this,' John said.

He had opened a cupboard on the opposite side of the room. It was fitted with hanging rails. Inside it were generations of clothes: coats, dresses, ballgowns, sweaters, skirts, and rack upon rack of shoes, each carefully stuffed with tissue paper, as if the owner might want them again at any moment. There were scarves, gloves, even handkerchiefs, underwear in separate sliding shelves, with small bags of lavender on each row.

John looked at her. 'Have you ever seen anything like this?'

'Nothing quite the same,' she said. 'Not preserved like this.'

'It's a shrine,' he said. 'He made a shrine to her.'

They went back out into the hall, the gardenia scent of the dead woman clinging to them.

They opened the door to the bedroom; the curtain half-way across the window, caught under the open sash, was the one that Catherine had been able to see from the front doorstep.

There was a double bed, with a red satin eiderdown and pillows with stencilled patterns of trailing roses. The wallpaper featured old English roses with double petals, red on white. It was an overtly feminine room, seemingly untouched since the early sixties. The curtains hung in elaborate swags and ruffles, yet more roses embossed on damask.

A large wing armchair stood facing the foot of the bed, its back to the door.

John went to it, looked at its occupant. Catherine heard him gasp. 'What is it?' she asked.

She moved to his side. He put out a hand, palm upwards, to stop her.

She noticed the photograph first, of the fresh-faced girl in the studio picture, a copy, framed in gilt. It was propped on the eiderdown close to the chair. Then Catherine saw the hands, their papery thinness, the white knuckles shining, lying curled in Mr Williams's lap, relaxed. The tips of the fingers were blue. All the space between the hands was soaked with blood.

Mr Williams's face was white, expressionless. His eyes were open, gazing at the picture in front of him, blue eyes the colour of a faded ceanothus flower. He had dressed himself in his best suit. The collar, ill-fitting, was clean. He wore his regimental tie, and the badge of a charity organization in his lapel.

Then Catherine saw the knife he had used: a small penknife with a mother-of-pearl handle, resting on his knees. He had cut his wrists and remained quietly where he was, waiting.

It was two o'clock in the morning when John gave up trying to sleep. He had been lying on his back staring at the ghosts of light on the ceiling, Catherine finally asleep beside him, his mind purposefully blank to the events of the day.

But it kept coming back, in rewind: the ambulance, the police. The body taken downstairs, the sound of footsteps in the hall. Cameras in the bedroom. He had been standing on the landing outside the room when they had lifted Mr Williams to put his body into the mortuary bag. John couldn't get over the plasticity of the arms and hands, even after rigor mortis had declined. The head had rolled a little. The shoes seemed so pathetic, laced and polished, the effort to be well presented now gone.

It had been so pitiable, such a wreck of an ending. But, then, all endings were pitiable in their way. Dignity was a label attached by the living, John thought. Something to soothe us, like babies afraid of the dark.

As a little boy, he had been afraid of the dark. Even when he was seven or eight, the light had to be on out-side his room. It hadn't helped much: in the light cast by the twenty-five watt bulb he had seen wraiths crowding to catch a glimpse of him; he had heard foot-steps, seen smoke stream along the floor. He couldn't be placated, even when it was explained to him that he had been dreaming. 'It just seemed as if you were awake,' his mother would say.

He wondered now, so many years later, in this dark room with Catherine breathing shallowly at his side, if he had ever put away the dreams of childhood. If he allowed himself, he could see them all now, massing silently at the edge of his sight. All the things he didn't want to look at.

He sat upright, swung his legs out of bed. This was no good. It would get him nowhere. In fact it would only make it all so much worse.

He kept seeing Mr Williams's face, the abdication in it.

He had his own choices, now, he thought. Piece by piece, painting by solitary painting, Mr Williams had sold his life over the years – had hated selling any of it, according to Catherine. Each little bit had been a wrench. Catherine had told him tonight that she thought that Mr Williams's giving her the last portrait by the Scottish watercolourist had been nothing more than a sustained goodbye, his ticket out of the world. It was the last thing he had loved, the last of the pieces that he and his wife had bought together. Giving it to her had been like writing a suicide note: even more graphic, in its way, than the knife resting on his knees.

I have a room downstairs, John thought.

He walked to the window, pulled back the curtain a little and looked down over the garden. It was a calm, starlit night. In the sky, he could see the Plough clearly, resting on its side, almost directly above him. The Seven

Sisters of the Pleiades. In Spain, they had seemed closer than this. He had learned all their names, once, and watched their slow procession around the sky over weeks and months. The miracle of received light, the flickering messages from old worlds. Candles to light the way.

In Spain he had begun to buy in earnest. Sometimes he had even come back to London to make a particular purchase. Probably at some point he had even been to Bergen's, and attended an auction, while Catherine had worked there. Strange, that she had perhaps been so close when he had been working so hard to fill the void.

He had poured objects into the starlit dark. He hadn't even kept them in the house but had hired a storage unit, a dusty flea-bitten place on the edge of Málaga. He would drive there with his treasure, wrapped and boxed, and he would put it with all of the others. Just another box among many. He couldn't have explained to a living soul why this worked. It was a kind of insanity, a mechanism of mourning. He put beautiful things into boxes and hid them away, and he would think of them under lock and key, in the anonymous yard on an industrial estate, among other people's furniture and stores. Hundreds of little lights under bushels that only he knew about.

He just needed to know that they were in the world.

When he had come back to England, bringing them with him, he had asked the removers to unload the boxes into the drawing room. Without unpacking them he had fixed the alarm system. Only then did he unwrap everything. It took him two days, because each thing carried a memory.

I made a shrine, he thought. I made a shrine, too.

Now the thought almost asphyxiated him. He dropped the curtain and stood gasping for breath, his hands on his hips, his head nearly on his chest. He looked back at Catherine, trying to distinguish her face in the darkness. As if in response, she stirred. There was a second or two of silence, then she called him. He went to the side of the bed.

'Can't you sleep?' she asked. She propped herself up on one elbow, pushing the hair back from her face.

He reached out and touched her. She was so warm. 'I'm going to sell everything,' he said. 'Everything downstairs.'

'What?' she said confusedly. 'What do you mean? Why?'

He tried to think of a reason that would make sense to her. 'I don't want to be like him,' he told her, and she grasped his hand, pushing back some of the shadows that stood by the door, in his way.

He wanted to trust her. He wanted to give it all away and turn his heart over to her, and he wondered – with the shapes of faces eternally at the door, their shifting selves getting closer now, smoke drifting along the floor of his memory – if he could trust Catherine Sergeant. Not just with these things, precious as they were, with all the days of the past that they represented, but with everything.

Every priceless secret thing that he had been entrusted with.

Eighteen

John had forgotten what London could be like. He stood at the corner of the Strand and Whitehall, in the unexpected heat of late May, waiting to cross the road. The traffic heaved, sweltering with impatience. Work was being done in Trafalgar Square, and everywhere was a mess: pavements up, red and white barriers across each intersection, pedestrians jostling for position at each set of lights.

The sky was the kind of blue that he had thought he left behind in Spain: turquoise, rippling with humidity. He glanced across and saw Landseer's lions at the base of Nelson's Column looking impossibly vast in the human tide that ebbed around them.

When he finally got into the square, he could see that a new piazza was being made in front of the National Gallery: there were going to be steps running to the entrance, sealing it off from vehicles. He felt a pang when it came to him that he would never again see a red London bus passing in front of the gallery. It was fixed in his mind as one of the archetypal London sights, like guardsmen passing down the east side of Hyde Park towards Horseguards, or the University Boat Race sculls going under Putney Bridge.

He walked up St Martin's Lane, past the theatre and restaurant where he had once spent most of his time, the cacophony of Leicester Square, the tourists streaming out of the Underground station. London was sweating in eighty degrees, and blasts of air-conditioning issued from every doorway. He shrugged his shoulders to loosen his shirt from his skin. Helen would love it if he turned up travel-stained: she would have something to say about it the moment he walked through the door.

He got to the restaurant late. It was just gone one o'clock. He went down the stairs. The place resembled an old cinema, thirties style, with gaudy columns and a brass handrail. At the bottom of the stairs, modern art flickered: neon in tangerine and red flashes. He had always hated it here, and it hadn't changed. Pretentious and cavernous. The faint chemical smell, like chlorine. Still, it was Helen's choice.

She was sitting at a table right in the centre, wearing a tiny dress that was much too young for her. The lime-green shoestring straps cut into her shoulders, he noticed, as he kissed her cheek. She smelt expensively overpowering; in fact, he thought, she was too much of everything – too much flesh, too much makeup, too many grimaces that passed for smiles. He knew that expression. His heart sank.

'How are you?' he asked, as he sat down.

'Fine,' she replied. She took a long draught of the gin and tonic she was holding.

'Hot weather,' he commented.

'Too hot,' she agreed.

The waiter came; they studied menus and ordered. She seemed older, he thought, but in this sort of phase she always did. 'Are you OK?' he asked.

'I just said so.'

'I got your message . . .'

She was looking down at the table; then, she reached out and put her hand over his. It was a sad gesture, as if she were gripping him for balance. 'Tell me about you,' she said. 'Have you sold the house in Alora?'

'No,' he replied. 'It's let out.'

'It's such a pretty place.' She had visited him there once, and stayed for less time than had been planned. She had been subdued then and if she had formed an opinion of the house, she had not shared it with him. Rather, he had thought that she was uncomfortable, restless. It had been last summer, and she had complained, on the last day, of feeling too hot. 'I'm suffocated,' was how she had explained it. She had left the next day in her hire car and, he had found out later, had driven not to the airport but further north, deep into the mountains and beyond.

'This place in Dorset,' she said, 'is that a cottage, too?'

'No, I went a bit overboard,' he admitted.

She smiled at him. She could be so charming and pretty when she wanted, he thought. 'I must come and see it,' she said.

'Yes,' he told her. 'Come whenever you've got a break at work.'

She laughed softly. 'Oh, I've had a long break,' she said.

'Have you?' His stomach had lurched – when he had heard the inflection in her voice. A packet of cigarettes lay by her plate, and she was turning a lighter over and over in the palm of her hand.

The food came. He took a mouthful; she picked up her fork. 'Listen,' she said. 'This is a bit of a crisis, John.'

There was no use anticipating whatever she had to say. It might be almost anything.

She had put down her fork without having taken a bite. 'I want to sell,' she said.

He felt the weight of this old battle descending on him, as if the past with her had come up and pushed him, an old belligerence made flesh, like one enemy manhandling another, prodding him in the chest. 'Why?' he asked.

'For the money,' she said. 'Why else?'

'You need money?'

He noticed her grip the lighter. She closed her hand right over it and clutched it, rubbing her thumb along the top. 'You need money because you've lost your job?' he asked.

'Yes,' she said. 'And other things.'

'Well, let me help you,' he said. He had done so before. 'How much do you need?'

'Look,' she said, and her voice rose, 'are we going to have this conversation till the day we die?'

'What conversation?'

She laughed breathily in exasperation. 'Oh, for Christ's sake,' she said. 'John, please, don't make me beg.'

'I just offered you anything you want.'

'But I don't want your money,' she said. 'I just want a piece of what is rightfully mine.'

'Helen,' he said softly, 'it isn't mine and it isn't yours.'

'Of course it is,' she snapped, her voice rising markedly. 'Of course it is! Keeping it at all is just so irrational. It's more than irrational, in fact. It's criminal.'

'No one knows.'

'For an intelligent man,' she said, 'you can be very stupid.'

He let a moment pass. 'You're right,' he murmured.

She registered surprise, mocking him with both hands raised, palms out.

'But not about selling,' he said.

The waiter came and took away the untouched plates. Helen lit a cigarette.

They sat in silence for a couple of minutes. She asked for another drink; it was brought, and she made a prolonged show of running her fingers around the rim. 'Look,' she said. She was flushed now. 'I really need some money, John. I'm not joking.'

'I can't—'

She pounded her fist on the table to cut short his sentence. 'Yes, you can,' she said. 'You must.' She straightened in her chair. 'There's no need to look at me like that,' she said. 'Why do you look at me as if I was ten years old? I'm thirty-bloody-eight, John. I'm out of work. I want to buy a place of my own. Have something of my own. I need money.' She sat back heavily and stared at him. Her voice had broken in the last sentence.

'What's happened?' he asked.

'Nothing.'

'Something's happened, besides losing your job.'

'No,' she said.

He knew that she was lying. He knew by the tone of her voice, the old lying, evasive tone, and by the look on her face. Bruised.

'. . . and in case you didn't know,' she was saying, 'property in London is expensive.'

'Yes,' he said. 'I do know.'

She spread her hands. Ash dropped from the cigarette on to the floor. 'I need the deposit,' she said.

'And you haven't got it?' he asked. 'You've earned a fortune these last few years.'

'And you're sitting on a fortune,' she retorted, 'which we could sell, and make both our lives easier.'

He felt a small tightening, like a cord being twisted, just below his collarbone. He took a sip of water. 'Tell me what's happened,' he said quietly.

She bit her lower lip. He waited. She held his gaze. 'I lost a baby,' she said.

'What?' He tried to take her hand, but she withdrew it from the tabletop.

'Don't be sorry for me,' she said. 'It was a termination.'

'Helen,' he said, 'Heeble, I'm sorry.'

It was his old childhood nickname for her. The reason behind it was lost in the mists of time; neither of them knew when or why she had acquired it. His unconscious use of it now, though, brought tears to her eyes, and her guard dropped. The defensive expression on her face cracked. 'Thirty-eight.' And she was rubbing at the tears running down her face. 'And so stupid.'

'Who is he?'

'An actor.'

John gave her his handkerchief. 'Have I met him?' he asked. 'Would I know him?'

'It doesn't matter who he is.'

'Was it his idea?'

'He didn't know.'

John frowned. 'Helen . . .'

She shook another cigarette out of the packet, fumbled over lighting it. 'I don't see him now.'

'I'm so sorry,' he repeated. 'What can I do?'

She looked at him.

'I can't sell the legacy,' he told her.

'Yes,' she said. 'You can.'

'It's a clause . . . not to sell . . . you know that.'

'Who cares?' she demanded. 'It was some bloody thing written over a hundred years ago. Nobody cares now. Some painter no one's ever even heard of, too. Nobody gives a bloody damn.'

'I do,' he said.

The cigarette smoke curled over her head. Through it, the neon art of the opposite wall flickered. He had seen this defeat, abandonment, before. He had seen it while she sat on the floor of her kitchen twelve years ago, knees brought to her chest, the empty brown bottle by her side.

What have you taken? he had asked her.

He had had to edge on his haunches towards her then. She had been looking at him as a cat looks at a mouse, waiting. That terrible smile without humour in it. He had been convinced that she would lash out at him if he came within two feet of her. Yet when

210

he took the bottle and read the label, she did nothing.

How many? he had asked. *Not all?*

Twelve years. So vivid that it seemed just like a few hours or days ago. The memory still frightened him. The shadow of despair had filled the small room. It was like being under water, such was its shifting, light-refracting quality; a pool in which they both swam. It had been just eight months after Claire's death.

In response to his telephone call from outside John Soane's house on the day Claire died, Helen had taken him into her rented flat, a company flat in the old GLC building, looking out over the river. She had been up then, talking quickly. She helped him organize the funeral, and he always put the two together in his mind, his dragging sense of helplessness and her staccato instructions, her agitation on the day of the ceremony. When the cars were late, she had been incandescent with rage. 'I got this show together,' she told him, when he asked why it mattered. 'It's not a show,' he had replied, stung. 'You know what I mean,' she had said, pacing the courtyard, watching the road. And then she had come back to him, all tears, all apology. 'You must think I'm a monster,' she said. 'I didn't mean it how it sounded.'

When the cars arrived, it wrecked him to see how many flowers she had ordered. Claire had liked things plain, not as the multicoloured show of the cortège. But he dared not say so: it would have sounded ungrateful. As it probably was, he had told himself at the time.

In the days afterwards, he had noticed – but only through this same rippling, drowned haze – that his sister hardly slept. Helen kept him company through the hours he sat up. He would try to persuade her to go to bed, and she would claim that she didn't need to rest: she was busy at work, putting together a series. She had told him of the disputes and meetings in the same repeated way: how she had prevailed over weaker opponents; how no one knew anything; how much the whole system depended on her. He felt as if he were on the tail of a whirlwind. She confused him. He followed her reasoning only slowly, as if he had been through an illness. As if he were still ill.

The down phase came with the accident.

He had heard it. He had been sitting in the window of the flat. It was only ten days after the funeral. He had been trying to work that morning, his notepad and book of phone numbers next to him. It had been raining, a fine drizzling mist blowing almost vertically along the water. He had found himself watching the dredger and the barges, thinking of when the river had been crammed with floating traffic, about the docks: the tea wharves, sugar wharves, tobacco wharves further east. He had been thinking about a story someone in the office had told him, of a father who worked in the docks during the war, loading and unloading timber. About the smell of the pine sap, camphor, cedar on his father's clothes. About being a small boy and hearing the drone of aircraft just before the sirens, seeing the searchlights open their pencil lines of light in the sky, and feeling the almighty blast of the bombs. A rain of little black splinters of mahogany on the ground the next day.

You only had to hear the road names to recognize the past: Plantation Wharf, Trinidad Wharf, Smugglers

Way, Jews Row, Cotton Row, Ivory Square. Their history had vanished, crumpled into the flat witness of street signs. He had been thinking of history torn neatly down the centre like a piece of paper: London before 1950, London after 1950; one world barely related to the other. The time of dockers and lightermen was now barely echoed in the dredger drifting opposite. He stood on one side of a neatly torn history, too: on the other bank of the river from him stood Claire, rapidly diminishing, the three-dimensional person fading into one-dimensional photographs and pieces of paper. All Claire was now could be summed up by the numbers that had identified her. Medical records. Bank statements. She had gone, like the ships and cargoes, leaving only a faint resonance.

And he had been considering – this just a sonar echo in the light-refracting pool, without any weight or seeming consequence, a pale thought – of leaving the flat, crossing the road, and looking down at the water. He had felt a clean, imperative need to put an end to the grinding wakefulness.

And then he heard the noise.

Apparently Helen, in her little Fiat, had been making a U-turn in the road. There was no room, of course. The road wasn't designed for the manoeuvre. She had cut across one line of traffic, and collided with a taxi racing along the inside lane. She wasn't hurt, but the passenger in the taxi was injured, and an ambulance was called. When John got to the scene, Helen was standing in the middle of the road, arguing with a policeman. The ambulance was next to her, and the patient was being stretchered into it. Helen looked almost ghostlike, in a grey suit, the rain having plastered her hair to her head. She was drenched, but she carried on arguing, refusing to do anything about her car, or even to give her name and address. It wasn't her fault, she kept saying.

Eventually he got her home. They had spent half the night in the police station. She was so wired, so frantic, that he had called her doctor. And that was when he had first heard the phrase 'bipolar disorder'.

Unknown to him, the older brother who had not been at home when she was a teenager, she had had it – or, at least, it had been diagnosed – since she was nineteen. A trace of it ran back through their family to their grandmother, whom John barely remembered. Helen knew what she had, but had never told him, or shown him her medication. He sat opposite the doctor in their high-tech minimalist kitchen, the symbol of Helen's success, her achievements, and listened to how her life would be: the highs and lows, the mania and depression that would make up her inner landscape. There was no cure. In the mania, she would be euphoric, optimistic, with inflated self-esteem, poor judgement and recklessness, and she would have difficulty sleeping. In the depression, she would have persistent feelings of sadness, guilt or fatigue. She would find it hard to concentrate, and think of suicide.

This last warning, delivered in a subdued tone, had struck John with horror. He had been feeling exactly like that today, he thought, just before the accident: he had been planning to walk out, to answer the lure that rolled just a few yards away.

It had taken him a few days to persuade himself that

he did not have the same illness as Helen. He made it his business to find out the names of her tablets and the regime she was supposed to follow. By this time, she was malleable, if not monosyllabic. She had plunged down the other side of the rollercoaster ride, and watched him with disinterested eyes. Day after day she phoned in sick at work.

Sometimes, in the down phase, she would make an effort to rally. He always thought that this was probably more poignant, sadder, than if she had just lain on the couch, staring into space. In these rallies she would dress with care, put on too much makeup and go out. Just walking, she would claim. But she would come back drunk or, worse, more strung-out, more tense than ever, with that horrible look of aggressive despair.

Now she was half-way down her third drink. 'Come and stay with me,' he said. 'I want you to meet someone.'

She frowned. 'Who?'

'Her name is Catherine Sergeant.'

Helen nodded slowly. 'So, finally.'

'Yes, finally.'

'Who is she?' Helen asked. 'What does she do?'

'She works for an auction house. A small local one. I met her when I sold a piece of furniture.'

'An auction house?' Helen repeated. 'What is she? A saleswoman, or something?'

'She's a valuer.'

'Of what? Houses?'

'No,' he said. 'Art.'

The air froze. Helen put down her drink. 'Art?' she repeated harshly. 'An art expert!'

'Not just paintings,' he said.

Helen laughed. 'You're sleeping with some bloody art expert,' she said. Diners at an adjoining table glanced in their direction. 'Well, hip-fucking-hooray.'

'Helen,' he said, 'stop it.'

'And I suppose we've had lots of cosy conversations about one painter in particular, have we?'

'Helen . . .'

'How old is she?'

'Why is that relevant?'

'How old?'

'She's nearly thirty.'

Helen laughed in earnest now. 'Thirty?' she repeated. '*Thirty!*' She raised her eyes to the ceiling. 'For God's sake, John.'

'You might be happy for me,' he said.

'Happy? You're sleeping with an art dealer twenty years your junior and it hasn't occurred to you that she might be interested in something more than your amazing youth and vitality?'

The gibe hurt him more than she could have guessed. She stared at him, evidently trying to read what she saw there. 'You're in love with her,' she stated.

He didn't reply.

'Holy shit,' Helen muttered.

'Stop it.'

'Holy shit.' And she smiled.

He hated that smile; it made his blood run cold. It made him really afraid. 'Helen,' he murmured, 'are you still taking paroxetine?'

'I never have,' she retorted. 'That shows how much you know.'

'What, then? Olanzapine?'

She shot him a venomous look. 'Why must you always do this? Why do you always bring it up?'

'Are you taking lithium now?'

'Yes,' she said.

'You're taking it regularly?'

'I wish you wouldn't treat me like a baby.'

'Have you taken it regularly this week, this month?'

'Yes, yes, yes! What more do you want? Yes.'

He didn't believe her.

'If you took an aspirin, why would I have to know about it?' she demanded.

'This isn't like taking aspirin.'

'It is to me,' she said. 'Now for God's sake change the subject. I didn't come to hear your bloody memorial lecture on bipolar.'

'It's important.'

Her colour rose. 'I think I'm in a better position than you are to know how important it is,' she said. 'And I don't need you or anyone to remind me.'

Long moments passed. The people at the next table lost interest in the conversation, and went back to their own. John felt winded, as if he had run for a distance or lifted a heavy weight. He was torn between pity for his sister and annoyance.

'So,' she said, eventually, 'this woman, Catherine.'

He wondered what was coming next.

'What does she know?'

'Nothing.'

'Nothing at all?'

'She's seen things I've bought.'

'But not the rest?'

'No.'

'Are you telling me the truth?'

'It wouldn't matter if she knew or not,' he said. 'Catherine is a genuine person.'

'Oh, it wouldn't affect how she thought of you?' Helen said. 'Not one little tiny bit?'

Helen had hit on the one fact that he had been hiding from himself: that he had not told Catherine everything about himself – about the burden that lay between himself and Helen, about the secret that he had managed to persuade Helen to keep for so long – because he was afraid that it would change whatever was between him and Catherine. Just as it had changed – poisoned – his relationship with his own sister.

'A genuine person,' Helen said. 'You'd stake your life on it?'

'I would, yes.'

'And all the rest?' Helen asked. 'You'd gamble it?'

They glared into each other's faces. John said nothing.

'So,' Helen whispered, 'you'd trust her with your life, would you?' She smiled, pronouncing each word with elaborate precision. 'I do *not* think so.'

Long moments passed while John sat looking at his sister.

'I'm glad you've kept some of your sense, at least,' Helen said. She lit another cigarette, called the waiter and asked for coffee. She complained about the food she had been given, that its presentation was unappetising. There followed a long conversation, a further consultation with the maître d'. She was doggedly insistent; apologies were offered. John watched it all, sickened with himself. He couldn't let go of it, and that was the truth. He couldn't let go for Helen, and he couldn't let go for Catherine.

He was in prison, chained with a century-old promise.

He looked at the clock. His chest hurt, his hands too – he had been clenching them. Slowly he unfurled his fingers. 'Come down to the house,' he said, at last. 'I still want you to come down to the house.'

She picked up her bag. 'Oh, don't worry,' she told him, pushing back her chair. 'Wild bloody horses won't keep me away now.'

Sketch to illustrate the Passions: Anger, 1854

It was thought that water could confine the anger of mania. Cold water, of course; plunge baths into which a man could be precipitated from wooden bridges, clothed or naked. Ice cold and pumped straight from the river, full of mud, it would leave him stranded up to his neck, until the flood door was opened. The patient could then be retrieved from the floor, as often as not on his knees by the iron grille of the gate, trying to find his way out with the retreating water.

Shocking treatments would restore sanity to deranged minds or, at the very least, the threat would calm a madman into submission.

As the second half of the century dawned, Dr Hood considered the new American treatments. He had an engraving sent to him of the Benjamin Rush tranquillizing chair, the patient bound by foot and arm restraints and a shoulder brace. A rod protruded at the back, to which was fixed a head restraint, a box, that was lowered over the patient's face. It was said that this was calming to those who suffered mania and, due to its efficiency, many were bound to it for weeks at a time.

There was, too, the Utica crib, a coffin-like bed made of latticed wood. In the New York asylums, those who raved worst were tied to it, and the lid shut so that they remained incapable of movement.

Bedlam had few such modernities, but in one of the lower rooms there was a gyrating chair, held in a frame very like a gallows. It was an eighteenth-century invention and, as such, inappropriate in the most advanced modern thinking. For that reason, Hood had never expressly prescribed its use.

The patient was bound to the chair, which was bound to a large spindle, turned by an attendant standing on a flight of stone steps. As the rod was pushed, the spindle revolved, and the patient spun round. Some of the oldest attendants took pride in how long they could turn the rod; in the days before Hood had arrived, the public would pay to watch those released from the chair, for none could walk except in circles. The tickets were bought at the main gate from a creature of indigo colour, leaning on a moneybox, like Cerberus guarding the mouth of Hell.

Naturally, the paying public had long since been banned from the hospital. It was not that they were inconvenient, rather the contrary: the amounts paid had been a source of needed income. But eventually the wards of Bedlam had become notorious for whores, plying their trade out of the rain. Amours of a kind inhabited every corner. It had been said that, at any hour in the day, a sportsman might meet with game for his purpose; Bedlam was as great a convenience to London as the Long Cellar to Amsterdam.

But that was long ago. The room that held the chair was locked; the inmates were no longer chained. Only the water treatments and the Rush chair remained, and now, in the 1850s, Bedlam instigated one of its greatest innovations: a treatment to calm delusions. Upon admission each patient was photographed, the purpose being to confront each man and woman with a true image of themselves.

Dadd had already heard about the photograph. One of the Clique had visited him, and brought him news of the fixing of image by Talbot's calotype. He had told him that in Regent Street photographic establishments had been set up, and that persons of quality attended them to record their faces for ever in potassium iodide and silver nitrate.

Dadd had thought about it constantly, sitting alone, his eyes watching the slow progression of light across the wall. This, then, was where the painter died, he considered. The reproduction of the face in art was obsolete; the painter's interpretation of the soul in the face was not required. Nor was it needed for landscape: in time, he thought, the monochrome plates would capture colour. There would be no need to paint mountains, or trees bent by wind, or bridges, or docks, or rivers. Sooner or later the photographic plate would take hold of the rushing water, paste it into chemical and seal it for ever.

Man had stolen time: he had placed it in a lens. He had command of the seasons, capturing them in every mood. And he had command of other men.

A chair was brought into one of the galleries, on the landing before the doors. It was an ordinary bentwood kitchen chair with a rounded back. One morning, Anne Mary Rivers was brought there, a girl of eighteen of good family. She sat with her hands clasped in her lap and her eyes raised to the ceiling. She refused to look elsewhere, and was photographed in this attitude, her hair dishevelled, a calico hospital gown barely covering her shoulders. She made no attempt to look at the photographer, and it is to be doubted if she knew he was there. The records showed the date of her admission – 1 June 1854 – and the date of her discharge, six years later. Nothing else was noted, and the years before and after vanished as if they had never been, and all that Anne Mary Rivers ever was, or became, was an eighteen-year-old girl on a cheap chair, her upwards-looking gaze that of someone in prayer.

Others came that morning. William Wright was newly admitted. Fay Reynolds, aged seventy, had been resident at Bedlam for twenty-five years. Wright, in a state of frightened shock, was a schoolmaster, and the only reason found for his despair was his involvement in a drowning the year before, when he had found a woman's body. Fay Reynolds had been perpetually in prison for prostitution before she refused to sleep, and sang to keep herself awake. They were treated with purges and water, and locked in calming rooms. Fay Reynolds died, and William Wright was released; neither received their diagnosis, respectively of tertiary syphilis and melancholia.

Dadd was brought to the chair just before twelve o'clock.

He did not know William Wright, but he looked at him carefully, thinking that he resembled his brother. Wright was weeping as the photograph was taken, clutching at his chest, whispering to himself.

'Who is this?' Dadd asked the attendant.

'He is a fellow of St John's College, Cambridge,' was the answer. Dadd was nudged in the ribs. 'There you are, Richard,' said the steward, thinking it a joke. 'You may talk to him in your Latin and he will understand you.'

Dadd stared at his fellow inmate. 'What is the matter with him?' he asked.

'He has basses and trebles in his head,' the attendant replied. 'That's my opinion, Richard. He is a musical scholar, and he has too many basses and trebles muddling his brain.'

More often than not, Dadd would close his ears to this kind of reasoning. He heard it all around him every day. That such-and-such man had been driven mad by drink, or by visiting foreign countries, or by some kind of sin against religion. He knew that Brigham believed his own illness had been brought about by sunstroke while he was in Egypt.

He did not know if it was the truth or not.

Lately, he had come to believe that Osiris had instructed him while his conscience was not awakened; that the murderous command had entered his head while he was sleeping, or distracted, and had solidified there to make his brain its own ungovernable place. That, if he slept now or did not apply himself to concentration, the command would rise again.

And so, for the last few weeks, he had taken to

awakening his conscience by trampling the floor of his sleeping cell. He stamped his feet until they were cracked and bleeding. They allowed him to do it for the first few days and after that they had called Dr Hood. Brigham had suggested a strait-jacket, of the kind that Dadd had worn when he had been admitted. But, after he had watched Dadd for some time, and asked him what he was doing, Hood concluded that the strait-jacket was not necessary. 'Richard,' he had said, laying his hand on Dadd's arm, 'you may rest from your labours. I believe you have vanquished the enemy. He is thoroughly flattened.'

Dadd did not hear the humour. He leaned away from Hood's touch. 'You had better go away,' he said, 'or he will set upon you.'

'Who will?' Hood asked.

'The Piper of Neisse,' Dadd replied.

At the time Hood did not understand; only later, in his study, did he find the reference in papers removed from Dadd nine years before. Dadd had written a manuscript poem, 'The Piper of Neisse, a Legend of Silesia'. In it, a young man is imprisoned for witchcraft, because he can make even the least agile men dance. He dies alone in his cell, and rises up from his grave each night, rousing the dead in phantom dances through the town.

A week later when Hood went back to see Dadd, the stamping had stopped. Dadd was lying on his bed, chest rattling with bronchitis.

'How are you?' Hood asked him.

Dadd had turned a perfectly lucid face to him. 'I am inhabited by both the piper and the god,' he said, 'but they have taken to sleeping.'

'Don't wake them,' Hood said.

Dadd's eyes had filled with tears. 'I have voices in their place,' he said. 'Voices that speak my thoughts aloud. What shall I say to them?'

'Tell them to leave.'

'I cannot,' Dadd said.

Hood had sat with him long after it became dark, listening to the silence that Dadd claimed was full of sound.

William Wright was taken away.

The photographer motioned that Dadd should be brought forward.

Dadd stood by the chair, looking intently at the apparatus; a large darkroom tent had been set up adjoining the washroom. Dadd gazed at the black folds of material, and at the darkroom plates.

'Is this calotype?' he asked.

The photographer smiled. 'Do you have knowledge of the process?'

'No,' Dadd said, 'but I have heard of it.'

'It is not calotype. It is collodion.'

Dadd put his head on one side. The photographer glanced from patient to keeper: Dadd was tall, and his beard was turning white; the hair was receding a little from his high forehead; the handsome eyes were piercing and intelligent. He resembled nothing more than an Old Testament prophet. 'Collodion,' Dadd echoed.

'That is correct. Also called collodium.'

'As in colletic, from the Greek, an agglutinant, a glue?'

The photographer paused. What little Greek he had once had was long since lost. Then his expression brightened. 'There is a kind of glue,' he replied. 'To be sure there is. Mr Frederick Archer has perfected it. It is a solution of gun cotton in ether. It is a sticky liquid with which we cover the plates.'

Dadd was silent. He was not used to conversation. He could hear his voices straining to interrupt his thoughts, and his body tensed.

The photographer had not noticed. 'Collodion is more sensitive to light than calotype,' he was saying. 'It has reduced the amount of time in which the image develops. It was necessary to wait many minutes with calotype. Now the image is ready in two or three seconds.'

'It is sticky,' Dadd murmured. 'To capture the image.'

'In a manner of speaking.'

'On glass,' Dadd said, looking at the glass plates.

'The collodion is spread over the plate. Then the plate must be sensitized, exposed and developed when it is still wet.'

'To capture the image,' Dadd repeated.

The photographer looked at him expectantly, still waiting for him to sit.

'I have captured images,' Dadd muttered, 'but they are not to be seen in the world. They are here.' And he tapped the side of his head. 'You cannot take your collodium to them. There is nothing to fix them but my own hand. And they travel . . .' He extended his arm, and pointed with the other hand down from his head, across his shoulder and along his arm to his fingers. '. . . They travel on thought,' he said. 'Which is not to be found in solution, or on glass plates, or in alcohol or *water or with Pyro-Gallic.'* He stepped towards the photographer. *'I have learned all your names,'* he said, *'and yet you cannot fix me, or my thoughts.'*

He refused to have his photograph taken.

He went back to the criminal quarters, and was quiet for hours. He would not answer Brigham's gentle questions. Only in the evening did he speak, ranting at the murder of portraits, of artists, of inspiration by the collodion plate. When the rage was finished he wept bitterly, hiding his face in the coarse pillow, drumming his feet like a child.

The next day, and the day after, he bore all the aspect of grief, unwilling to eat or to wash, throwing his food on the floor in what seemed to be desperate mourning.

He was locked in his room.

On the fifth day, he began to paint.

The watercolour was almost structural, sculptural, in its strong contrast. At the top left-hand corner a house was seemingly ablaze; in the bottom right, a forge. Two figures stood by the fire, their bodies and faces whitened by the glare. A third face was barely visible in the shadows, staring into the flames.

In the inscription, winding under the heel of one of the figures, he wrote, 'Sketch to illustrate the Passions. Anger, by Richard Dadd, 17 October 1854, Bethlehem Hospital, London.'

He gave it to Dr Hood, who kept it on the wall facing his desk, and stared, too, into the white-hot flames, at what they had consumed.

Nineteen

It was coming towards the end of the sale when Mark Pearson first noticed the woman standing in the doorway. He had no idea how long she had been there – it might have been all afternoon. She was slight, but striking, with cropped hair, and was swathed in an enormous silk coat. The crowds had thinned a little since lunchtime; it was the second afternoon of the sale and they had now sold over nine hundred lots. The last was English and continental furniture, John Brigham's dresser among it. He glanced at his watch; the final lot was number 983. He estimated that it would take another forty minutes.

The saleroom was very hot. They had opened the top windows, but that had only increased the flow of sultry air; eventually they had opened the back delivery doors, and the bidders had a view out into the marketplace and the hills beyond. There wasn't a cloud in the sky.

Amanda had taken telephone bids all day; she had just finished, and came over to him as the bidding for the last lot was completed.

'Robert is here,' she whispered.

Mark took his eyes off the woman in the coat and followed the inclination of his wife's head. Robert was standing in the doorway too, watching Catherine as she took the bidding.

'How do you think he looks?' Amanda asked.

'Indifferent,' Mark said.

It was true. Robert seemed bored, leaning heavily against the door jamb, and loosening his tie. He stepped aside as the woman Mark had noticed earlier edged past him and walked slowly down the central aisle, looking from left to right for a place to sit.

Catherine saw the woman, and the catalogue in her hand; eventually, she sat down and began to fan herself with it. At first Catherine thought she was bidding; she glanced at her again, then went on. After a moment or two, she was aware of her sitting forward occasionally to peer at various items, her expression noncommittal. Catherine felt that not only the items, but the whole saleroom, was under inspection.

It came to the final ten lots.

'Lot 972,' Catherine said, 'a Dutch walnut and floral marquetry bureau, inlaid with various woods and enclosing a fitted stepped interior. A thousand pounds?'

There was silence.

'Five hundred, then.'

Within a few seconds three or four dealers were bidding against each other. The pace slackened around three thousand.

'Three five?' Catherine asked the nearest man.

'Three two.'

'Three four?' But there was no responding bid.

'For the first time of asking, at three thousand two hundred . . .'

'Three five,' said the woman.

Catherine looked at her. 'New bid in the centre of the room,' she acknowledged. 'At three thousand five hundred . . .'

'Three six,' said the dealer.

'Three seven,' the woman responded.

A murmur went round the room. Some of those who had been leaving halted at the doors. The dealers, all familiar to one another, craned their necks to see who the bidder was.

The man – it was Stuart, whom Catherine and Mark knew well – was studying his catalogue and glaring, aware that he was up against a private bidder, and annoyed that the price should be forced higher. 'Eight,' he snapped.

'Three thousand eight hundred,' Catherine glanced back at the woman. She was met with a direct stare, and a smile that surprised her. Then, a shake of the head.

'Staying at three thousand eight,' Catherine confirmed. She saw that Stuart had coloured. The woman had seemed so laid-back that he had assumed it had been nothing more than a whim for her to bid – which had cost him six hundred pounds.

'Going now at three thousand eight hundred,' Catherine said.

She glanced once again at Stuart's competitor. There was something vaguely familiar about her. Suddenly the woman's smile broadened. 'Four thousand,' she said.

The dealer gave up and returned to his chair.

'Any advance on four thousand?'

There was no opposition. Catherine brought down the gavel. 'And the name?'

'Brigham,' was the reply.

Amanda, standing at the rear, grabbed Mark's arm. 'What did she say?' she whispered.

'Brigham,' he repeated.

They looked at each other. 'It's his wife,' Amanda said.

'He hasn't got a wife,' Mark told her. 'She died twelve years ago. Catherine told me.'

'Well, he might have remarried.'

'She could be anything,' Mark told her. 'A sister, a cousin . . .' He looked anxiously at Catherine. She had paused only for a second, then passed on to the next lot. The woman was sitting back in her chair, apparently relaxed.

'She doesn't look bothered,' Mark said.

'Is she supposed to?'

'Well, if she was his wife, and had come here to find Catherine,' Mark whispered, 'you might expect her to look a bit more thunderous than that.'

It took just half an hour to complete the sale; in all that time the woman did not move.

When Catherine had finished, she left the podium and, as she walked down the aisle, the woman stood to meet her. She held out her hand. 'I'm Helen Brigham,' she said.

Catherine returned the handshake. 'I'd just about worked it out,' she said. 'It's nice to meet you. John didn't mention that you were coming.'

'I hadn't told him,' Helen said. 'It's a surprise. He asked me the other day. When he was up in town. We met for lunch.'

'For lunch,' Catherine repeated.

'I'm dying to see his new house,' Helen said.

Catherine could see no resemblance at all between this small, dark-haired woman and her brother. John was tall and ascetic-looking, thin, sometimes to the point of appearing drawn; this woman was quite different. 'And you live in London?' she asked.

'That's right.'

There was an awkward pause. Catherine was still trying silently to work out on which day John had met Helen. He hadn't told her about it. 'Well,' Catherine said eventually, 'you bought a lovely piece.'

'You think so?'

'Yes, of course.'

'But not as nice as anything John has.'

'Well . . .'

'I expect he's shown you the entire collection.'

'I've seen . . . yes,' Catherine agreed, bewildered.

'All his secrets,' Helen said. 'Every one?' She lowered her voice. 'My God, you must have been thrilled.'

They were interrupted by Mark and Amanda.

'This is John's sister,' Catherine said. *All his secrets. When we met for lunch.* She gazed at Helen's profile as she turned to Amanda, at the thick silk collar, the theatrical colour of the coat; the cruelly cropped hair and the pale face beneath it. 'This is Mark Pearson, and his wife, Amanda. Amanda, this is Helen, John's sister.'

'Do you have a house down here you're thinking of

furnishing?' Mark asked. 'You bought a lovely bit of nineteenth century.'

'No,' Helen said. 'The desk can go to John's for now.' She looked around her at the room, and at the customers, now filing out. 'You have quite a set-up here,' she said. 'John said it was a small venture, but this is big.' She returned to Mark. 'So, Pearsons is yours.'

'Not exactly,' Mark said. 'Catherine and I are partners.'

Out of the corner of her eye, Catherine saw Robert coming towards them. He had grown tired of waiting: impatience was written all over him. She tried to signal that she would come and talk to him, but he was making his way past the last of the crowds, and Mark had already turned. Politely, he held out his hand.

Helen looked from one to the other enquiringly.

'Helen,' Catherine said, 'this is Robert Sergeant, my husband.'

There was a second's pause. 'Really?' Helen asked. 'How interesting. I'm John Brigham's sister.' She extended her hand, and Robert took it.

'Robert lives in London too,' Catherine said, lost for any other way to explain herself. There was an almost palpable tremor of embarrassment.

'Whereabouts?' Helen asked.

He named a street. Catherine had no idea where it was. It was the first time he had ventured the information that he had a flat, an address, rather than a hotel.

'Near the Cavendish?' Helen was saying.

'Not far.'

'I know it.'

'Robert's mother lives in Bedford Square,' Catherine added.

'Does she?' Helen murmured.

Robert extracted his hand. 'I need to have a word with you,' he told Catherine.

They excused themselves, Catherine moving back to the podium, Robert following. They stood between the wall and the display cabinet, where two customers were waiting to receive their purchases. The steward glanced at Catherine; he was holding the receipts book for her to countersign.

She turned her back on him. 'What did you want?' she asked, her voice lowered.

'Should I know who John is?' Robert asked.

'He's a customer,' Catherine said.

'A customer.'

'What did you want?' Catherine repeated.

'I've been into the estate agents,' he said. 'They had two people interested before I walked out of the door. They want to see the house tomorrow.'

'Tomorrow,' Catherine echoed. 'All right.' And she was thinking, *All his secrets . . . all his secrets . . . you must have been thrilled . . .*

'Can you be there during the day?'

'What?' She was distracted. 'Oh, I don't know. I haven't looked at my appointments for tomorrow. I can be, I suppose. Are you going back to London?'

'Tonight,' he told her. 'Now. In fact, an hour ago if this sale hadn't taken so bloody long.'

'You should have left a message at the desk.'

He said nothing. He glanced back at Mark, Amanda

and Helen. 'Who is John Brigham?' he asked again.

She ignored him. 'I'll see to the house,' she said.

He put his hand on her arm. 'I went there today,' he said. 'They wanted all the stuff about council tax and water rates. I couldn't remember. I went to check in the study.'

She held his gaze.

'You aren't living there,' he said, 'are you?'

'It's nothing to do with you where I live,' she replied.

'The other night,' he said.

'What about it?'

'The other night you led me to believe . . .' He stopped, took a breath. 'And here was I, thinking all sorts of things.'

'What are you talking about?'

'I was thinking . . .' he said. And he laughed a little. 'I was thinking how much I had hurt you. I was feeling guilty.'

'You should,' she told him. 'You started all this.'

'Guilty about you living by yourself. I was thinking about the bureau. And Rye.'

'It doesn't matter now,' she said.

'That's right,' he agreed. 'And it didn't matter then, crying about Rye.'

Catherine felt herself colour. 'What do you mean?'

'You lying to me.'

'Lying?'

The steward touched Catherine's shoulder. 'I'm sorry,' he said. 'If you would just . . .' He held out the receipts book. She signed; he returned to the cabinet; all three people standing there stared at the couple alongside them.

'I'm not talking to you here,' Catherine whispered. 'And I'm not discussing something like this.'

'You really had me going,' Robert said. 'I was sorry for you when you've got someone else.'

She made to turn away from him. He caught her elbow. 'You didn't waste much time, did you?'

She pulled away her arm, furious. 'You've got a bloody nerve,' she hissed. 'What does it matter to you? You don't want me, Robert. You left me for someone else, remember?'

'There isn't anyone,' he said.

There was a beat of astonishment. 'What?'

He stayed silent, his lips pressed tightly together in a kind of grimace. Then he seemed to take hold of himself: pushed back his shoulders, put his hand into his pocket and took out a business card. He grasped her hand, opened her fingers and pressed the card into her palm. 'This is the estate agent,' he said. 'Ring them.'

'Robert . . .'

He went back to the group in the centre of the room.

Helen was in the process of writing a cheque. She signed with a flourish, and handed it to Amanda. Catherine watched Robert talk briefly to Mark; then Helen touched his arm. He lowered his head to listen to her, and eventually nodded.

They went out of the room together and, at the door, Helen turned back to look at Catherine.

She didn't lift her hand or smile. She simply looked, just once, before leaving.

Twenty

That evening John drove into town. He had been waiting at Bridle Lodge for Catherine; when she didn't come home after the sale, he paced the house for a while, then rang Pearsons.

Amanda had answered the phone.

'Hello,' he said. 'It's John – John Brigham. Is Catherine there?'

'No,' was the short reply.

'Is she on her way?'

'No,' Amanda said. 'At least, I'm not sure. I think she went home.'

'Home?' he echoed. 'To her house, you mean?'

'Yes.'

He tried to analyse her tone. 'Is she all right?' he asked. 'Her mobile's switched off.'

'Do you want me to give her a message if she rings here?'

'No,' he said hesitantly. 'No, that's OK. Thanks.'

He had tried her house phone, which rang and rang. For a while he thought she must be out. Then, after the sixth or seventh attempt, he became convinced that she was there but not picking up. He got into his car.

When he pulled up in the quiet street where Catherine lived, he saw that although the house was in darkness her car was parked in the drive. He walked up to the front door and knocked. There was no reply, so he knelt down and tried to look through the letterbox. The hall was just a blur of grey. 'Catherine,' he called. 'Are you there?'

A premonition ran through him. It was like being doused with cold water. He got up, looked round the side of the house, went to the gate, and opened it. There were no lights here, either. The little garden was empty. He knocked on the kitchen door. 'Catherine,' he called.

He tried the handle and found, to his surprise, that it was open. As he stepped inside, he saw her belongings scattered on the worksurfaces: her jacket, the car keys. A cupboard door hung open.

He looked to his left, into the little dining room, and was shocked to see Catherine sitting bolt upright in a chair, perfectly still. Her eyes were closed and her head was tilted slightly backwards, in an attitude of wariness or aversion. It was only when he took a step towards her that she stirred. 'Jesus Christ,' he muttered. 'What on earth's the matter? Why are you sitting here in the dark?'

She got up and walked towards him. 'I must have fallen asleep,' she said. She ran a hand through her hair. 'What time is it?'

'Nearly eight,' he said. 'I've been ringing this number.'

'Have you?' She spread her hands. 'I came back to

239

check on some things Robert said we had to have to hand for the house sale, some papers . . . I was up in the study.' She paused.

'What's wrong?' he asked.

'I . . . Helen came to the auction,' she said.

'Helen?'

'She walked up to me and introduced herself,' Catherine continued.

'I had no idea she was here.'

'Hadn't she rung you?'

'No.'

'She said you'd asked her.' He tried to read her face. 'When you met her in London. Was it a secret?'

'No. Of course not.'

'But you didn't say you were going.'

'She rang me last week and asked me to meet her.'

'You didn't mention it.'

'I wasn't sure if I should go,' he told her. 'Helen . . . Helen can be difficult.'

She moved to the other side of the room, and switched on the light. In her face, when she turned, was the one emotion he had never wanted to see: doubt.

'There's no secret,' he repeated.

She gave a small, tight smile. 'That's funny,' she said quietly, 'because that's the opposite of what Helen told me.'

'About what?'

'Secrets,' she said. 'In fact, I was trying to remember exactly what she told me,' she continued. 'She said something about the collection. Your collection. And

240

then she said, "All his secrets." And she asked me a question. She said, "I expect he's shown you the entire collection? All his secrets. Every one?"'

He put his hand to his head. 'Helen is . . . There is this thing about Helen . . .' he began.

But Catherine's voice had risen. 'And then she looked at me, and she said, "My God, you must have been thrilled." In a whisper. That I must have been thrilled.' She was staring directly at him. A questioning inflection hung in the air. 'I wonder what was supposed to have thrilled me,' she murmured.

'Catherine . . .'

'Why didn't you tell me you were meeting for lunch?' she asked. 'What was so private about it?'

'Nothing,' he said.

'You went all the way to London. You must have been gone all day – the day Mark and I were cataloguing until eight or nine o'clock.'

'Yes,' he said. 'Wednesday.'

'But . . .'

'Catherine,' he said, 'can we go home? Can I talk to you at home?'

'Is it so serious?'

'I'd rather be at home.'

He lifted his hand and held it out to her, but she didn't respond. She had kept her eyes on his face. 'What was so private about it?' she repeated.

'I didn't want to worry you.'

She frowned. 'And why would I be worried?'

He sighed exasperatedly. 'You're right,' he said. 'There's no reason. It's me who's concerned.'

'Why?'

'Because . . . you have to know Helen.' He held out his arms to her, but she was still frowning.

'I'm missing something,' she said. 'I don't understand what's going on.'

'I want to tell you,' he said. 'Let me tell you at home.'

She sidestepped him, and he noticed an empty tumbler on the table next to her. Now that he was near her, he could smell the whisky on her breath. She didn't drink: she barely touched a glass of wine, let alone spirits. 'How long have you been sitting here?' he asked.

She turned away. He came up behind her, wrapped his arms round her. She twisted against him, and slowly pushed him off her. He was suddenly aware of more than just a few inches of space between them. He felt the gulf open as surely as if he were standing on the edge of a precipice. 'Oh, no,' he murmured. 'Don't think that.'

But she voiced his fear. 'You're keeping something from me,' she whispered. 'Something important.'

She walked past him, out into the kitchen, the way he had come. She opened the door and went out into the courtyard. He followed her, and found her taking deep draughts of air. The pain in his chest was thin, tight, like the tip of a blade between his ribs. He tried lifting his head, pulling back his shoulders. He was breathing, but getting no air. As he listened to Catherine's breaths, it felt strangely as if his breath depended upon her; if he put his mouth to hers, she could breathe for him. He tried not to think of this image of himself as a parasite, taking the air out of her throat. He looked at her profile – arched neck as she tipped back her head and gazed up at the cloud-strewn humid sky – with the ivy of the fence behind her, variegated patches of shade – and felt her stepping away, through a door, through a skewed perception of him.

'I'll tell you everything,' he said.

'I thought I could trust you,' she murmured. 'I thought this was different. That *we* were different.'

'You can trust me,' he told her. 'We are.'

'I've had things hidden from me,' she said. 'Why is that?'

'I won't hide anything,' he said. He wanted to beg her.

'Robert hid his feelings,' she continued slowly, 'and his plans. Now you.'

'Tell me what you want to know,' he said. 'I haven't a secret from you.' He corrected himself: 'I won't have a secret from you.'

She crossed her arms, and gave an almost imperceptible shake of her head. 'Family secret,' she said. 'Helen was talking about some sort of family secret. Did you hide it from Claire, too?'

The pain became more refined, a single hot line from the base of his throat to the centre of his chest.

'I thought she was talking about the porcelain,' Catherine said. 'But she wasn't. She was talking about other things, wasn't she? I got the feeling that she thought I was interested in . . . whatever it is. That I was pleased to have found out. Perhaps it's something she thinks I'm trying to cheat her out of.' She was closer to him now, one hand at her throat, gazing at him intently. 'What is it, John?' she demanded. 'Money that you and she inherited?'

'Oh, God,' John said. 'Please, darling.'

'Am I wrong?'

'Helen says a lot of things. She doesn't see the world straight. She—'

'What is the secret?' Catherine persisted.

She had dropped her arms. The garden pressed in on him: he could smell the copper taint of a shrub close by, something with ink-dark leaves. Somewhere nearby, a street away perhaps, a dog was barking intermittently. He saw a light in a neighbouring house.

He felt the world flicker, the images and sounds compact, as if everything had been caught in some vast net and pulled upwards. Catherine's face and body swayed towards him. He put his hand to the wall, and dropped his head to his chest. The collapsed darkness became a minute tapestry of detail: the ragged arc of lichen under his fingers, the grit of the brick, the shuffling of the stars between clouds.

He saw the magician under Dadd's fingertip, extending his arms to hold the mottled wings and clasped hands; he felt the touch of dancers' feet, little more than drops of rain, over his shoulders. The girl in the green-glass mirror stayed where she was, looking into the glass with disappointment.

'Why can't you tell me?' Catherine asked.

'I can,' he said, 'I don't want it.' He straightened up: the garden rebounded like a flexed photograph, a piece of celluloid. 'There isn't anything I wouldn't give you,' he said.

She jerked back from him. 'Give me?' She gasped. 'I don't want anything from you.'

'I didn't mean—'

'You think I want to take this thing from you?' she said. He heard the deep hurt in her voice. 'You think that's what I'm interested in?'

'No! no!'

'Don't you understand?' she said. 'I don't want anything from you. Nothing!'

'Catherine—'

'I don't want your house,' she cried. 'I don't want your money, I don't want your family or its secrets. I don't want any of it!'

'Catherine . . .'

She put her fist to her temple. Her voice fell, for a moment, to a hitched whisper: 'This is so like Robert.'

Panic rushed through him. He tried to catch her arm, but she stepped quickly out of his reach. 'Don't you think I'm sick of people and the way they hold on to their bloody possessions?' she said.

'This is different,' John whispered. 'Only you would know how different. Even Claire didn't really know. I told her, but I never showed her.'

Catherine's hand dropped to her side. 'I don't care,' she said. 'Don't you understand? I don't care what it is. I don't care if it's the bloody Crown Jewels.' He saw, to his horror, that she was crying. She wiped her face with the heel of her hand. 'I just wanted *you*. I wanted the world the way you saw it. I wanted the seeing . . .'

That word, 'seeing', cut a piece out of him.

She was still talking.

'But now I find that wasn't right,' she said. She walked past him, within an inch of him, without touching. 'And . . . you know what?' she asked herself. 'I was thinking just now, when I was sitting here, that you

245

must have talked about me to Helen. And you must have discussed me, and you let her come to the conclusion that I couldn't be trusted—'

'No!' John interrupted. 'Catherine, it wasn't like that.'

'Well,' she said dully, 'whatever it was.'

'Please don't do this,' he said. 'Please.'

But she had stepped on to the threshold, and now half turned towards him, her hand on the door frame, her face obscured by shadows.

'Please come home with me,' he said. 'Catherine, please.'

'I'll ring you tomorrow,' she said, her voice heavy with disappointment.

'Darling . . .'

'Some time tomorrow,' she repeated.

She went inside, and he heard the key turn in the lock.

Lucretia, 1854

Two women were in his mind.

It had come to him through the gossip of the prison that there had been a murder in the women's cells.

He had been thinking of Lucretia, the martyr, the heroine, the faithful partner, whose virtue had been taken, and he started to paint her in browns and purples, taking the knife from the folds of the cloak across her shoulders, and pointing the tip at her breast.

They said in the prison that the women had not known each other, that they had been brought in separately and merely formed an alliance through others who knew them both. The tongues that wagged told of jealousy, sprung from their knowledge of a man and his possessions, to which they both felt claim.

He took his mind from their degradation and into Lucretia's bare shoulder, her eyes lifted to heaven, her hair streaming over her neck. He painted the skin very white, luminous, the background dark, the folds of her garment intricate. Strength in the posture, determination of death in her expression.

'What has happened to the murderess?' he asked the steward one morning.

'She is confined,' was all that the man would say.

And confinement it would remain for the rest of her days, unless it could be proven that the woman was not mad but cunning. He heard the whispering, as though it was transmitted through the brick, heard it flowing in the random utterances that passed for conversation in the darkened hallways. They muttered that she had come into the prison only to find her mark, to rid the world of her enemy and reclaim her inheritance. He dreamed vividly of the point of the knife, and he painted Lucretia's knife very pale against the dark cloak, her left hand that grasped it almost floating and she unaware of her intention. He painted her boldly, like a man, so caught up was she in her husband's imagined disgrace, so oblivious to his forgiveness.

He closed his eyes as the paintbrush laid on the folds of the garments.

He was trying to recall the female faces of his family. His mother, now faded so far into obscurity that he could not recall a single detail of her face. Yet he remembered Mary Anne, elder to him by three years. It had always been said that she resembled her mother, and perhaps there he could keep the memory of them both, two coins pressed from a single mould, with her intense, sympathetic gaze, the curls at her temples, the lace cap that covered her head. There was an anxiety in her look, he thought. Was that a manufactured recollection – her anxiety for him reflected in his memory? He wondered if she ever thought of him.

And then Maria Elizabeth, who had married his friend John Phillip.

Or so they had told him.

Phillip was a painter: would he have painted Maria? Would he have painted them together? Would John Phillip have perhaps painted Catherine, his brother's wife? Was there an image of them all somewhere that he might be allowed to share?

Dadd opened his eyes and gazed at Lucretia. He knew, in a passionate instant, that he wanted to see his sister. And his sister-in-law. He wanted to see Catherine. He wanted to know if there were children. No one told him of his family. He was in a parallel world to theirs, yet he yearned to hear and see them, and he sat still in front of the painting now for more than an hour, until the steward came to disengage the brush from his fingers.

'*I would like to see my sisters,*' *he told the man.*

'*Your sisters, sir?*'

'*My sisters,*' *he repeated. And when there was no reaction other than a smile, he shouted,* '*Are you deaf? Are you as raving as those you pretend to shelter? My sisters! My sisters!*'

It was late in the evening when the senior steward came to him.

Dadd was sitting quietly, having taken the laudanum.

The man told him that Maria Elizabeth, the youngest, the sweetest, the most untouched of all the family, had been committed to an asylum in Aberdeen.

His sister had tried to strangle her youngest child.

It was likely, the man told him, in the softest tones – did he think Dadd would leap up and strike him? Did he think he would strike the walls, injure himself? He had no strength to do such a thing, he had no strength at all – that, like him, she would never leave the place where they had sent her.

Just at that moment, he wanted badly to be back in Dorset, driving out of Dorchester South station, as he had a hundred times after a business trip. It seemed like a distant paradise now. There were just two sets of traffic-lights to get out of town and up on to the long, straight drive towards Beaminster, out on the breezy tops with green valleys stretching down at either side of the road. He wanted to be back in his home town, with its crooked, sloping square. But that route was forfeit.

He wouldn't pass the black-on-white 1940s signposts hooked crookedly on to the verges any longer, or take the left-hand turn down the hill towards Pearsons, its roof showing red among a haphazard jumble of sandstone and slate tiles. He wouldn't pass through the great banked edges of the lane, with its cow parsley and beech trees, braking carefully at the dog-leg turn where the frost always lay in winter, and the rain collected in one of the field entrances. He knew only too well that it had been his own decision, premeditated, careful – or so he had thought at the time – to come back to London. But he missed the past; he missed the peace. He missed looking at the patterns of things: leaf shade on the road, the peculiar chalk ridges and circles in the crops, the quiet of his own back garden.

For some unfathomable reason, the corner of the garden came into his head now in vivid detail. He propped his briefcase on the railing and leaned on it. A line of taxis drew up alongside him, rattling, panting like dogs, waiting for the lights to change. *Like dogs. Beset by dogs.* Where the hell had that come from? What a thought. He withdrew to the garden, where he had made a seating area last year, just wide enough for a bench. He had put up a little fence and painted it. His first practical project: he had been proud of it. Catherine had planted a climber; he tried to think what it was. A kind of clematis with a magenta flower. But the pleasure of having made it, of having completed the work, had been disproportionately huge to him.

He felt a pang of territoriality. It didn't belong to him any more, not in any real sense. They had had an offer on the house already; the estate agent was keen to complete. Someone else would sit in the corner by his fence. He felt ridiculously, almost childishly, cheated. He wanted to snatch back that part of his life – take the turn on the downhill lane, sit on the garden seat, watch Catherine planting the climber in the rain.

He pushed himself away from the railings and walked down Lombard Street.

The flat was in a marble-faced block at the back of Bishopsgate. It was functional. That was the best that could be said of it. It hadn't been designed to be lived in long-term. He reached it now, stepped out of the throng of the pavement crowds and into the building's little foyer, then walked up the three flights of stairs.

He let himself in and went through to the bedroom. He took off his jacket, and lay down on the bed, sighing with exhaustion, feeling the smothering stuffiness of the room. He thought of Catherine as he had seen her two days ago. She had been different, he thought. There was no doubt about it. Different in the way she held herself. Quieter, calmer. There had been an air of confidence about her that he did not recognize. And then, closer to her, he had seen that, after all, his leaving had left a mark on her. It gave him no satisfaction to see the direct, assessing look on her face when she talked to him, as if any preconceptions she might still have harboured about him had been swept away. She had looked at him as one stranger might look disinterestedly at another, and he saw that she was also older. She had always seemed rather childlike, but that had gone.

He looked at his watch. Five forty. There was nothing to eat in the flat. He wondered what to do. He could go down to the Greek sandwich bar on the corner before it closed. Or cross back over the bridge and sit in one of the pubs south of the river that he used to drink in before he got the train at Waterloo. Sit near Tate Modern and watch the river go by; go in and eat, perhaps.

He smiled to himself. If Catherine had been with him, there'd have been no doubt where they would eat: it was always galleries, galleries, galleries.

When he had first met her – on the least beautiful, least painterly station in London, Liverpool Street on the day of a train strike, and later in the crowded queue for the phone, before either of them possessed a mobile – she had struck him as rather fey, to be protected. On that first meeting, she had been wearing a black coat with the collar pulled up round her ears. He had noticed her thin wrists and pale skin. She had been shivering. He had bought her coffee; and that had been the beginning.

She had hardly spoken about her work at first. Indeed, she had kept it from him: she had said she worked at Bergen's, and let him imagine that she was a receptionist. She seemed exactly like that: a girl from the suburbs who was good at looking attractive and being polite. He had liked her modesty.

She had had barely a word to say about herself; they had spent most of their first meetings talking about him. She would draw him out – it was not that he wanted to monopolize the conversation. But then he had seen her do that with other people, clients. She would let them speak, and glean whatever she wanted from them. She was a careful, pragmatic listener. When you had finished talking, she would know all about you. And you would know nothing of her. Or very little.

That had been the attraction for him. She had struck him as unknowable, distant. The princess in the tower. He supposed he had barely given her any credit: he had been flattered by her intense gaze, her questions. He courted her. An old-fashioned word, but he had liked it all. This quiet girl. Buying her roses – her face had flooded with pleasure when he had given them to her that time. She wasn't used to being looked after: she had been alone since her parents died. She had gone through university alone.

For some reason – it turned out to be inaccurate – he had imagined that this was the same as his loneliness, the withdrawal he had experienced because he didn't want to be near his mother. Not wanting to be near, and not being near – he had thought it was the same thing. Of course it wasn't. He had isolated himself from the incessant amateur dramatics of his mother; Catherine had been separated from a woman she adored. They were both alone, and he had thought they were of the same mind because of it.

He knew within a couple of weeks that she had fallen in love with him. 'I can't think why,' he had told a colleague.

The woman had smiled at him. 'You're a handsome chap,' she had said. 'Clever, reliable. Women like that, Robert.'

Had Catherine liked it? Perhaps. Everything had been all right at first. It was only after six months or so that he realized – with terrible misgiving – that Catherine was much more than he had supposed. That the fey and fairy-like exterior he had fantasized about hid a vein of steel. She was fixed and intent. She knew what she wanted. She was deeply a part of her job; she was visual; she had a perfect memory.

And it was then, just before they were married, that he discovered he had not paid enough attention while Catherine was paying so much. He had gone on in his straight line, doing his work, being a dependable partner, earning a vast salary that he thought she admired, when it had hit him that Catherine was his equal – more than his equal, for she had something that he did not, and would never, possess.

It was not, in fact, a quality he envied.

She gave everything. She handed her whole self to him, to the steadily growing edifice of their being a couple. She gave it concentration. She wanted to get to the heart of him. And he felt that acutely, as if he were under some insidious form of attack.

Suddenly he understood that she was a woman who would inhabit him, colonize him, turn him over to her rule. She would want to *know*. She would want to *see*. And it was this curious, persistent, undermining *seeing* that he couldn't stand. He resented it. More than that, he feared it. He feared handing himself over to her. He feared her intensity. And the very thing that had first drawn him to her began to repel him.

When they had been married a couple of months, he had recognized that she would always want what he didn't want to give. There would always be some way in which he would not defer to her. She would always feel herself held at arm's length. He couldn't help it; he did not even feel it was his fault.

He felt, if he were honest about it, that he had been artfully suckered into giving, or being asked to give, what he would not relinquish. He felt that somehow she had lied to him. She had seemed safe and quiet, but she was nothing of the sort.

There had been one night when they had been sitting together, reading, when she had looked at him with such a glance: more than loving, it was a look of complete happiness. A smile like that should not worry anyone – it sounded odd, now, to say that it could – but it *had* worried him. It had shown him her complete abdication of herself. An amazing ability. He knew he'd never master it. He'd never feel it. More importantly, he'd never want to feel it. The idea made his blood run cold.

He imagined himself – he remembered the feeling so clearly – being dragged into giving himself away. And the moment he felt that he began to move back from Catherine. And in time she began to understand. She would never reach him. He would always be apart. He would keep his precious sanctuary.

Perhaps that was where the lessening had started –

that was the perfect word for it. There was simply less of everything. Less conversation. Less toleration. She stayed with him, of course, but he saw the resentment creep in. In the end, in the months before Christmas last year, they had barely spoken to each other. The silence stood between them – that, and her conviction that he had failed her.

He thought of her like one of her paintings, one of those detailed Victorian canvases, the large ones that she knew so much about, with a host of characters. She admired painters who had devoted such care to detail. And he hated them. He hated the very idea that one person could consume another like that, every particle of them, each inch of cloth, every fleck of skin or strand of hair, and the patterns of the carpets under their feet, the flowers on the wallpaper behind their heads, the reflection in the glass that they held in their hands. It was almost cannibalistic, this greed to replicate another human being.

Sighing, he got up and began to take off his travel-stained clothes. He folded the suit jacket and the trousers, putting them aside carefully for dry-cleaning. Then he walked to the shower, and spent several minutes under the stream of hot water, feeling the needle-like stream on his shoulders and back. He put his head under the hot water and let it douse his face. And all the time she was in his head, in the pictures that played there.

He had seen his mother the previous weekend; felt that he ought to take her out, now that he was here. He had offered to take her to tea at Fortnum's, but had got little thanks for his trouble. The moment his mother had sat down she was complaining. 'Jesus Christ,' Eva had muttered, rolling her eyes in the direction of a group of laughing young women at a neighbouring table. 'It all gets worse.'

He had ordered tea. His mother was wearing a rather absurd fifties-style shirtwaister with voluminous skirts. 'I remember that dress,' he told her.

'It's like me,' she had said. 'Moth-eaten.'

Above them the ceiling fans had whirred. Their noise and movement increased Robert's sense of disjointedness with the afternoon. He was not where he wanted to be, even after all his efforts to break free. He realized, with dulled disgust, that he would probably never break free of his mother, and, through her, his wife. Both women clung to him like webs.

As if reading his thought, Eva spoke up: 'Have you left her for good?'

'Yes.'

'I'm glad,' Eva commented. 'She was no fun at all.'

He couldn't look at her. Eva had taken a long draught of her tea. 'Paintings,' she said. 'All she ever talked about. I should like a bit more than that, myself.'

'A bit more than that?' Robert asked.

'A bit of fun,' Eva said. 'Like your father and I had.' She fingered the material of the dress. 'Nine years in Singapore,' she mused. 'A party every night. Every hour a happy hour. That was when the British knew how to live.'

He had stared at her, noting her cruelty and selfishness. The cruelty now over Catherine, her selfishness in the past. She and his father had stayed in the Far East for those nine years of his childhood, ostensibly working for some tobacco concern but, in reality, pleasing themselves, making him feel the outsider, prey to their tempers, their continual arguments, until the bubble burst and the capitalists, colonists, came home. Even then he had had enough of his mother's screeching and clinging.

He looked at her again and realized how much his dislike of Catherine's single-mindedness, her clinging attachment to him, was a reaction against the woman sitting now in front of him, wearing the elaborate necklace he had given her for Christmas. It had originally been for Catherine, a surprise, until he realized that he was going to leave her; then it had seemed absurd to give it to her.

Seeing his mother wearing it now he felt uncomfortable, as if she were wearing a trophy of her daughter-in-law's dismissal.

A doubt had sprung into the back of his mind, a terrible, sickening doubt, that he had confused Eva with his wife, painted Catherine in Eva's colours.

Now getting out of the shower, he heard his mobile ringing.

He walked back to the bedroom, and picked it up, expecting his office to be returning his earlier message.

'Hello. Remember me?' said a female voice.

He knew it, but couldn't place it. 'I'm sorry . . . ?'

'It's Helen,' she said. 'Helen Brigham.'

He had run Helen Brigham to the station the other day, and given her this number when she had wondered if the train would run on time. She had seemed so anxious that he had said he would help her if she was stranded – although what he could have done, staying in a local hotel, or why Helen Brigham wouldn't have rung her brother, were thoughts that had not occurred to him until afterwards.

'Hello,' he said now, still puzzled.

'Well,' she said, 'I'm standing on Cheapside, looking down Bransgore Street. Which number are you?'

He paused. She was in London – but, then, she lived somewhere to the east. 'Is there a problem?' he asked.

'No,' she said, 'but I need to talk to you . . . if it's convenient.'

'I see,' he replied.

'Is it?'

'Yes,' he said. 'Of course.' He gave her the number of the flat.

Five minutes later, she knocked at the door. He stepped back to admit her, and she ran her eye over him, taking in the wetness of his hair. 'I've disturbed you,' she said.

'No,' he told her. 'I just got back from a trip.'

'I was on my way home from work,' she said. 'I wondered if you could tell me something.'

He led her into the tiny sitting room. 'A drink?' he asked.

She shrugged.

'Coffee?'

'A glass of wine would be nice,' she said.

A few moments later he brought it from the kitchen. She held up her glass in a joking gesture of celebration. 'What shall we drink to?' she asked.

'I've no idea,' he said.

'Life and its strange twists,' she said. 'Life as a footnote.'

'I'm sorry?' he said.

'A footnote,' she repeated. 'You know, the little bits they put as a backstop to text. A sort of afterthought.'

'Why would you think of yourself as a footnote?' he asked, perplexed.

'Don't you?' she asked. 'Left behind while they move on.'

'Are you talking about Catherine?' he asked.

'Yes.'

'But she didn't leave me behind,' he said. 'I left her.'

Helen lowered her glass, which was already half empty. She considered him. 'You left her,' she repeated.

'Yes.'

'Why was that?'

He frowned.

'I have a good reason to ask,' she said.

'What reason?'

'She's living with my brother,' Helen said. 'I would like to know what sort of person she is.'

Robert took in the information 'living with my brother' slowly. He took a sip of his wine. 'What difference does it make?' he said. 'They're both adults.'

'She's very young,' Helen commented.

He thought about it. Catherine was three years younger than he was; this woman was probably six or seven years older than him, nearing forty. Although it was hard to be sure. She was very pale. Her hands were veined, the skin dry, the knuckles unpleasantly prominent. If she was coming home from work, he thought, she was dressed very casually: jeans, T-shirt, sandals. He noticed that her feet were dirty, as if she had walked a long way. The jeans, too, were not very clean. She looked like an ageing child. Rather sad, too:

he had seen that the other day as she sat beside him in the car.

He realized that he had been inspecting her, and blushed.

'Is she good at her job?' Helen asked. 'This . . . art valuing, the auction business.'

'Yes,' he said.

'Does she specialize?'

'Victorian things.'

'Paintings?'

'And sculpture.'

Helen Brigham stood up. She put down her empty glass, walked to the window and gazed out at the office buildings.

'Is there a problem?' he asked.

He saw, then, that she was crying and felt a burst of frustration – exactly that, not sympathy but frustration that she should come here and burden him – before he joined her.

'Can I do anything?' he asked. 'What is the matter?'

Her hands were over her face. 'She'll take it from me,' she whispered. 'It's all I have for the future.'

'Take what?'

Her hands dropped. 'Does she have any money?' she asked suddenly.

He was lost for words. Helen had been to the auction rooms. She had heard Mark Pearson say that Catherine was a partner in the business.

'You see,' she said, 'I have to protect my brother.'

He was astounded. 'Protect him?'

'From fortune-hunters.'

Robert laughed, taken by surprise.

'It isn't a joke,' she said. 'People do such things, you know.'

'I'm sorry,' he told her. 'And I don't think you need to worry.'

'Shouldn't I?' she asked. 'Why not?'

'Because . . .' He wondered how he could explain it. 'Because Catherine wouldn't be interested in that sort of thing.'

She made a disbelieving, sardonic face. 'Everyone is, at some level. Everybody wants what they can get.'

'Not Catherine. It wouldn't occur to her.'

'It might,' Helen said. 'If she found something worth keeping.'

'I don't understand you.'

She crossed her arms over her chest, hugging herself.

'Did you ask your brother this?' he said.

'No,' she replied. 'I didn't go to the house. I didn't see him.'

'Why not?'

'Because . . .' She shook her head. 'It's hard to explain. He would think I was overreacting. You see, I asked him a while ago . . .' She put the knuckles of one fist to her forehead and rubbed the skin. 'I think it was last week,' she murmured. 'I asked him . . . I'm worried . . . I can't sleep . . . I need money . . .'

Robert was embarrassed. He could see the tears slowly descending, tears that seemed to have more life than the papery skin beneath them. 'I'm sure he wouldn't deny you help,' he said.

She glanced at him. 'He wouldn't?' she asked, as if Robert had more access to John's motives than she did. 'He wouldn't keep it back because of her?'

264

'I don't know your brother,' he reminded her.

'Neither do I,' she said. 'I don't know anyone any more.' And she dissolved into real sobs. There was nothing he could reasonably do but put his arms round her. 'You can't trust anyone,' she said, her voice muffled against his shoulder. Then, she raised her face to his. 'Isn't that true?'

'I don't know,' he said, disconcerted by the desperation on her face.

'Did you love her?' she said. 'Did you love Catherine?'

'Yes,' he said.

'And she loved you? Once, I mean. You loved her once, and she loved you?'

'Yes,' he said, feeling uncomfortably that it was not quite the truth.

Helen Brigham's fingers tightened round his upper arm. 'But you can't trust that,' she whispered. 'Not even that.'

She moved her hand up his arm, along his shoulder, then pressed her mouth to his. He was taken aback, yielded for a second or two to the insistent pressure, was almost tempted to respond, until he felt her fingers exploring his face. The intimacy jolted him backwards. For a moment he caught sight of her, eyes closed, mouth slightly open. Something about the fleshiness of her lips, the stale smell of her, overwhelmed him. She opened her eyes.

'I'm sorry,' he said. She looked disoriented. 'Come and sit down.'

She did so.

'Are you all right?' he asked. Because it seemed to

him that there was patently something not right about this situation, this woman, but he couldn't fathom what it was.

'Yes,' she said. 'I'm all right.'

'Do you think,' he ventured, 'that perhaps you should go and see your brother and talk this over with him?' He cast about for something positive to add, some piece of useful advice. 'And perhaps Catherine.'

'You want me to go and see Catherine?'

'To set your mind at rest.'

'You want me to go and see your wife and my brother?' she repeated.

'It's only a suggestion.'

'Can't you help me?' she asked.

He was thoroughly confused now. He felt that he wanted to wash the taste of her off his face, but couldn't think of a reason to excuse himself. 'I'm sorry,' he said, 'but with what?'

'Can't you speak to Catherine?' She put her hand on his knee.

'To say what? I don't understand. What would you want me to say to her?' He moved back on the couch, gently disengaging himself from her reach.

She saw the movement, and stood up abruptly. 'I can see you don't want me here.'

'Helen, I—'

'I'm sorry to have wasted your time.' He tried once again to speak, but she held up her hand to stop him. She went to the door, and paused there, her hand on the latch. She looked back at him. 'You talk to Catherine,' she said softly. 'You talk to your wife, and you tell her . . .' She stopped to inspect him, his expression. 'Are you listening to me?'

'Yes,' he said.

She opened the door. For a second, she paused on the threshold, one hand lingeringly caressing the other, smoothing her fingers, wrist and forearm.

'I'll talk to her,' he promised.

She looked down at her arms, then slowly around the almost empty, anonymous room. 'Tell her to keep away,' she murmured, 'from my brother.'

Songe de la Fantasie, 1864

Richard Dadd was transferred to Broadmoor Hospital, a purpose-built asylum for the criminally insane in Berkshire, on 23 July 1864.

He had been in Bedlam for almost twenty years.

They had anticipated that there might be some difficulty in persuading Dadd to move from his familiar cell, but he had taken the news calmly, almost without reaction, and spent several days filling the portmanteau that had been given to him, asking for small lengths of cotton in which to roll his paintbrushes, and which he also used to wrap his volumes of poetry.

Brigham had noticed, on the morning of the day of departure when he went earlier than usual to check his charges, that Dadd was sitting on his bed with a book open on his lap.

The painter looked benign. It was hard to believe that he was a fantasist, a schizophrenic, a murderer. Dadd was forty-seven years old, yet he looked much older. He bore little resemblance now to the photograph that had been taken of him only five years previously. After his prolonged weeks of grief, he had finally allowed his image to be recorded, and had been shown at his easel, where he was working on Oberon and Titania; an imposing man, broad and bulky, his eye fixed on the photographer, not the lens. His hair had still been dark, then, with only a few traces of grey. Now he looked as if shock had overtaken him: his hair was almost completely white.

The physician's opinion was that Dadd had reached a sudden – if delayed – acquiescence at his circumstances. After his photograph had been taken, Dadd no longer raged, or took to violence, even of argument. 'He is improved in temper,' his notes ran, 'though still holding his old convictions.'

'What are you reading?' Brigham had asked him, that last morning in London.

'Resolution and Independence,' Dadd said, holding out the book.

'William Wordsworth. "My whole life I have lived in pleasant thought . . ." Brigham smiled. 'Well, sir, there's an idea for you.'

"My old remembrances went from me wholly, and all the ways of men," Dadd read.

'Well, that's good. Old remembrances are no use to us, sir.'

'Are they not?' Dadd murmured. He picked up the last piece of cotton fabric, closed the book, wrapped it, and held it to his chest.

They brought the carriage that was to take Dadd and four other inmates at eleven o'clock.

Dadd was silent until he reached the last flight of stairs, and could see the patch of yard, the rims of the wheels, and the horse's hoofs on the brick driveway. He held on to the handrail and stopped.

'We'll move on now,' Brigham said. 'Last few steps, sir.'

But Dadd would not move. Tears were in his eyes as he stood rooted to the spot. They began to fall: slow, heavy tears.

'There's nothing to be frightened of,' Brigham said. 'Come, sir, there's a fine new building waiting for you at the other end. A fine view of woodland. And there are terraces to walk upon. It is a better place than here, Mr Dadd.'

'I have had to leave it,' Dadd whispered.

'That's right, sir,' the man encouraged. 'That's right. You must go.'

Dadd turned to him. The tears were splashing on the fustian jacket. It was the same one that Dadd had worn twenty years before when he had been admitted. 'You will have it,' he said.

'Have what, sir?'

'The canvas they will not let me take.'

There were more than forty paintings in the locked storeroom next to the physician's office.

'You have seen me working on it,' Dadd said.

The attendant nodded. He took out his own handkerchief and wiped Dadd's face. Suddenly Dadd was searching in his pockets. He pulled out a piece of paper. 'I wish to write,' he said.

'There's no time,' Brigham said. 'The driver is waiting. You must take the train in forty minutes.'

'Give me a pencil,' Dadd said.

As he looked into the other man's face, Brigham felt

nothing but pity. What a life wasted, he thought. He had sat and watched him many times, working on his drawings. Sometimes Dadd would spend all day producing a little thing, a face, a hand, a branch of leaves. And then he would screw up the paper and throw it away. Brigham had picked up many of them. He kept them at home, carefully smoothed out and held flat under a travelling trunk that his wife filled with linen. One or two had got damp, and the children had taken some, but he still had a good number. He had an affection for the peculiar chap; he thought his drawings very fine. Sometimes in the morning, if the man had had a poor night, Brigham would sit with him and listen to the horrors that had inhabited the dark.

He took a stub of pencil out of his jacket, and gave it to Dadd, who scribbled hurriedly for a few seconds. He handed the note to him. 'You take this, Edward,' he said, using the attendant's Christian name for the first time. 'You give that to Mr Neville and tell him that it is to be seen to.' His hand closed on his wrist. 'You take it for me,' he said. 'You have been kindness itself to me. You are a fine, stirring fellow. You are Polyphemus.'

'Indeed, I am not, sir.'

'From the idylls of Theocritus, the lover of Galatea.'

'I don't doubt it. But I am not he, sir.'

'It has taken me nine years,' Dadd said. 'It is called The Fairy Feller's Master Stroke. I have nothing else to give you.'

The attendant smiled. 'I cannot take that, sir,' he said, 'for you have given it already to Mr Haydon.'

Dadd stared at him, baffled. 'The Master Stroke?' he repeated.

'Yes, sir.'

Dadd looked down the stairs, to the splashes of sunlight dancing on the road. 'I shall paint you another,' he said. 'I shall paint you a copy. And you must take some of the others that they have here.'

'It doesn't matter, sir.'

'Oh, yes,' Dadd murmured, pressing his fingertip into the centre of the piece of paper that he had already put into the attendant's hand. 'I shall certainly paint you another, Mr Brigham.'

The carriage pulled out of the yard. It rattled slowly down the long driveway and out into Lambeth Road, towards the oldest settlement of London at Lambeth Palace.

At first the blinds were closed, pulled down so that the patients would not be disturbed; but, after less than a mile, it was thought that the noise from outside, which could not be drowned or lessened, was more disturbing if no sights accompanied it. The blinds were raised, and Richard Dadd saw London for the first time in two decades.

They went down to the river, to Westminster Bridge. It was thought that the horse ferry across at Lambeth would be too slow so they passed, in a roaring slew of carts, carriages and pedestrians, over the span. Halfway across, Dadd leaned forward, looking to his left. 'What has happened to Westminster Palace?' he asked.

'It was burned down,' he was told. 'They are rebuilding it. There will be a great clock tower on the bridge.'

Dadd stared at the half-raised Pugin and Barry edifice, hidden behind its scaffolding, on which men were ant-like dots working between the beams. He saw the empty gaps for windows, the horses drawn up with loads, dozing in the mid-morning heat. Dust drifted across the Thames, whose surface, muddy and churning, was clogged with river traffic.

The carriage turned right, along Horseguards, then left along the Mall and Constitution Hill. Dadd showed no interest in the street to the right of them, Pall Mall, where he had first exhibited at the British Institution, a young man of twenty-two, a coming talent, a genius, a person to be courted. Only two years later he would produce Titania Sleeping and Puck, both bought by Henry Farrer, when Farrer was the dealer with the most commercial eye and had forecast great things, a place in the public eye, fame and fortune. But all that past had vanished: Henry Farrer would not recognize Dadd now.

The carriage emerged on to Hyde Park Corner, where the traffic ground to a halt. There was some sort of hold-up along the road, the driver called down, that they could not pass. After ten minutes or so, one of the attendants got out and negotiated a passage for them along the Serpentine Road through Hyde Park, people shrinking back to let them through.

Dadd sat forward on the edge of his seat. He had drawn the Serpentine, that sinuous stretch of water, more than once. He caught sight of the Long Water and, beyond it, the pretty little dogcarts and broughams passing along West Carriage Drive. He blinked rapidly; his sight was not what it had been. He had stared for too long at paint only six inches from his eyes. He could not focus on the rolling waterfalls of colour. Two *children were running alongside the carriage, each with a handful of gravel, which they threw at the wheels; he tried to lean out of the window to look at them, at the liveliness in their faces, but he was pulled back, into the shade.*

They passed out of Marlborough Gate into the morass of traffic again; the green was left behind; ahead, new buildings shone white, faced with Isle of Portland stone. Dadd breathed heavily: the impact was too much. Yet he had to remember. It was all he would see before he was locked away for the rest of his life. It was all he would have to paint. He must remember how it looked, so much busier than before, so many more people. He must remember. It would vanish within minutes. He tried to place the perspective of the sky against the city, the people against the pavements, the jolting motion of the broughams, the fluttering of women's pale dresses, the dancing of a horse's movement, the writhing blocks of humanity in the street. It almost choked him.

And sound, more than anything: the wall of voices, the echo of the trees and water, the hollowness of the park, the stagnation of the street, the blackening circles of the chimes of churches . . .

They were at the railway station. Dadd was given a small cup of water, in which laudanum was dissolved. He was helped down the steps and out into the baying mass of Paddington, into Brunel's massive terminus for the Great Western Railway, running from London to Bristol: a hugely vaulted iron-girder roof with decorative iron ribs, held up by cast-iron columns.

The noise now was a living monster, another Bedlam.

Men dragged luggage on wheeled carts, racks of leather, bands of brown. The sound of the iron wheels assaulted him, smothered him, the awful metallic clanging next to him as he was half walked and half dragged by the attendants, beside the train. Dadd dared not look up: already the glittering windows, the brass on the finishing, the open sashes where, here and there, a body hung out, calling, waving at whatever was behind him, frightened him beyond belief.

He tried to look upwards instead, disoriented, nauseous: he had never travelled by train. The sight of the engine at the front, on the very point where the track curved out into the light sent him into a paroxysm of terror.

He was bundled through the smoke and steam; they were late; the train was about to leave. Strangers side-stepped him and grimaced. He could not bear it. The world was a blazing star; he had been swept up in switching parallels of light and dark. The crowd howled at him; he moaned as he was hauled bodily into the belly of the beast, and sat in the allotted space, shivering, weeping, his hands over his face.

When he reached Broadmoor, Dadd showed no interest in his new private room; no interest in the belongings that had been brought to him. Even a violin had been purchased, and was waiting for him on a little writing-table.

It was remarked that he was quiet, peaceable with his fellow patients; but the diagnosis did not touch him. It was not calm at all. It was retreat. It was indifference to the ordinary world. He was an exile.

In time, he was roused to sit up, dress himself and eat. He sat with others, in the day rooms, hands folded in his lap, or placed exactly on his knees. He said little, because he knew that he could not communicate what he knew or that it would not be accepted. Life did not exist in what his senses told him, in what he received in the lies of sight and hearing.

The real world, a thing of beauty, had to be guarded, he knew; shut up firmly against its parody. The real world existed not outside himself but inside, gifted to him by old gods. The real world vibrated under glass; he could hold a magnifier to the paper, and see it. Just the smallest door led through to that world, the real world hidden in the invisible grains of cotton and wood, flattened and processed into paper and canvas. The real world hid there, between the strands of fabric and grass. Somewhere deep in its heart was the truth.

He sat next to the window, with its view of the woodland, but he did not look out.

He kept his promise. He painted a copy of The Fairy Feller's Master Stroke, for Edward Brigham.

And called it Songe de la Fantasie, his place of safety.

Twenty-two

It was ten o'clock in the morning when Catherine found him. John was sitting in a corridor outside the cardiac-care unit, his mobile phone in his lap. In the process of dialling a number, he stopped when he saw her walking towards him.

She halted in front of him, her expression one of frustrated fury. 'Peter Luckham told me,' she said. 'He rang and asked how much longer he should look after Frith.'

John switched off the phone.

'You weren't going to tell me?' she said. 'Nothing? *Nothing?*' She was flushed and out of breath from running. 'I have to wait to hear from somebody else,' she said. 'Peter had to ring me! How could you?'

'I'm sorry,' he said. 'The last time I saw you—'

'You've been in hospital two days, and Peter Luckham has to tell me.' She spread her hands in appeal. Almost to herself she muttered, 'God, *God.*' And to him, 'You really thought I wouldn't want to know this?'

'Catherine,' he said, 'you told me you would ring me. When you didn't . . .' and he gestured to the mobile phone.

'I know what I said,' she whispered. She was beginning to catch her breath. 'What are you doing sitting out here?' she asked abruptly.

'I'm about to leave.'

'They're letting you go? Have they finished?' she asked. 'What tests have they done? What did they say?'

'Catherine,' he said, 'this is something and nothing.'

'Peter said you rang an ambulance two nights ago!'

'Yes, I did.'

'When exactly?'

'About three in the morning.'

'After you came to see me, that same night?'

'Yes.'

'Oh, God,' she repeated, more softly now. 'And that's something and nothing, I suppose? You could have just picked up the phone to me. You think I'd not try to help you? What? That when I finally heard' – there was a flash of sarcasm – 'I wouldn't give a damn?'

'I didn't know if you'd want to hear from me.'

She gasped. 'You fool,' she said. 'You bloody, bloody idiot.' He stood up, still unsure of her. She looked away from him, evidently collecting herself. 'Look, if nothing else, tell me. What have they said? What have they told you?'

He looked away up the hall.

'Aren't you going to say?' she asked. 'What is this? A state secret or something? Tell me!'

'It's angina,' he replied.

'Angina,' she repeated. 'Like . . . stress?'

'Not really.'

'What, then?' He didn't reply. She spotted the small holdall at his feet. 'Is this yours?'

'Peter brought it.'

She sat down next to him, two seats away, twisted in the chair to face him. 'John,' she said, 'please tell me what they said.'

He was trying not to give in to the relief and fear that had dominated the past forty-eight hours. He always felt so horribly vulnerable in a hospital ward. He just wanted to go home – had made himself popular this morning by demanding to be discharged. In the end he had signed a form to say that he was discharging himself. They had put him here to wait for his medication.

He tried not to look directly into Catherine's face.

'Intractable angina,' he told her.

'I don't know what that means.'

'It's . . .' He massaged the fingers of his left hand with those of the right. 'I've had it some time.'

'You have?' She was aghast. 'Since getting back to England?'

'Before that.'

'But how long?'

'Several years.'

She was scanning his face. 'Is that why you came back?'

'Mostly.'

'All the time since I met you?' she asked. 'All the time I've known you?'

'Yes.'

'But you could have an operation, surely?' she said.

'Something to help. There's loads they can do, isn't there?'

'I had an angioplasty in Spain,' he told her, 'but the condition's called refractory angina.'

'A bypass,' she said. 'You could have one. I used to work with someone who had a bypass. It worked like magic.'

'You can't operate on this kind,' he said. 'Some people called it stubborn angina, and that's what it is. Fucked-up angina. You put a stent in one place to open up the flow, and it closes down somewhere else.'

'I've never even seen you take a tablet.'

'I have beta-blockers, calcium blockers. I used to take statins. Sotalol. I still take nitrates.'

There was a long silence. She was baffled by his off-hand attitude. She had heard of beta-blockers, but not statins or sotalol. She couldn't even guess what they might be. Over John's head, a luridly coloured poster on the wall extolled the virtues of exercise and healthy eating. It wasn't as if he was overweight, she thought. He didn't smoke. It didn't make any sense.

An auxiliary passed with a trolley of drinks, and turned into a side ward. They listened to her talking to the patients, good-humoured banter passing back and forth.

'What did you think I would do?' Catherine asked him. 'Why didn't you tell me all this? Did you think I would leave you or what? Did you think I couldn't grasp it, that I wouldn't understand?'

'I don't think about it,' he said. 'I hate these places. I hate the whole subject. That's why I didn't tell you. I just don't think about it.'

'It's not a good enough explanation,' she said. 'It's rubbish.'

'It's my problem,' he said.

'Well, thanks for the vote of confidence.'

The ward sister was walking towards them, holding a pharmacy package. She gave Catherine a little nod of acknowledgement, and handed the parcel to John. 'I don't suppose I need to tell you about these,' she said.

He stood up. 'No.'

'You need to come back to see the consultant.'

'All right.'

'I rang his secretary,' the nurse continued. 'She said you didn't attend last week.'

Catherine looked accusingly at him.

'I will,' he said. 'Thanks.'

They walked out; he held the door open for her. It was a blustery day, clouds scudding across a patchy blue sky. On the hospital steps, John stowed the medication in his jacket pocket.

'I'll give you a lift,' Catherine said.

'I can get a taxi,' he said. 'I was about to ring for one when you arrived.'

'You bloody won't,' she said.

He started to walk away. She watched him in astonishment, then hurried after him. 'What is it with you?' she demanded.

'Nothing,' he said.

'Look at me,' she told him. 'Look me in the eye. You haven't looked at my face since I got here.'

Reluctantly, he did so.

'What is it?' she said.

'I didn't want you involved in all this.'

She gave a gasp. 'And I'm not involved?'

'I'm not such a good bet, Catherine. It's not fair on you.'

He set off down the slight slope towards the town. He walked with a curious, crooked gait, shoulders hunched, as if he were warding off a blow, or defending himself against one. At the next junction he waited while several cars negotiated the narrow entrance into the public car park; the last one was a private cab. He hailed it, bent down to talk to the driver.

She ran down the path and snatched his arm. 'How you bloody dare to do this! How you bloody dare!'

'Look—' he said.

'No! You look, John! You're not getting away that easily. You wanted me to live with you, and you wanted me there every moment of the day—'

'I thought it was what you wanted,' he said.

'It was,' she told him. 'What did I do? What was so bad that you shut me out?'

'I can't explain,' he said. 'I don't know.'

'You can't tell me that you're ill? You can't tell me whatever it is, this thing with Helen, you just . . .' she cast about for the words '. . . just cut me off?'

'I've been alone a long time,' he said.

'And that's a reason?' she replied angrily. 'OK, that is a reason. It's a reason to want someone with you, to want to be loved, never to be alone again, not to slam the door in their face.'

'I didn't want to load you down with it all,' he said. 'It's my problem.'

'Shit,' she retorted. 'It's all so much shit, John. You didn't trust me.'

'No,' he said. 'That's not right. I don't trust myself. I don't know what to do.'

She gazed at him, frustrated and confused.

All around them the busy access road moved, awash with patients and visitors, delivery trucks. They stood on the corner, a small oasis.

As he looked at her, he thought that perhaps he had just one more year, or two years – a man his age might expect twenty-five. What would two years be? It hardly rated as a miracle. Not for a man of fifty. Two years with Catherine. Two years, eight seasons.

Eight seasons with Catherine.

He pressed his lips together, but his mouth turned down despite his efforts to control it. *Fuck it*, he thought. *Don't start crying in front of her.* And he made himself laugh with the stupidity of it. 'Jesus,' he muttered. He felt in his pocket for a handkerchief, realized he didn't have one.

'What are you going to do?' Catherine asked.

'About what?'

'About this,' she said. 'There must be something. Some operation.'

He opened his mouth to repeat the constant thread, *arteriosclerosis, inoperable refractory angina*, then thought better of it. He hated the words. They were stuck inside his head. He wished that he could somehow climb inside and pull them out. Once heard, never forgotten.

He looked at Catherine and she saw the reply written in his expression. She lost colour; stood stock still.

He had asked his GP for a prognosis two months ago.

'You need to rest,' he had been told.

'Is there any other treatment?'

'A form of gene therapy is being tried in the USA. A growth factor injected into the heart.'

'Can I have it here?'

'I'll look into it.'

They'd regarded each other, John trying to read between the lines of what he'd been told. 'Can I walk any distance?' he'd asked.

'Yes, of course.'

'How far?'

'However far you feel is OK.'

'Play sport?'

'Perhaps not wise.'

Well, he wasn't wise. Being wise was as good as being an invalid. It wasn't what he'd wanted – it was a long, long way from what he'd wanted – so he'd worked on the weir gates, hauled the timber into trailers. He had walked four miles one morning, before he met Catherine, hoping that, on the frosty day in March, with the first sun through the trees, and the first green centimetres of the bluebells showing above the soil in Derry Woods, while everything looked so promising, so good, the first bright day of the spring, that the nagging, exhausting ache would shut his heart down there and then. He couldn't be wise and sit and wait. He would rather put a gun to his head and be done with it.

And then Catherine had come to the house. And it wasn't an easy decision any more. It wasn't the same choice. It was no longer a matter of walking the pain down in Derry Woods. He had made a little deal with himself. He would take his medication, and not walk too far or do any heavy work. He decided to restore the stairway in the Lodge: a small, intricate job, not too taxing. All the time lying to her by not telling her. He bartered being wise against loving her, and prayed to God that he wouldn't die in bed.

Now he felt a guilty regret. 'I'm a selfish man,' he told her. 'I wanted you.'

She put her arms round his neck. She didn't cry, but her breath was a shallow flutter against his face. After a minute or so, she drew back from him, took her keys out of her bag. 'I'll take you home.'

He took her hand. 'Don't take me,' he said. 'You'd take a sick person. You'd help them. But I don't want your help. I don't want nursing. I just want you to come back to the house with me.'

She nodded. 'All right, John,' she said.

Twenty-three

That night they went up to Derry Woods, starting across the fields from the weirs on the river when the dusk was so deep it was almost dark. The paths were dry underfoot, with chalk showing through as they rose. It was warm, humid, the heat of the day still hanging in the air. Under the beeches, the gloom deepened. Frith was far ahead, thrashing through the undergrowth.

They had last been here three weeks before. Then it had been the first week of May, and the new leaves on the trees had been a high, bright colour, dazzling, closer to yellow than green. The beeches, strung out in a long line down the hill, formed an unbroken green tunnel; below them, just above the water, under a haphazard mixture of hawthorn and scrub, wild garlic had covered the ground, its waxy leaves open in a peeled-back display, giving off a powerful, almost rancid, wash of scent.

They looked back now the way they had come, over the tops of the trees to the hills beyond, now just a line of darker shadows on the far side of the valley. Bridle Lodge had vanished; they could only guess at the line of the river. All was silence in the upper reaches of the valley. Only in the land below, probably somewhere in the Lodge's own garden, blackbirds were in competition in the twilight.

They stood in silence, his arm round her shoulders.

They had got back to Bridle Lodge at midday. John had unlocked the front door, and walked straight to the alarm panel outside the drawing room. He had turned to Catherine and held out his hand. 'Come here,' he said. 'I want to show you.'

He'd keyed the alarm; they'd gone in and closed the door behind them.

John went to the desk on the far side near the windows. He opened a drawer and brought out a sheaf of papers. 'These are the invoices I could find,' he said. 'I went through it all when I got back from you the other night. They go back about ten years. Other things, I can guess where I bought them and when,' he said, 'but some . . . the little bits, some of the Bow, I don't know . . . but I'm going to sell them all.'

She'd walked over to him, trying as best she could to take in this information. 'Let's take it to London,' she said eventually. 'If you really want to sell, you may as well get the best price you can. And it wouldn't feel ethical to put it through Pearsons.'

He'd taken her hand in his, pressed it to his mouth.

'Or you can think about it some other time,' she said. 'If you really want to sell, there's no hurry . . .'

'Yes, there is,' he had replied. 'I want all this to go.'

'It's such a lot, John. You'll want to keep some of it.'

He'd dropped her hand. 'Helen wasn't talking about this when she mentioned secrets. She was talking about something else.'

He took her to the window-seat, and positioned her there, facing into the room. He watched her for a second over his shoulder, then walked back to the centre of the room, lifted aside the gateleg table and moved its contents on to the floor in front of the sideboards. Then he got down on his hands and knees and rolled back the rug. The floor looked smooth, oak floorboards with an almost black patina.

'This took me a hell of a long time,' he was saying to her. 'I almost gave the game away when I first met you, talking about lifting floorboards.' He ran his hand over the floor. 'I wanted it invisible,' he murmured. 'I took up the boards and cut them. It was January, those weeks when it never stopped raining. When I'd eventually made the compartment, the boards had expanded. I had to wait until they dried. I put them in the kitchen near the stove . . .'

She was staring at him, mystified.

'Here,' he said. He tried prising a board with his fingertips. It wouldn't budge. He got up, cursing, went to the sideboard and took out a small screwdriver. Catherine propped her elbows on her knees.

A few moments later he had removed two boards; from out of the cavity beneath them, he took a metal box. It was about two foot by three, shallow, an architect's steel drawer from a plan chest that had been fitted with a steel lid. It took some manoeuvring to get it out, and, when he had succeeded, he laid it flat on the floor in front of her. 'It used to be in a bank.'

'What is it?' she asked.

He said nothing.

The drawer was divided into two compartments: one small, one large. He opened the smaller one and put some A4 plastic file covers on the floor. Inside each folder was a brown paper envelope.

'I've wrapped them in a couple of layers of acid-free,' he said.

He stood up, and brought the folders to her. There were about twenty, she estimated. Next, from the same drawer, he brought her a pair of cotton gloves. She put them on.

'Open them,' he said.

She laid the pile next to her on the window-seat, and took out the first. It had a word and a date on the left-hand corner, *Night and Day, 1864*. She drew breath sharply, and looked at him.

'Open it,' he repeated.

She took out the acid-free paper, and the drawing wrapped inside it.

A pencil sketch lay in her lap. The half-circle, looking like the template for a stone carving or plinth, was inscribed on the bottom right-hand corner: 'Richard Dadd, 1864'.

'But this is in the Ashmolean,' she said softly. 'They bought it just before the war.'

'This is a copy,' he told her. 'Dadd made a copy.'

For some seconds she stared at it in astonishment, then looked at the folders next to her. He held out his hand to take the first. Wordlessly, she picked up the next and opened it.

'*Port Stragglin*,' she said. 'Oh, my God.'

She had written a seminar paper on this watercolour. It had been painted in 1861. On the original, Dadd had written a poignant inscription, '*General View of Part of Port Stragglin – the Rock and Castle of Seclusion/and the Blinker Lighthouse in the Distance/not sketched from Nature.*'

She turned the envelope over again and looked at the date on the outside: 1865. 'He redrew them?' she murmured.

'Everything he had to leave behind in Bedlam,' John said, 'or gave to anyone else.'

She looked again at the drawing. '"Not sketched from Nature",' she murmured. 'He used to draw such beautiful things, his flowers and trees, like pre-Raphaelite paintings, or Surrealist . . . and that phrase, "not sketched from Nature", because he was out of sight of a garden . . .' She held up the drawing. 'I always thought this was perfect,' she said. 'The rock and the town, the ships in the harbour, their rigging, the chimneys on the houses. The towers that follow the road up the rock. When you first look at it, it's impossible. Nowhere on earth is made like that. To get a whole world on a little piece of paper just seven inches by . . . I don't remember, seven inches by four?'

'Five,' John said.

'So this is exact,' she said.

'Exactly the same size.'

She sat back. 'My hands are shaking,' she said. She closed her eyes. 'This was what you were talking about. This is what Helen wants.'

'No,' he said. 'She hates them. She wants to sell them. She wants the money.'

'And she thinks I want to sell them, too,' Catherine murmured. She frowned suddenly. 'You're not going to?'

'What do you think?'

'Well, this alone . . . What would they make if you sold them? I don't know . . . it's impossible to say. Ten thousand? Twenty, thirty? They never come on the market. I think the British Museum has the original of this. There are some private owners,' she continued, thinking aloud. 'In America. There's one in Connecticut . . . the Tate has some, and the Victoria and Albert Museum . . .' She looked back at the drawing, and again at John. 'But mostly,' she said, 'when you see a catalogue, it just says, "Whereabouts unknown". There might be a picture, a copy or a photograph taken years ago, but no one . . .' She took a breath. 'No one knows where they are now,' she said. 'They vanished.'

John had replaced the first drawing in its envelope.

She gazed at him. 'John, how many have you got?'

He inclined his head towards the next folder.

She opened it.

It was *Mother and Child*. 'Oh, God,' she whispered.

'It's the clothes,' John said, 'the incredible folds. Just too much material, and too much shadow. They're brilliantly eerie. The overstatement. It's as if Dadd's mania, his obsession, is right here.'

'And the bird in the background,' she said, smiling now. 'Such a strange bird, with its puffed-out feathers.' She put her head on one side. 'It's peculiar to see it so small,' she said.

'He almost miniaturized this one.'

'It's quite a big painting,' she said. 'Oil on canvas. It came up for sale in the nineteen fifties.'

'Nineteen sixties,' he said.

She glanced from one to the other. 'How could he remember them all?' she wondered. 'Everything's the same. It's as if they've been photocopied.'

He took *Mother and Child*, and gave her the next.

Ten minutes later, she took them all to the empty table and spread them out on it. John said nothing else. After some time, she turned to him. 'There's nothing else?' she asked.

'I have eighteen paintings,' he said, 'and fourteen miniatures on enamel.'

She said nothing. She didn't move.

'*The Child's Problem*,' he said, '*Bacchanalian Scene, Cupid and Psyche, The Pilot Boat, The Flight of Medea* . . .'

'Oh, shit,' she said. 'John.'

He burst out laughing. 'That's not an academic response, Mrs Sergeant.'

'Oh, yes, it is,' she retorted. 'You've got a copy of *Bacchanalian Scene*, in miniature?'

'Yes.'

'On enamel . . .'

'He tried out all sorts of things in Broadmoor,' John said. 'He painted a drop-curtain for the theatre, and scenery for their plays, and lanterns. He engraved glass . . .'

Catherine had gone back to the window. She stood with a hand over her mouth, gazing out at the garden. 'Eighteen paintings,' she said.

'Yes.'

'Copies?'

He smiled at her. 'You're doing a great job of keeping calm,' he said.

'Copies or not?' she repeated.

He went to the metal container, opened the larger compartment and took out a canvas bag.

'These were always rolled,' he said. 'My father said they were never framed. So . . .' he pulled the drawstring . . . 'some have cracks. They all need attention. They need restoring, and frames, and . . .'

He pulled a painting from the bag, and held it out to her.

'What is it?' she asked.

'Unroll it.'

The first thing she noticed, among all the other faces, was the magician. Dominating the centre of the picture, he sat with his arms outstretched. Catherine gasped, leaned forward. She studied the magician's face, then back at John. 'He's different,' she said. 'Look at this . . . look at him.'

She got up and tilted the painting so that it caught the light. Her eye ran over the whole. It was like *Songe de la Fantaisie*, in that some of the flowers were in bloom where they had only been in bud, or were invisible, in the original painting. The grassheads that trailed across the picture were in seed, their minute petals open. 'They're all different,' she murmured. 'Every one.'

The fairy queen of *The Fairy Feller's Master Stroke* was standing directly above the magician, and now looked out of the picture, instead of turning her profile

293

to her partner. The dragonfly trumpeter was walking straight for the viewer, wings outspread. Every face in the picture was looking straight out, some with the fixed stares of *Bacchanalia*, others merely curious.

Catherine's fingertip brushed the two girls beside the magician.

John had come to her side.

She lowered the painting. 'It's you,' she whispered. 'The magician is you.'

He glanced at the portrait. Even the colours were changed; the greys of the original had become powder blue, the ground under the Feller's feet was bright yellow. The people in the picture were flourishing, growing, moving. There was light in their eyes. It was as if the artist had caught them in the act of dancing, running. The skirts of the girl with the mirror floated outwards, her feet were lifted: she was flying, for a moment, on the wings that extended from her shoulder-blades.

'Look into the mirror,' John said.

It was Catherine's face. Someone else was leaping out of the reflection, close enough in colouring and dress to be the girl who held the glass, but not close enough. She was someone else, transcending the mirror, passing through it.

Catherine didn't take her eyes off the painting. 'This was what you meant,' she said. 'When you told me to look at the girl with the mirror, you meant you had seen this. You had seen who was in the mirror.'

'You,' he said. 'That's what I couldn't get over when I first saw you. You're in the mirror. He saw you in the mirror, and painted you.'

'You're serious.'

'Of course I am,' he said. 'Why not? He saw other worlds, vast enough to be *Port Stragglin*, and so small that even today you'd have to find them with a magnifying lens.'

'But it's impossible,' Catherine said.

John moved so that he was behind the painting she held, looking straight at her. 'Of course it is,' he said. 'But then again, is anything truly impossible? Where are the boundaries?'

'You cannot seriously believe that he saw me,' she said.

'No, I can't,' he answered, 'but I believe he saw a version of the world, something that runs alongside us. Another reality.' He nodded at the painting. 'They used to call them fairy pictures,' he said, 'as if they showed something that wasn't there, wasn't alive. But,' he shrugged, 'there were people all over the world saying that they saw these images, just as he did. A whole industry grew up on the back of paintings like this. It was the fashion for years.'

'But they didn't really exist,' Catherine said.

'Maybe not. And you can look at a picture like this and say that nothing Richard Dadd painted really existed. After all, what was he? A madman locked up for most of his adult life. A man who could take a knife to his father's throat and think for the rest of his life that he had done the right thing. A man who heard voices . . .'

'But you think it existed?' Catherine said.

'If you're asking whether I believe in fairies . . .'

'You do.'

'No,' John said. 'But I believe that someone like Dadd knew a world we couldn't begin to imagine. Who's to say what's living in that world right next door to us – right inside us, with the things we never acknowledge, or we learn to ignore?'

'Otherness,' Catherine murmured.

'What?'

'The otherness of things,' she said. 'I've heard it described that way.'

He looked down again at the painting. 'What else do you see?' he asked.

She was shaking her head rapidly from side to side. 'I see your face in the magician,' she told him.

'Ah,' he told her, 'but that's not magic.'

'Why not?'

'Because this painting was made for my great-grandfather, Edward Brigham.'

Her mouth fell open with shock. Then light dawned in her face.

'He was Dadd's attendant in Bedlam,' John said. 'He looked after Dadd for nine years. And in those nine years Dadd painted *The Fairy Feller's Master Stroke*.'

'Which he gave to the senior steward at Bedlam, Mr Haydon, who liked *Oberon and Titania* so much that he asked for something similar.'

'And when Dadd got to Broadmoor,' John said, 'he painted this copy, a copy that isn't a copy because it's better.'

'And put Brigham's face into the picture.'

'And yours,' John said.

She laughed a little, too amazed to do anything but stand clutching the painting.

'Don't you think it's a better picture?' he asked.

'I don't know,' she said. 'I can't really string together a coherent thought.'

'I think it's better,' he said. 'It's more optimistic.'

'I can't think,' she murmured. 'Take it from me.'

He did so, and she sat down abruptly. 'This isn't happening,' she said. 'You've got the eighteen water-colours,' she said, 'and the miniatures, and this, and . . .'

'Eleven others.'

'Eleven other oil paintings, in there?'

'Yes.'

'Copies of ones I'd know?'

'Five copies. Six originals.'

She put a hand to her forehead. 'You have six Dadd originals?' she said. 'Oils?'

'Yes.'

'How do you know?'

'What?'

'How do you know they're originals? You mean they've never appeared in any catalogues, any references?'

'They're mentioned in his journals of Syria,' John replied. 'They're all paintings of Egypt, Syria and Greece.'

She said nothing. She watched as John carefully, slowly, replaced the painting in its weatherproofed canvas. 'They have to be kept better than this,' she said.

'I know.' He stood by the container. 'Do you want to see the rest?' he asked.

'Tomorrow,' she said.

'OK.' He replaced the container, put back the

floorboard, the rug and the table. He eyed her warily. 'Are you all right?' he asked. 'You don't look too good.'

'Are you surprised?' she said. 'I can't believe you've got all those under your floorboards.'

It was fully dark now, and yet there was still a kind of light in Derry Woods. They sat on the dry, warm ground, and waited for Frith to come back. In a few minutes he appeared, running full pelt through the trees, catching scent of them when he was almost upon them.

'Where have you been?' John asked him, as the dog lay down beside them and rolled luxuriously on his back.

The sky was empty of cloud, Catherine saw. She had the same sensation she'd had as a child, of falling upwards through the stars. She reached for John's hand.

'I want to give Helen something,' he said. 'She needs money.'

'Why don't you sell them all?' Catherine suggested. 'You'd make a lot of money. Perhaps a million – more. Helen could have half of that.'

'Is that what you would do?' he asked.

'They aren't mine,' she said. 'It isn't my choice.'

'But is that what you would do?' he repeated.

'If I was desperate for money I'd have to.'

'But imagine you weren't. What then?'

'I don't know.'

'Keep them?'

'I really don't know,' she said.

'Pass them on to your children?'

'If that was what had happened before, then . . . yes.'

'But I haven't got any children,' he pointed out. And he was silent for a while. Then he said, 'My father kept them all his life. He never told us about them. He left them in his will. It wasn't as if he didn't need money in his lifetime. But in the original bequest there was an instruction not to sell them. Dadd gave them to Edward Brigham on the understanding that they would never be sold.'

'But you talked the other week about selling everything,' she said.

'I meant the porcelain,' he told her. 'At least I think so – maybe I suppose, then, that I meant the Dadds too. But now . . .'

'Now what?' she asked.

'It doesn't seem right,' he said. He sat forward, knees drawn up, arms crossed over them. She could just about make out his profile. 'I have to think of these things,' he said, 'Helen and the paintings. I can't just leave them. They have to be sorted out. I've been living for too long with my head in the sand, trying not to think about it. I have to decide.'

'Not just yet, though,' she said.

He squeezed her hand in reply, and she had a sudden crushing longing to stay out in the dark, never go back to the house. Things were not the same in the light: they were clearer, more cruel. In the dark, you could pretend you were invulnerable, that the world would stay away from you.

'Helen's never with anyone for long,' John was saying. 'She's had a lot of relationships, all ending badly.'

'I'm sorry,' Catherine murmured.

'Nothing lasts long with Helen,' John said. 'She has a lot to hide.'

'Hide?' Catherine shifted forward too, so that she could see his face a little better. 'What do you mean?'

'She has bipolar disorder. Dadd would have known it as mania. A few years ago they would have called it manic depression.'

Catherine looked at him in the shadows. 'Oh,' she said. 'I see . . .'

'She hides it,' John said. 'Even hides her medication. When I lived with her for a while in London, after Claire died, she had an accident. She took time off work. The firm's medical officer came to see her. It transpired that she had never told them about the bipolar. She was asked to resign.'

'That doesn't seem fair,' Catherine commented.

'People aren't always fair when it comes to psychiatric illness,' John said, 'but she hadn't disclosed it. They called it a breach of trust.'

'What did she do then?'

'Got a job abroad. Moved around. She came back to London after a few years. But I don't think she ever really got over being fired,' he said. 'She bore a grudge about it – she does that,' he said, quietly. 'You may have noticed.'

Somewhere down the hill they heard a noise. Next to them, Frith sat up, ears pricked.

'Don't you dare.' John laid a hand on his collar.

'What is it?' Catherine asked.

'Deer, I should think.'

A breeze had picked up, carrying the sound of more than one animal moving slowly through the land below them. They listened to the steady progress, moving from west to east. They had caught sight of the large buck and the small group of does once before, late in the evening like this – they had left Frith at the house. They had come round a bend in the path, in the dip where the beech trees ended, and found the buck standing motionless in front of them, his head towards them.

A storm had been brewing out to sea, twenty or so miles away; late at night, it had blasted over the house, a spring thunderstorm that shook the glass in the window frames. But for now it was a current in the air, a darkening of the sky.

The muscles had flickered along the buck's flank. The does had come out from the cover of the trees and, one by one, had passed over the path and into the denser shrub. The buck had stayed perfectly still as they crossed, his gaze passing back intermittently to John and Catherine. Then, in seconds, he, too, was gone.

Catherine wondered if the same group was now below them. She thought of that other night, and of walking back to the house, coming to the open section of the fence that gave a view of the village and the fields, and of seeing the storm coming over the hills.

The branches of the trees, sweet chestnut and oak, had lifted, the wind had picked up, and as they stood looking at the rolling indigo of the cloud, drops of rain had splashed on their faces and clothes. Not the storm, but its first few messengers: fat, cold drops in the rising wind. As beautiful as a summer day, the sight of the clouds coming and the trees rolling with them, the sky multiplying and changing.

Now the noise of the deer was receding. The scent of

the woodland rushed up to Catherine on the heavy night air. 'Isn't that strange?' she murmured. 'I can smell something citrus. Oranges.'

'It's Douglas fir,' John replied. 'There's a little copse of them about a mile away, up on the top towards Bere Regis. Their needles smell of oranges and lemons.'

'It must remind you of Spain.'

'It does.'

'Why don't you go back?' she asked. 'Put the paintings back into the bank and go to Alora. Lie in the sun.'

'Would you come with me?' he asked.

'Of course.'

'I can't ask you to do that,' he told her. 'And I can't put the paintings back into the bank.'

'But why not?'

'Because Helen is co-trustee,' he said.

'What difference does that make?'

'Why do you think I took them out in the first place?' he asked. 'I was afraid she would just sell them one day.'

'But she can't!'

'I took them out, anyway. I considered selling them.'

'Does she know?'

'No,' he said. 'And she's not going to.'

'But what if she went to the bank and found they were gone?'

'She won't,' he said. 'At least, I hope she won't. She's never been there in all the time we've had them. I only took them out in January, when I spoke to her after I'd left Spain. She sounded very hyper and destructive.' He paused. 'She was having problems with the man she was seeing.'

'If she finds out now,' Catherine said slowly, 'she'll come gunning for you.'

They stopped. Frith was whining pitifully, desperate to plunge after the deer. John clipped on his lead. He stood up, and held out his hand to Catherine.

'You still haven't answered the question for me,' he said.

'Which one?'

'What would you do with the paintings if you didn't have children?'

She felt the texture of his hand in hers, the precious warmth of his skin, the pressure of his fingers. 'If Helen had children,' she said, 'they would have to pass to them, to your nieces or nephews.'

'They would never get that far,' he told her. 'They would be sold before her children were born.'

'You can't be sure of that,' she said.

'I can.'

She looked back down the hill. 'Then donate them to someone,' she decided. 'Donate them to the nation. That's all you can do.'

'To lie in storage for the next hundred years?' he asked.

'No,' she told him. 'To be loved. To be seen.'

The Crooked Path, 1886

They told him strange things that year.

Dadd had many visitors, encouraged by the stories that he had become calm. They brought the world with them, the teeming world with its myriad complications, its popular thoughts, the taint of its cities.

They told him that, flooded with migrants, London was now twice the size it had been when he was first confined to Bedlam; its immensity was famous the world over, by far the largest city on Earth.

It had more Irishmen than Dublin, more Roman Catholics than Rome; it had spread out into Highbury and Hornsey, Brixton and Balham. Places that Dadd would have known in his youth, at the time of his initiation into the Clique as elegant and a place for gentlemen, were now slums: Holloway, Islington, Soho and the Strand. Holloway had become a wasteland of marshalling yards for the railways, and on the empty grounds between the lines Hell was reproduced daily; here, bones were boiled, rags sorted, and contractors brought their piles of dust.

The railway, thought a blessing, was also the city's blight. Until ten years before, the fields of Gospel Oak, Kentish Town and Chalk Farm were cattle pastures and watercress beds; but then came the North London Railway, the Tottenham and Hampstead Junction Railway and the Midland Railway, turning the fields into shunting yards drifting with coal smoke. The district of Primrose Hill, which to Dadd had been as secluded from the city as anything in the distant countryside, was now cut in two by the Euston line.

Dadd listened to the pictures his visitors painted. He had not liked the railway on the one occasion that he had ridden on it. It was not simply the noise, after the silence of his life, it was the surrender to all things mechanical, physical and seen. It seemed to him that each man put his faith in only what could be quantified. God had become a Gothic mockery. There was no room for the small, uncelebrated detail. He preferred the retreat of his own world, and was glad that he was not forced to take part in the other, which men called reality, outside Broadmoor's walls.

The one story that truly haunted him was of the underground railway. The new District Line in London ran from Paddington to South Kensington, then east to Blackfriars, where it burrowed. They had started what they called deep-hole boring, where the carriages would be cable cars. Already they had gone beneath the City and Stockwell, like rats in drains and sewers, running greased along their tunnels, silent under the feet of those swarming above.

One particular feature, one particular horror, invaded Dadd's sleep. It was the single tube tunnel under the Thames between Tower Hill and Vine Street, on the south side. It had already been open for fourteen years when Dadd heard of it: one thousand, four hundred feet long and only seven feet in diameter, lined with cast-iron sections. When it was opened, a small passenger car ran on a little two-foot track, hauled on one endless cable by a steam engine on the south side of the river.

He kept thinking of the little car, crammed with passengers. It would rattle, straining at the weight of its load over the narrow track. A man could reach out and touch the sides of the shadowy tunnel. He would feel as if he were encased in a long iron pipe, the rivets on the walls passing within eighteen inches of his body. Rivets and sections that kept out the enormous width and weight of the water above.

This was Hell in the world. This was the place of the wide-eyed demons he had seen for years. A man-made coffin, stinking of wet, smoke and the sweating bodies of others.

But the funicular carriage had lasted only three months. Then the car was removed, and the tunnel opened to pedestrians. Every year, lit by gaslight and stepping between the still-existing train tracks, one million people crossed the river underground.

He thought of those people. The million faces lit by the gas; the hundred million breaths exhaled in the fetid air. He thought of them descending the timber staircases every day, with barely room to move with ease. He thought of what might happen in the case of fire or flood: water filling the iron pipe; flames rolling along its length, and only the timber staircase left as a route to the daylight.

In an effort to climb out of the thoughts, he began to paint precipices. Mountains soaring above water; paths curling between breathy heights. He dreamed of standing on the top of the highest mountains, where even the colours had dropped away.

He painted The Crooked Path in September, a dry month after a dry summer. Vertical lines ran down the right-hand side of the picture; sheer rock faces. On the highest, balanced somehow on the narrowest of ledges, two soldiers from different millennia were engaged in a life-or-death struggle. Directly below them, three figures gazed away from the battle, out across the open country. Two were hunched and veiled; the third seemingly indifferent.

He wanted to show that they did not care about the struggle happening above them: enclosed in their stony corner, there was nothing to show how they had found their way to the spot. He called it The Crooked Path, but there was no path, no route or road through it. Those who battled above had nowhere to go with their eventual victory; those who sat below would never make the attempt to go on or back. Isolated, stranded, every figure was in the prolonged act of breathing their last.

Two visitors came from the Chalcographic Society. Dadd did not remember their names.

'Where is the path leading?' one asked him. 'I should say that The Crooked Path is a rather inaccurate description. There is no path to speak of.'

Dadd bore the comments with indifference: they did not see, despite their inspection. Perception was a craft. Opinion was a facile pretender.

'How many people have you drawn below?' the second man asked. 'I count three bodies, but five faces.'

He looked at the man. The fifth face was well hidden, peering from the folds of the garment. The year before he had painted 'Fantasie de L'Harème Égyptienne', and he had put a face there, just to the left of the centre: shrouded in a cloak, the dark skin and eyes peer out, mere fingernail cracks in the whiteness of the scene, touches of charcoal in the gouache.

'There are witnesses in grains of sand,' he said. And he smiled broadly at them, waiting for their response.

But they did not see. Between the rocks, under the empty ledges, next to the feet of the soldiers, under the hand of the waiting travellers below, inscribed on the sheer faces of the mountain, were hundreds of eyes.

That was what came at the end of a journey: the watchfulness of the gods.

He took himself out of his room and asked to walk on the terraces. There, for the rest of the day, he went backwards and forwards, feeling the watching eyes upon him, looking at the earth as it dropped away.

Twenty-four

All the windows of Catherine's house were open; it was the first thing Amanda noticed as she parked the car in the drive.

Catherine answered the door to her knock.

'What's going on?' Amanda asked.

'I'm cleaning,' Catherine said.

Amanda pulled a face. 'I find it a rather pointless occupation,' she joked. She stepped inside. 'What's the occasion?'

'We have a buyer,' Catherine told her. 'I'm clearing my things out.'

'Everything?'

She indicated the piles of towels and bedding. 'Yes.'

'Clothes, furniture?'

'I'm stealing one of the firm's vans. They're coming after lunch.'

'Ah,' Amanda said. She put down her handbag on the couch. 'Stealing. I must remember to tell Mark.'

Catherine switched on the kettle and put her hands on her hips, preoccupied. 'This seemed like a good time,' she murmured. She started making up another cardboard box, taping the edges in place. Then picked up, folded and packed a couple of towels.

'So,' Amanda said, 'you're moving in with John?'

'Yes.'

Amanda watched her friend. 'Are you OK – really?'

Catherine glanced at her questioningly.

Having seen that there was going to be no immediate answer, Amanda went into the kitchen and came back with the tea. 'Tell me all about it,' she said, 'or not, as you wish.' She poured the tea into the mugs; stirred two teaspoons of sugar into hers. 'I've eaten two bars of chocolate and four biscuits in the last hour,' she mused wryly. 'There's not enough sugar in the world for my system. I'm coming back as a man next time.' She glanced at Catherine. 'Do you think you might be rushing all this?'

'All what?'

'With John.'

'You think I'm making a mistake?'

'It's early days.'

'It doesn't feel like early days.'

'Just because you have to leave this house doesn't mean you have to move in permanently with John,' Amanda said. 'You could come and live with us.'

'You *do* think I'm making a mistake.'

Amanda shrugged. 'He's a lot older than you.'

'I know that.'

'And you're in a fragile state of mind.'

Catherine laughed shortly. 'Oh?'

'Come on, darling,' Amanda said. 'Your husband

leaves you without a word . . . Or, rather, with just a bloody stupid little note . . .'

'And then I meet John.'

'Exactly,' Amanda said. 'And his deranged sister.' Catherine paused at the word. 'Oh, you don't know,' Amanda said. 'Her cheque bounced.'

'For the bureau?'

'The same. So I don't think we'll ship it up to John's house, if it's all the same to you.' She looked at Catherine narrowly. 'You don't seem surprised.'

'Maybe not.'

'Has she done this sort of thing before?'

'John told me she had little money.'

'Well,' Amanda observed drily, 'he might have told us before we accepted a bouncer from her.' She sighed. 'But back to a more important subject,' she said. 'You and her brother.' She finished her tea. 'You're a bit too old to go off on one like this.'

'Like what?'

'All starry-eyed.'

'You're wrong.'

'OK, I'm wrong. If you like.'

'My head's not in the clouds. In fact, it's anything but.'

'Ah,' Amanda said, raising an eyebrow.

'John's ill,' Catherine said.

Amanda took this in slowly. 'But not seriously, surely?'

'Heart disease.'

'Is he waiting for a bypass?'

'No.'

'A transplant?'

'No,' Catherine said. 'He's not a good candidate.'

'Jesus,' Amanda breathed. 'I'm sorry.'

Catherine sat down, and now slumped in her chair, gazing past Amanda through the window to the garden.

'Is that why you're moving up there?' Amanda asked.

'It seems pointless to be anywhere else.'

Amanda was touched. 'Look,' she said, 'isn't there anything?'

'Some sort of treatment in the USA,' Catherine said. 'Gene therapy. A growth hormone injected straight into the heart.'

'Well, can't he have that?'

'He asked his GP. I told him to go straight over there, never mind the GP.'

'And will he?'

'I don't know,' Catherine said quietly. 'He seems resigned. It's as if he's waiting.'

'For what?'

Catherine said nothing. Eventually, she took a deep breath. 'You know that my father died when he was fifty.'

'Yes,' Amanda said. 'But not of a heart attack?'

'No,' Catherine said. 'The funny thing was that he used to have this recurring dream. I've been thinking about it. He used to dream that he was standing on the top floor of a building, outside, at the edge. He used to say that he could see the stone coping running round the edge of the barrier. It was four or five feet high, and he had climbed up on it, and was looking down.'

'How horrible,' Amanda said. 'Sounds suicidal.'

'Except that he wasn't,' Catherine told her. 'He was

the most cheerful man, and I always used to think it was strange to dream of what seemed to be a suicidal drop. But that wasn't the most peculiar part.'

'What was?'

Catherine smiled faintly. 'He used to say that one day he would jump,' she said. 'He would *have* to jump.'

'And that's not suicidal?'

'No. He said he knew it was something he would have to do. Like a routine task ahead of him, a project – an academic exercise, almost. To see if he could do it. To see if he would.' She was looking past Amanda, remembering. 'And on the day he died,' she said, 'I thought, He jumped. Just that. He jumped.'

'Perhaps it was a premonition?'

'Do you believe in them?' Catherine asked.

'It's a funny old world. I wouldn't say that anything was impossible.'

'You think he'd somehow seen what was going to happen – had a feeling for it?'

'Maybe.'

'A feeling represented by the dream?' Catherine asked.

'Yes.'

Catherine paused. 'I had the same dream,' she said.

Amanda blinked. 'When?'

'Last night.'

'Exactly the same?'

'I was standing on a precipice and I stepped off. I woke up falling.'

'My God! How horrible.'

'It was.'

'But you can't think this is a dream like your father's?'

'Why not?'

Amanda shuffled forward in her seat so that she was closer to Catherine. 'Because there's a different interpretation,' she said severely. 'You're worried about John. It's linked in your head with John, and your brain produces that image – the jumping-into-thin-air image. It's just association, not premonition.'

'OK,' Catherine murmured. She looked up from her clasped hands. 'You're right.'

'You've been here by yourself, thinking this?'

Describing the dream had brought it back. The dreadful, skin-crawling sensation of stepping from the height into nothingness; the vertigo, the rushing of air. The rock faces gathering speed past her face. She had woken with her hands and face tingling fiercely.

She had got up in the dark – scrambled, horrified, out of John's bed. It had been early, just after five. She had gone to the window and stood, leaning with her hands on the sill, to wait for the first light to touch the garden. She must have remained there for almost an hour, because she was too frightened to turn back and see that it was not her dream of falling but John's.

She was afraid that she had dreamed it for him. The more she thought of it, the more likely it seemed.

Straining in the darkness to hear, she wasn't sure that she could make out his breathing. She became more panicked with every passing second; she became convinced that she would turn and see him lying utterly still. Go over to him. Find him cold to the touch. It happened to people. She had read about it. Most heart-attacks struck in the middle of the night. She had dreamed the terrible dream because he had put it into her mind as he left her.

The dawn came up imperceptibly. At one moment it was pitch black, and then, it seemed in the next second, she could see the filmy outlines of the trees, the terrace. In the next, she saw the water-meadows, the mist moving through them from the river. A tawny light, somewhere between grey and russet, made the fields full of autumn for a while instead of summer. Then – after only five minutes of watching – the grass was the pale, pale green of when it first grows, almost translucent.

She had turned. He was lying on his side facing her. His hands flexed. Then he sighed. She had felt absurd. This longing, and fear, this complicated feeling, went so far beyond the thin words she could ever use to describe it. And she knew that there was never going to be enough time.

Yet she needed no time at all, because she already knew him. It was nothing to do with age, with the man he was, with the Dadds. Even with those points of contact and understanding. It was something else. A recognition. The second – perhaps the third – time she had seen him she had recognized him. A surprised and sudden conviction, utterly unlike what she had felt for Robert. She had been committed to Robert, but it had been mechanical compared to what she felt with John. There was no effort in being with him, no compromise, no matter what Amanda thought.

She knew that if she looked up at Amanda now and told her this, she would be met with some ironic comment. Amanda was a lot of valuable things, but she was not in the least romantic or even imaginative. Catherine could never tell Amanda or Mark – or probably anyone else – what she felt. That she simply had the satisfaction of being in the right position, like an actor moving to cue on a stage. She already had her script; she was already in the action of the play. The lines were written.

And when John had looked at the girl in the mirror, she had understood what he was saying, and the relief was almost tangible. She had found the other world at the right hand of the magician.

She felt Amanda's hand on her shoulder. 'Darling,' Amanda said, 'nothing will happen to John.'

'No,' Catherine said. 'No.'

'You must get him to go for this gene therapy, whatever it is.'

'I will.' Catherine rubbed a hand across her eyes.

'Get him on a plane,' Amanda insisted.

'Yes, I will,' she said, and she returned Amanda's smile.

But she already knew that she wouldn't.

Because they had already stepped off the edge. They were already falling. Through the air, through the glass.

Twenty-five

'I need to talk to you,' Robert said.

Catherine had answered her mobile as she had pulled into the drive of Bridle Lodge that afternoon in the Pearsons van. John was waiting for her: the door opened, and he came out, dressed in paint-speckled jeans and T-shirt. He had waved; she had picked up the phone, gesturing to him that she would answer it.

'Where are you ringing from?' she asked Robert.

'The motorway,' he said. 'I'm at the services near Ringwood.'

She was surprised: he was only forty miles away. 'What are you doing down here?' she asked.

'It's Saturday,' he said, 'and I need to see John about Helen.'

Catherine stopped short in surprise. 'Helen?' she said. 'Why?' She gazed at John through the windscreen. 'He's right here.'

'And I need to speak to you. About us.'

Catherine's heart sank as she watched John walk over to her. Behind him, the gilder who had been helping with the final stages of the stairway, the restoration of the panels, came out, easing his back, shading his eyes to look across the drive.

'I'm busy right now,' she said.

'I wouldn't ask if it weren't important.'

'Robert, I'm unloading my half of the furniture from the house.'

'Where?' Robert asked.

'At Bridle Lodge. John's house.'

John had come up to the side of the van. She opened the door. 'Hold on a minute,' she said to Robert, and covered the handset. 'It's Robert,' she told John. 'Something about Helen?'

John appeared puzzled. 'Tell him to come here.'

'You're happy with that?'

'Why not?'

She put the phone back to her ear. 'Robert, come to the Lodge.'

Silence. 'OK,' she heard Robert say. 'Give me the directions.'

He arrived within the hour. In the mean time, there had been a flurry of rain, hard and swift, splattering the windows of the house and darkening the grass. They had rushed to bring in the furniture – the van was half unloaded – and it was stacked temporarily in the hall. Robert got out of the car and walked across to her stiffly.

'Robert,' she said, 'this is John.'

John held out his hand; Robert shook it.

'This is about Helen?' John asked.

'Is she here?' Robert asked.

'No,' John said.

'Have you seen her in the last week?'

'No – not for a while.'

'What's happened?' Catherine asked.

Robert looked at John and back to Catherine. 'She came to my flat in London,' he said, 'and she's been ringing me.'

'About what?' Catherine asked.

Robert ignored her. 'She's been ringing me every day this week,' he told John. 'Sometimes five or six times a day.'

John was silent.

'I have only met her twice,' Robert said, laying heavy emphasis on each word.

'She isn't well,' John muttered.

'That I had gathered,' Robert retorted, giving him a look that plainly demonstrated he thought Helen was her brother's responsibility.

'I've asked her to come here,' John said. 'She hasn't returned my calls this week.'

'Come inside,' Catherine said.

She had indicated the house; the furniture was just visible through the open door.

'Can I speak to you alone?' Robert asked, and walked away across the gravel, slowly, pointedly, his hands in his pockets.

Catherine looked at John. 'I'm sorry,' she said.

'Go ahead,' he told her. 'I'll wait.'

Catherine followed her husband, catching up with him at the edge of the terrace where he had stopped.

'Doesn't he care about her?' he asked.

'Of course he does. You don't understand what's gone on.'

Robert laughed shortly. 'Well, she hasn't much time for *you*,' he said.

'Me?'

'You shouldn't be here,' he said abruptly.

'What?'

'Getting between the two of them.'

'That's my choice.'

'One you've made very quickly.' There were a few seconds' silence. 'Lovely place,' he commented.

'Yes, it is.'

'You've landed on your feet.'

She was affronted. Behind her, she heard John go into the house and close the door. She looked at her husband. The same old Robert. Neatly dressed. Scrubbed and polished, like a clean floor. He was always so tidy, everything in its place. Every emotion battened down. Now she saw that he was neater, tidier, more closed off than ever. 'A cage of a face,' she had told John.

He had laughed. 'That doesn't make sense.'

'Doesn't it?' She had laced her fingers across her own face. 'Like this,' she had explained to him. 'His whole body is like . . . a fence, a barrier. He becomes solid. Literally immovable.' She perceived that John thought she might be exaggerating.

She wished he could see Robert now. In profile, he was unnaturally still.

'This must take a lot of looking after,' Robert was murmuring. 'A proper estate. You should see where I'm living in London,' he added, as if to himself. 'A rabbit would turn it down in favour of a hutch.' And he smiled, raggedly. 'Has John really not heard from her?' he asked.

'No.'

'Can you be sure?'

'Yes,' she replied.

He made a move to sit on the terrace wall, then realized it was still wet from the rain. 'Is he like her?' he asked.

'In what way?'

'In . . . temperament.'

She shook her head.

Robert was standing very upright, his chin lifted. He looked rather like a man who had been insulted in some subtle way that had only just occurred to him. She ran the tip of her shoe along the bottom of the wall, then bent to pick up the few stray leaves that had collected there. She rolled them into a ball.

'Catherine,' he said, 'you should make your decisions more rationally.'

She was astounded that he felt he could still speak to her like that. 'Like you,' she said. 'I should be more like you, and your rational decision to walk out without discussing what you were doing.'

'You're resentful,' he mused. 'That isn't you.'

'You're wrong,' she told him. 'I'm not resentful at all. Not any more.'

'This is Brigham's influence, I suppose.'

'What do you mean?'

'Cold,' he said.

'John? You couldn't be further from the truth.'

'Mark Pearson told me.'

'That John is cold?'

'Something like that.'

Catherine tilted her head to look at him. 'John is not cold,' she said. 'He's nothing like you.'

Robert's body language spelt surprise, as if she had slapped him.

'That's right,' she said. 'He doesn't keep his feelings on a bloody drip-feed.'

'What are you talking about?' he demanded.

'Drip-feed,' she repeated. 'Like having a bag of saline attached to your arm. Just a little drip of feeling now and then. You might as well keep a graph.'

'That's not true.'

'Isn't it?' she said. 'You've never been there, Robert, not wholly there, not heart and soul.'

'I came here to help you,' he said, 'with the problem of your lover's sister, who, if you must know, is bloody tormenting me . . .'

She put her hand to her head, as if to block out the sound. 'I don't need your help,' she said. 'I'm amazed at you.' Then, she dropped the hand. 'No, I shouldn't be amazed,' she said. 'I don't want to be having this conversation.'

'And you think I do?'

'I don't know where Helen is,' she said, trying to take her voice down a pitch or two, 'and neither does John. If you'd like to come inside for a cup of tea, talk to him . . .'

Robert stared at her. 'Talk to the man you're living with?' he said.

'Robert, I've asked you,' she said. 'You don't have to accept. If we could help you, we would. But we haven't seen her, she hasn't been here. If there isn't anything else . . .'

She made a move to go. He grabbed her elbow. 'It's *we*, is it?' he asked. '*We*, as in a partnership?'

'Let go,' she said.

'And here I am,' he muttered. 'I expect you think I'm a hard-hearted bastard of a husband.'

'I never said that.'

'More or less.'

'You don't have the remotest idea what I think,' she retorted. 'You were always ten paces back.'

'And that's a fault?'

She was amazed. 'How can it not be?' she demanded. 'There isn't a worse fault!'

'Yes, there is,' he replied.

'Name one,' she said. 'Name one worse than not loving your wife. Or saying that you do, but never giving her your heart. Keeping her at arm's length.'

'Lack of control.'

She put her hands to her ears involuntarily. 'You are unreal,' she said. 'You're a two-dimensional picture of a person, do you know that? Lack of *control*!'

He snatched her wrists, brought her arms to her sides. 'Have you any idea what it's like to lose a sense of proportion?' he asked. 'I lived with my mother,' he said. 'Do you know how destructive it is when one person inflicts their selfish fucking egotism on people around them?'

They paused, she with her back to the house, he still holding her wrists.

'There's a difference,' Catherine said, in a low voice, 'between losing control and being in love.'

'There's no difference at all.'

She looked into his eyes. 'Is that what you did?' she asked. 'Kept control?'

'Yes,' he replied.

'To keep things straight, to keep them secure.'

'Yes,' he said.

'I loved you,' she told him, 'and you kept back a piece of you, all the time.'

'Then we balanced out,' he said. 'It was a perfect partnership.'

She saw that he believed this. It was necessary for him to believe it.

'You don't have a pre-ordained mission to keep the world in order,' she whispered.

He let go of her wrists.

She would never forget this conversation. She would never forget that he had kept back a small percentage of himself from her by force of will, believing it to be right.

'Then I come here,' he said, suddenly, 'and see my things being brought in to him.'

'Your things?'

'From my home, into here.'

'We agreed. I haven't got anything we didn't agree upon,' she protested.

She couldn't read his expression. He seemed to be struggling with some inner possession, trying not to let go, trying not to sink. All at once his face crumpled and she saw part of him she had never witnessed: unguarded, unprotected. 'I made a mistake,' he said.

For a moment, she thought she had misheard him. 'What?'

'I should never have left.'

'You lost control, perhaps,' Catherine said ironically.

'And this is what happens when you do,' he retorted.

'It's impossible,' she told him. Suddenly she felt sorry

for him. 'If you think there's some way back, there isn't,' she said quietly. 'There just isn't, Robert.'

'Why not?' he demanded. 'Nothing that's happened is irreversible.'

'John,' she said. 'There's John.'

'Nothing that's happened here is irreversible.' And he repeated himself slowly.

'You want me back?'

'I want my life back,' he said. 'It can be repaired, Catherine.'

'We didn't *have* a life,' she said.

'What are you talking about? We spent years together. We were married – we're still married. Perhaps you've forgotten that.'

'No,' she said.

He seemed confused. 'You really think we didn't have a life?' he asked.

'Not the kind of life I need.' She glanced back at the house.

'Oh,' Robert snapped, 'and that kind of life is here with John Brigham.'

'Yes,' she said levelly.

'You've known him for two minutes.'

'I've known him all my life,' she said.

Robert burst out laughing. 'Oh, Christ,' he said. 'Now I've heard everything.'

She said nothing, simply held his gaze.

He was grinning at her. 'And it's nothing to do with money, and nothing to do with him having a half-a-million-pound house . . .'

Her face became stony, frigid.

Robert took a step towards her. 'He's twenty years

older than you,' he said, 'and looks thirty years older. What's the matter? Waiting for him to keel over? Good strategy. Whole bloody estate falls into your hands. Don't suppose he's left it to Helen?'

She turned on her heel and walked away from him, back to the house, then heard him coming after her. 'Catherine,' he called. 'Catherine.'

She had reached the doorway. 'You'd better go,' she told him.

'Catherine,' he said. 'I'm sorry.'

'Goodbye, Robert.'

'Look, I—' He stopped himself. 'Catherine, I'm telling you – I've made a mistake.'

She didn't reply.

'Don't you remember . . . when we went to France, and before, before . . .'

She put her hand on the door. 'What good did it do you?' she asked.

'What do you mean?'

She was trying to keep a rein on her temper. 'Holding a piece of yourself back and keeping me at bay. It did you no good at all. Look at you.'

He flinched.

She sighed. 'This is insane,' she whispered. 'It doesn't matter any more.'

'We can start again.'

'Because . . . what? Life's too hard to handle? Is that it?'

'And is he so very different?' Robert demanded. 'You'll find him difficult, I can guarantee that. Do you suppose that Helen's character doesn't run in a family?'

'Oh, no,' she warned. 'Don't begin on John. He's nothing like her.'

'He'll become like her. He'll show his true colours.'

'No,' she retorted. One hand was clenched against her chest.

Robert was watching her. 'Everything comes down to this,' he said. 'You can fall in love, or think you do. You can go off on your fantasy tangents and see life through rose-tinted glasses. But it comes back to this eventually. Love burns out, and that's the fact of the matter.'

'That's not true,' she said.

'It is true,' he insisted, temper rising. 'You loved me once. Where is it now? Those things mean nothing in the long run.'

'You're wrong.'

'I'm not wrong,' he said. 'It'll be the same with John.'

She shook her head.

'Pragmatism holds the world together,' he said, close enough to her now for her to feel his breath on her face. 'Not infatuation.'

She turned away her head. 'There's no way,' she murmured. 'I'm sorry. No way.' She was trying to turn the door handle.

'You'll see that I'm right,' he said.

'No.'

'I'll change,' he said.

'You can't.'

'It doesn't matter about this sale,' he said. 'We'll buy a nicer house. One that you choose.'

'It's not about houses. How could it possibly be about houses?' She shook off the hand he had laid over hers.

'And I won't say a word about Brigham,' he said. 'It'll be as if he had never existed, I promise.'

She was choked with fury, hand on the door handle. She stared at the brass of the lock, and the distorted reflection of her face in it.

Robert went to his car, got in and reversed savagely out of the drive, spraying gravel in his wake.

As she watched him go, she heard footsteps in the hallway, and John opened the door.

They said nothing.

She stood trembling; he took her hand. Then they walked away, through the rain-drenched garden, down between the trees, picking their way finally past the dark red heads of the peonies that lay flattened, drooping their dark red bodies out of the border and down against the pale brick of the path.

Flora, 1882

The visit came late in 1877: an art journalist from London who had been paid to see the once-genius at work. Dadd had seen him standing in the hall at Broadmoor, looking at the dining areas and the view of the gardens. He had been in a rectangle of sunlight, which turned his black clothes rusty. Round-shouldered, portly, hat in his hands, he seemed deep in thought.

When Dadd was introduced to him later in the super-intendent's office, he knew that the man was not a gentleman. His collar was yellowed, the bands of satin on the coat lapels were worn. His demeanour was all turned down: a downturned mouth and downturned eyes. His hands were clasped oddly, one across the other.

Once Dadd had painted a man like him, nearly thirty years before – the little man who scrapes his shoe out-side the drawing-master's door. He had called the picture Insignificance or Self-Contempt – Mortification – Disgusted with the World. *And it was the world that* bore down on the little man's shoulders, the enveloping cloak of the rusty-black world that hung over his shoulders in the sunlight. So the first question he had asked him was 'How is the world?'

The journalist had snatched a glance at the attendant: apparently he did not know if any information could be given. 'The world is running apace,' he said at last.

'After what?' Dadd asked.

The little man smiled. 'Oh – all kinds of miracles.'

Dadd leaned forward. 'Have they a name?'

'The transmission by telegraph . . . the phonograph . . . the light globe.'

Dadd inclined his head. 'What is a light globe?' he asked.

'A filament . . . a vacuum . . . that creates an artificial light.'

'By what means?'

'I am not sure,' the journalist confessed.

Dadd's eyes ranged over him.

'I hear that you have painted wall murals,' the journalist continued, 'and the theatre curtain, here in the hospital.'

'Yes.'

'You have painted on cloth, for the curtains and scenery?'

'Yes.'

'And the subjects?'

'The stars, the planets,' Dadd said. 'The rising of the sun.'

'I have never seen a sky of yours,' the journalist said. 'I have seen very many figures, and landscapes.'

Dadd considered this truth. 'I have looked for another world under my feet,' he murmured.

When the article was printed just after Christmas that year, the little man in the rusty-black coat had called Dadd's paintings 'melancholy monuments of a genius'. It was better than the last review, in which the journalist had called them 'curious freaks of fancy'. However, Dadd was not troubled: he never saw the articles. They were kept from him in case they disturbed him.

He thought for a little while about voices transmitted by wires, and preserved in wax, all of which seemed to him the product of sickness, a worse sickness of mind than he had. And the names were so curious. The phonograph. The telephone. How did a man press a voice into wax, or thread it along a wire?

Birds hung on wires. Sometimes, when he was a boy, farmers had killed and hung crows on wires at the edge of woodlands, or on field gates, as a warning. He thought of the world's voices hung on gates, hanging head down in the air, strangled and rigid, knotted and tied.

Flight was harnessed like this, and the same with voices and light. A voice, or an illumination, a man-made sun or star, compressed into the hand, balled into a chemical. It was odder than looking in a mirror and seeing a familiar room reflected backwards. All the world was going in the same direction, encapsulated, imprisoned, reduced.

It seemed that man's sole intentions were to tie creation to a gate. Put the sun in a glass globe; put a symphony on a wax cylinder. But nothing extra was gained, except perhaps a little space, an empty space that had been filled by the persons who owned the voices, the musicians who played the instruments. It provided a space where once an audience had sat in a concert hall, or a man read aloud in his own room. It prolonged and extended a single moment, making it both small and rootless, no longer identified with a particular place.

Music hurtled around in the sepia reproduction of the world, the photographed and recorded world, losing the value of the moment because it could be seen and heard over and over again. There was no more advantage in being present. The moment could be preserved and played back to you. The experience of passion could be replicated and shared a hundred thousand times, exactly the same in the hundredth telling as it had been in the first. No progression, only replication.

He wondered if they had taken into confinement the men who had created the false miracle; if they, too, languished into old age. He did not know. He had not asked, so astonished had he been that such a sad little man could create such fantasies, or believe them if they had been told to him.

He imagined his own voice encapsulated, then played back to him. It was simply the expression of what his mind had been telling him for decades: that there were voices let loose in the world that clung to false bodies and inhabited minds. Voices that took on the sound of a man's own.

Soon, he thought, sitting before a blank wall and staring at its face, the world would believe in its own bodiless, formless ghosts. It would hear them. It would transmit them to others, and every man would allow himself to become convinced of their reality. Soon the whole world would be barred and caged, and the asylums would be opened, because there would be no distinction between the lunatic and the rest of mankind.

There was not so much difference, then, after all, between the madman and the sane. There was not so much difference between the artist and the lunatic. They bled into each other.

A month later, Dadd was told that Rossetti had died.

Dante Gabriel Rossetti, named after an angel, who had, in turn, painted angels. A man who did not need platinum or iridium, zirconium or magnesium to illuminate his faces. And yet even Rossetti had been tormented in his way: the man had exhumed his dead wife to retrieve a book of poetry he had written, and thereafter retreated into his addiction to chloral hydrate. Rossetti, who had painted the same beautiful face of his model over and over again, and called it Proserpine, La Ghirlandata, and Venus Verticordia.

Dadd resolved to paint his own beauty.

He called her Flora, and she was as real as Elizabeth Siddall, Rossetti's muse. His model was Florence, the wife of the medical superintendent, whom he saw at daily intervals. He asked if he might paint a fresco of her, in the way of the old masters. She was a kindly woman, of a sweet nature, and implored him to paint in her own hallway, so that she might see the picture as soon as she came into the house.

Into her figure Dadd poured his privacy: the reality of imagination that could not be reproduced more than once. This was a reality that could not be copied any more than his own inner vagaries could be repeated.

He painted her on a large space, six foot by ten, directly on to plaster, using the fresco techniques he had learned forty years before, colour mixed with water on fresh plaster. He painted every flower of the field in perfect detail: delicate pink sainfoin, bird's-foot trefoil, wood vetch with its orchid-like flowers and delicate trailing vines; white melilot, red clover, hare's foot. In her hands Flora held a cornucopia: a blaze of cowslips, cuckoo flowers, dame's violet; wild columbines, straight thin stems topped by a hanging purple bloom.

He painted her like a May Queen, garlanded, crowned. He remembered his father telling him about the Garland King of Derbyshire, carried on horseback through the town, covered with flowers and foliage, a Green Man come to life. A festival older than time, as old as the woods, as old as the peaks. Beltane translated to May Day. He had seen villagers Beating the Bounds, walking the parish boundaries on May Day, with willow or elm wands in their hands.

He thought of the ingrained connection between the land and what sprang from it, and it rolled down the brush to dance across the wall: Quaker grass, ragged robins, harebells, celandines. He drew the grasses particularly, just as he had drawn them carefully across the Fairy Feller: beautiful wall barley, with its head of fine hair; marram grasses, stately spear-carriers; meadow foxtail; timothy; and the hairgrass, so delicate, so full of movement, pulled by the slightest breeze, rippling across the wall under Flora's naked feet.

When it came to her face, he had more difficulty. Rather than the superintendent's wife, he had a sudden need to paint Catherine, but no image came. Eventually, he painted a fairy's face with his own striking dark eyes.

She sang out of the picture, calling, calling, the sun rising at her back, the fields filmed with promise of heat, the trees dark with full leaves, the river running through the fields behind her.

The fresco took eight weeks. When he had finished, Dadd retired to his room, lay down on the bed and stayed there. He called it an idleness; he told his physician the same. 'I am very idle,' he said to the doctor, who was summoned.

His heart and chest were examined. 'There is some congestion in his breathing,' was the doctor's verdict. 'Nothing more or less than I might expect in a man of sixty-five.'

Dadd lay on his back, hands crossed at his waist, eyes closed: an icon of sleep, a prophet in stone.

In his dreams, he saw himself astride the echoing Earth, painting the planets and stars on the backcloth of the sky, with Catherine at his side.

Twenty-six

Helen pulled her car over to the narrow patch of ground alongside the road. She looked ahead for a while, to the few flint-and-cob houses on the lane that climbed the hill. Then, she got out slowly, in laboured movements, and walked down to the bridge.

Beyond the span, the river spread out into water-meadows, and became shallow and fast-running; here, by the bridge, it was much deeper. She leaned on the parapet and looked down into the four or five feet of water. It was clear above the chalk and pebbles, and looked cool. She watched the eddies, the ripples, the bright green strands of weed lazily streaming from their roots. She ran her hand along the stone, felt the cracks with the tips of her fingers, passed her flat palm along the lichens, their corrugated edges.

As she stood there, a family came along the river path. She heard their voices first, then saw them between the trees, a couple and three children who were at the water's edge where the weeds were thickest. They had a dog with them, a little spaniel. It quivered on the bank, then plunged in after the stick that the biggest boy had thrown. Helen watched the tableau for some time: all five following the swimming dog, waiting for it to return, framed by the trees, the low-cut hedge, the flat fields beyond turning to hay.

She let them pass her, smiling at them. The sun beat on the back of her neck; she went down on to the path and into the shade.

She was deathly tired from the driving, the miles of road. So tired that she would have willingly lain down right now; she looked at the river and wondered how much of a relief it would be to be swept downstream, gliding like Millais's Ophelia between the reedy banks and shallows. She wanted, at least, to dip her body into the cool water, sink her head under for a second, feel the water in her mouth, on her neck, running over her eyes and through her hair. She was so exhausted. The oblivion would be beautiful, if just for a minute. Or an hour. An hour in the Millais painting.

It was twenty-four hours now since she had gone into the merchant bank at the top of Walbrook. Her heart had been beating so fast with nervousness that she had thought she would faint. The last time she had visited the place had been twelve years ago, when Claire had died, and she and John had transferred the paintings there from their father's bank; it was more central for them both. She remembered the interior only vaguely, a gilt-and-black mausoleum that had been partially modernized, combining the Corinthian marble with smoked-glass security screens.

She had given her number and references; shown identification. Nothing in the way that the staff looked at her had prepared her for the truth. They had acted as if they didn't know. And that had struck her with venom when she had come back out into the foyer after visiting the vault. They were smiling at her, the wicked smile of the conspirator.

She had broken back out on to Walbrook gasping for air, and randomly turned south. When she had got to Cannon Street station she had found herself walking towards the Embankment. She went on for miles. In the sweating heart of the City, all the way along the river, all the way across Bloomsbury, up Kingsway, until she had stopped on the steps of the British Museum and sat down among the crowds there, feeling beaten by deception, betrayed.

John had had only to tell her. That was what she kept thinking. John had had only to speak to her. He needn't even have asked her permission; he had had simply to tell her. But he hadn't. He hadn't bothered to ring, or write a letter. That was what devastated her most, that he hadn't trusted her enough to let her know his decision. He had taken every single painting, every single drawing. He hadn't even left the miniatures, and she had once told him that even though she hated all the rest – my God, how she loathed them, the eerie and ugly little fairy world, all its grotesque detail – she liked the little pictures, the ones on enamel, some no bigger than a thumbnail. She liked looking into them. It was amazing how deep they seemed, how three-dimensional. You could gaze into them for ever and still see something new.

But he had taken even those, pocketed them like a thief. That was exactly it, she had thought, sitting between the ranks of students and families spilled over each other, buffeted by the noise and the unremitting sunlight. He had stolen from her. He had taken them all away, hidden them and never said a word.

She hadn't gone home. She had hired the car and driven down here, to the green south with its endless open downland, its chalk flanks. And it was here, last night, in the dark, that she had stopped the car in a lay-by, almost crawled to the verge and vomited into the grass, pressing her palms hard into her eye sockets, blinded by white flashes, black lines.

The day had broken into this dancing, streaming ribbon. She heard them talking to her, not loudly enough to distinguish the words, just talking. That rambling soliloquy in the background that she had learned to tune out came down, a mothy blanket bubbling with sound.

She never took lithium any more. Lithium, the great healer. All the medication was pointless. It cracked her teeth, it thinned her hair, it made her put on weight. More to the point, it made her – that, and everything else they prescribed – truly suicidal.

There had been one time in London, after the accident with the car. She had been going somewhere – some interview for an employment agency. She had been standing on the station at Chancery Lane. It was supposed to be one of the deepest stations on the Underground, and she remembered feeling its depth, how far down she had come. She could recall the oppressive atmosphere. She had waited a long time for a train. There had been a delay posted up on the electronic board. And then she had felt the train coming, the rush of air along the tunnel, and she had been seized by a sudden thrill of release. She could jump. She could fall on to the line. It wouldn't take much. And the realization that she could do this, that she had the power to stop the weight, the unbearable weight of dread and nausea, just by taking a step or two forward and falling . . .

She had glanced up the line. The rails were so uncomplicated. It would be blissful to feel the push of the metal, the almighty crush. Just a second's impact.

The train rushed past her. The noise charged through her. She had stood and waited, then stepped inside the carriage with everyone else.

But it had been so tempting. Flooded with desire to cut herself free, she had sat quietly in the seat and fixed her eyes on the floor.

She had never told John, or anyone else. Having been fired for not disclosing the bipolar, she had never mentioned that again in any conversation, let alone a job application. She let people think she was moody, if that was what they wanted to think. She let them think she was difficult. It worked: her staff retreated from her. No doubt they talked behind her back, but she didn't care about that. At least it made them do what she wanted. They were wary of her, careful not to offend her, not to light the fuse. She saw it in their faces.

By the time she met Nathan, she had accepted that she was shut up in her own world where she made the rules. In her manic phases she had been to bed with whoever she wanted: men she had only known for a few hours, even a few minutes. It was in a manic phase that she had started the relationship with Nathan, in a flurry of desire and possession that now she could barely remember.

Since the termination, she had gone down like a stone, further down than ever before. Some days she didn't get up at all. She had wanted it to be different with Nathan. She had wanted to be a different person. She had firmly believed – my God, she had believed with her whole being – that she had turned a corner; that she had control of it. Because she loved him. She allowed herself the picture of the family, the house, the future; the vision of herself at the centre of an ordered life. She would be calm. She would change. Nathan had been her last chance to change.

It had been now or never. She was in her late thirties: time was running out. Her options were getting fewer. She had wanted to give up what she had been before, the way her life had habitually run. She had wanted the whole idyllic scene, the children, the home, the neatly made beds, the cupboards full of linen, the fresh flowers in the hall, the whole picture she had painted in her head. She had wanted that world, her imagined world, her particular sweet fantasy where she had control of the characters.

She could master the illness; she would conquer it. And for a long time – it seemed like the longest time of her life – she had fought the familiar plucking fingers of the lowering mood, pulling her back to the siren call of the abyss, the stroking seduction of the dark.

Now she sat on the ground by the river and stared ahead without seeing.

It hadn't worked. In a down phase like this, the world was a slowly rotating carousel, getting ever slower. She was the only rider, and everyone else stood outside, just passing slurs of shape.

John was less than a mile away now, she knew.

If she walked straight up the lane past the cottages, she would come to a crossroads. A left turn would take her back into town; straight on would bring her to the edge of the woods. There would be a gate in the lane, and the beginning of a long drive. That was the entrance to Bridle Lodge. She knew because she had driven this way the night before, at midnight, parked her car and looked for the house between the trees. There had been no lights. She had toyed with the idea of walking up there in the dark, a shadow among shadows. Breaking in perhaps, through a door, a window. Finding what he had hidden from her.

But, in the end she had decided against it. She would see him in daylight. She would face him. She would ask him why he had done it. She would have her explanation.

She had turned the car round and driven aimlessly, eventually stopping in a picnic area – just a rough wood table and a clearing – in the hills above the Frome valley. She had slept in the car.

'Are you OK, love?'

She jolted at the sound of the voice.

A man was looking down at her. He had his little dog by the scruff of its neck so that it wouldn't run past her.

'Yes,' she said, shading her eyes. 'I'm fine.'

'You're feeling all right?' he persisted. 'Anything I can do?'

She got to her feet, brushing herself down. Why was he asking her such a thing? Did she look out of place? She hadn't considered it. Standing there, the canopy of the trees reflected in the quick-flowing river, the watery reflections crossing over the man's face, the little dog dancing in his grip, she swayed momentarily.

He put out his hand as if to steady her.

'Is there anywhere nearby to stay?' she asked.

The man was frowning. She was puzzled: surely that was not an unusual question to ask. They were in the heart of holiday country. The county was dotted with hotels and guesthouses.

The man gestured over his shoulder. 'There's a bed-and-breakfast just up the road,' he said. 'House with a yellow sign, on the left. You'll see as you go up towards Derry Woods.'

'Thanks,' she said. She patted the little dog, then walked back along the path. Behind her, she knew that the man was watching her every step of the way.

The guesthouse was where he had said it would be. They had a room. Helen brought in the only luggage she had – a carrier-bag that held a hairbrush and a few toiletries she had bought that morning.

As she mounted the stairs behind the woman who showed her to the bedroom, she felt her feet drag. Fatigue swept over her; her knees buckled with the effort of climbing. Everything went grey: the old familiar grey, as if all the vibrancy had washed out of the world.

She found it hard to listen to what was being said to her. She just wanted to lie down. She said something to the woman, she couldn't remember what – thanked her, probably, said the room was nice, it didn't matter.

When the door was closed, she laid down on the bed, fully clothed.

She was sound asleep when, half an hour later, the brief rainstorm scattered its heavy drops against the window.

Tlos in Lycia, 1883

It was dark; he was trying to remember the route they had taken when he had been a traveller forty-one years ago. He had been a young man then, barely twenty-five. A young man of promise, whom the whole world had forgotten. Whom the whole world believed was already dead.

Dadd stirred in his bed, turning his head towards the window. His eyes opened briefly and he looked at those assembled in the room: he thought he glimpsed Brigham, whom he had left behind in Bedlam. The physicians Monro and Morrison. Even Sir Charles Hood seemed to stand behind them, although that was impossible: Hood had died in 1870; Dadd had been told that his paintings that Hood had owned had been sold at public auction. They had been dispersed, as the man himself had been dispersed, as he himself would soon be dispersed into the grains of sand and strands of grass that he had painted as his own memorial.

He did not even know who had bought them. He had

been told that someone had paid a hundred and thirty six guineas for Oberon and Titania, *and that, at least,* had amused him. He had often thought since of his ghastly Titania glowering for ever on a stranger's drawing-room wall.

Dadd closed his eyes on the company. They were ghosts, all.

He took himself back to the journey, to the warmth of the long-lost day. Lycia, on the edge of the Mediterranean. They had come through Greece, Caria, Rhodes, and were now passing south, in a country whose name was like a whisper, a lover's endearment.

They had been climbing all day, and now passed along the ridge of the low mountain. The valleys, gentle, undulating slopes, were full of olive trees, but where they walked was sandy, the rock showing through the soil. As they rounded the shoulder of the hill, he saw the temple, a whitewashed dome rising incongruously from a field of thyme and grass. He stopped to wonder at it, and the scent overwhelmed him; not only thyme, but rosemary, and, as they descended to the little church, roses lying nakedly on the ground, trailing sparse petals, yet triumphantly seducing the senses, a strong, clear signal in the hot sun.

The priest was sitting in front of the single room, on a bench in the hot sunlight. As soon as they reached the door, Dadd could see that this was no more than a single space carved into the hillside. It was dark and, in even starker contrast to the outside, damp with what seemed to be a little stream of water issuing from the rock. Candles had burned down in the wall sconces, until the last of their light was shimmering in pools of *wax. There was no gold here, no treasure; the crucifix was bleached wood and had been nailed together. He remembered the grain of it. Wood from rosemary, twisted and fissured, like Christ's tortured hands upon the cross.*

He had gone again to the door, and stood at the very edge of light and dark, on the point where darkness met the aching noon. Lying in his bed now, he thought he had never left that place. He had been standing ever since on that point, on that equinox, dark at his back, light at his feet, and a thousand worlds between the two.

His mind ran back over mornings when the sun had barely crept into the Bedlam cell; of days, later, when more light was admitted. He remembered the window being altered. He remembered the birds in their cages. He remembered the year when he had at last allowed himself to be photographed and the time he had spent looking at himself, an image within an image within an image, for he was more than the man in the picture, and the painting behind him was more than strokes on a page. They thought that they had incarcerated him, but in fact they had freed him: he had travelled much further than the average man by virtue of what Monro, Morrison and Hood were apt to call insanity.

He had been freed to walk through his own subtle paranoias, to illustrate his own hell, to design his paradise. He thought of Port Stragglin with its parapets and mountains, its physically impossible gradients and fortresses, which he had conquered in his mind. He was a landscape of impossibilities and triumphs. He had done the impossible: held the world in his hand, created others, crushed what he did not need.

He was the purveyor of magic, the sorcerer, the Medusa, the Tiresias, the father of demons. He was delicate and kindly: he had spent a year painting the tracery of insects' wings. He had painted a dragonfly, a satyr, a bower of roses. He had painted murder. He had painted knives within the reach of a child's hand, and nightmares on that same child's face. He had drawn tiny Gardens of Eden, and populated them with horrors. He had been king and emperor, soldier and thief. He had made empty canvas bleed and sing; run with music. Score a line on flesh; leap with seething ingenuity.

He felt his hand being lifted.

He opened his eyes. A doctor leaned over him.

'Will you take a little of this?' the man asked, and held a glass to Dadd's lips. The liquid was a little cloudy. He drank it.

'Laudanum, for sleep,' the doctor murmured.

Dadd watched the man's fingers on his wrist and looked with objectivity at the hand splayed beyond: his own right hand that had made so much in life, now inert.

It may have been hours later, when they had lit the gaslight in the corridor, and he could no longer see their faces, that someone asked, in a quiet voice beyond the door, if he were still alive.

He dropped his body, weightless as it was, lighter than air, and walked away. The wall crumbled, and he was standing in a crowd of familiar faces. He looked around himself: the grasses leaned across the whole picture. He reached up and touched the nearest, coarsely twined in the stem.

He began to smile. He laughed with delight. The sound bubbled out of him, and the community in front of him turned: the king and queen and all their courtiers, the pirate, the woodsman, the scholar, the insect trumpeters, the fairy feller himself, who, for the first time, turned his face on his creator, and dropped the axe to the ground.

It was real, after all. Everything imagined was real.

He had not lived in darkness, he had not died in fantasy, or been in prison, or lost his reason. He had been alive. He had seen it. He had heard it. And it was not false, but thrived. He had touched them. They had come to him. Universes in thought, multiplying souls. He had known, always, that they had been there, and that he was not out of the world but within it, on that threshold of light and dark, on the invisible meridian.

He leaned back, letting them course through him; galaxies burning in a filament of thread; voices singing through wires. Every impossibility, every possibility.

When he looked back to them all, the girl with the green-glass mirror was already smiling.

She stepped down from the shelter of the magician, and walked towards him, holding out her hands.

Twenty-seven

There was nothing to do but go forward.

John took a step across the insubstantial divide, a faint filmy border between this world and sleep. He had woken when it was still dark, and stayed awake, listening to Catherine's breathing and his own. He had matched hers for a while, copying the cadence, watching her barely visible face in the darkness, intending to get up and open the window. He wanted to feel the fresh air on his face.

But as he turned on his side, the room seemed different, peculiar; it was like looking at a shoreline, the soft little waves breaking at his feet, a humid mist clinging to them. The room, the window, had receded. A kind of softly humming exhaustion came in with the tide; he closed his eyes.

As he moved away, he saw his feet at the water's edge, then the flickering of passing lights, like reflections. There was a dazzle that reminded him of a long-lost journey; the train ride he sometimes took across the river into work in London. There had been a bank of poplars planted next to the railway line, perhaps two or three hundred yards of trees. On sunny mornings, if he closed his eyes, he would see their images dancing on his closed lids; and the effect would be strange, hypnotic and disturbing, a computation that his brain couldn't manage. One morning he had heard someone on the train say that it was the kind of effect that triggered migraine, a strobe dancing behind the eyes. He felt that now; a moment of cinematic frames rushing across a lens.

Then the water was gone, and he was standing on solid ground.

He saw a central patch of red first, pale rose-red, almost pink, describing a long, slow arc. It was a piece of cloth falling to the ground. He looked beyond it, narrowing his eyes, straining his vision: out of a moss-grey bank shapes appeared, then faces. Eyes turned on him, eyes with incredible intensity. He saw a hand raised in the foreground, and the flash of metal, touched by the sun and turned gold; gold, too, in a strip across the ground as the light intruded on the gloom.

Then, one by one, the flowers were illuminated like lesser suns, all the way along the bank and stretching upwards. He saw that it was a dense hedgerow, and the flowers were dog-roses and daisies, the petals intricately picked out so that he could almost feel their texture from looking at them.

Stillness . . . then the picture fell apart, as everything began to move. It rotated and changed. From the bank figures emerged, of all shapes and sizes: a sea captain, staff in hand, cloak across one shoulder; a woman with a ruff of thick lace above a scarlet coat; working men, countrymen in smocks and gaiters, a boy in a green jacket, a man with a grizzled face and a cap crushed far down over it. They had all been posed stiffly between the leaves, and now they moved over the green, the grasses, the remains of nutshells, scattered in thousands of pieces just beyond the strip of sunlight.

He stared harder into the centre, where the cloth had fallen, and saw the magician looking at him, one hand raised as if in warning, a smile on his face.

The man began to stand up, and John saw how tall he was, how broad, overshadowing all the other eyes, faces and figures that were now running towards him. And then the figure in the bottom centre of the picture turned, holding the axe over his head. It caught the sun again, and flickered once, twice, as dazzling as the disjointed images from the past, the poplars from the train window, jumbled on the blade. John saw him coming, the axe weaving in the air.

The man was smiling, the magician's hand was upraised, and, as he watched, rooted to the spot, he saw, through the dancing, racing lights, the magician's hand fall.

He woke, gasping.

Catherine was holding his arm. 'What is it, John?' she was saying. 'What is it?'

He was still seeing the rushing crowd of faces bearing down on him.

She got out of bed, and ran round to his side, opened the drawer in the bedside table, took out the medication.

He put his hand over hers.

'You must take it,' she told him.

She gave him a glass of water, and he swallowed the tablet obediently. They waited together, she now sitting on the side of the bed, and he half sitting, half lying, hand fisted against his chest. When his breathing had slowed, she took his hand and closed her fingers around his.

'What was it?' she asked.

'A dream.'

'A nightmare?'

He shook his head. 'It was *The Master Stroke*,' he said. 'They were all moving. They were coming towards me.'

She sighed. 'You're worried about the paintings.'

'Maybe.'

'Do you want to go to London, talk to someone?' she asked. 'Or we could just take them, if that's what you want.'

He looked down at their joined hands.

'John,' she murmured, 'I want you to do something.'

'We'll go,' he said, 'and take them.'

'I'm not talking about the paintings now,' she told him. 'I want us to go to the USA. I want you to see this surgeon . . .'

'No,' he said.

'It could make a real difference,' she said. 'You don't have to listen to anyone in this country. There are other options.'

'No,' he repeated.

There were tears in her eyes.

He wanted to explain to her about the light. How he kept dreaming about it, standing between light and dark at first, then the rushing, changing light of this morning's dream, but most of all the sensation that had first swept over him that morning, that he had felt now several times: the sensation of drowning in the hazy sea, softly, without struggle.

'I can't understand you,' she was saying.

He turned her face towards him.

'If I'm not suitable for gene therapy, they'll just try another angioplasty,' he said, 'or cut me up with epidural catheters. Do you know what they call those things? Subcutaneous ports for medication. A kind of hole in my chest. No, thanks. I don't want to risk being a guinea pig over there.'

'It would stop the pain.'

'It might, it might not. It might set up an infection and trigger a heart attack.' He started to get out of bed.

'John,' she said.

He got up and raised her to her feet, wrapped his arms round her.

'You've got to do something,' she whispered. 'Not just . . . nothing.'

He pressed his face to her, the sweet smell of her, then lowered his head and kissed her shoulder.

'Promise me,' she whispered.

He lifted his face, and held her at arm's length. 'I'll tell you where we'll go,' he said. 'We'll go to Segura de la Sierra.'

He smiled: she was staring at him, puzzled, frowning. He put his arms round her waist, kissed her, drew back and gazed into her face. 'We'll drive up there one morning,' he said quietly, 'before the sun is up and it gets too hot. We'll drive up through the mountains. There's a village, and a little castle – you have to ask for its keys in the village, and you let yourself in, as if it were your own house. You can stand and look down, all the way to the valley.'

'John,' she said. 'Don't.'

'Or Cazorla,' he murmured. 'It looks just like *The Crooked Path*. Did I ever tell you? There's a fortress right on the peak.'

He could see himself and Catherine there, perfectly clearly, as sharp as a memory: he could see them driving the long, spectacular road through Cazorla, Segura, Las Villas, through the thick woodland where he had once seen ibex. He could see himself and Catherine at Ubeda, in the beautiful churches, and at Baeza, the Renaissance town, Moorish and full of medieval splendour, in the white and gold cathedral in the Plaza Santa Maria.

He could see them in absolute clarity and detail; he could feel Catherine's arm linked in his, their shadows ink-black against the harshness of noon. He could feel her lying in a white room heavy with heat, naked, the full length of her pressed to him, feel her mouth and touch. The image blasted through him, incredibly vivid, a drench of intoxication, and he knew in that same second that they would never be there, or that she would go alone, and lie in a room like that alone, or walk through Baeza alone. And that light was rushing outwards, leaving the soft, ensnaring waves around his feet, and the inexorable pull of the sea; and that it was inevitable, a moment passing in the world that would take him with it. Just as everything in the paintings had passed out of the canvas and lived. He would exchange that experience. He would pass through the paintings and into the whispering ocean, into nothingness. It was just a movement, a necessary passage. Just as the figures in the painting had turned towards him and begun to rush from their places.

And he could see something else, too.

He could see that he had lived.

And that this had been truly living, and that this was what it meant: that he had been more than alive, to be with her.

They went downstairs, and the house felt stifling, even so early. They opened all the windows and doors, grateful when a light breeze blew in.

'I've never known it so warm at this time of year,' Catherine said. She walked on, turning to smile briefly and anxiously at him, as she went into the kitchen.

He was standing by the stairs when he heard the car coming.

He waited, listening to the speed as it made its way up the drive between the trees. He walked to the open door and stood leaning one shoulder against it, shading his eyes. He saw it come into view and Helen was at the wheel; he saw her expression; knew before the car even stopped, before she even got out, what had happened.

She strode towards him across the gravel and he had time to think, No, not yet, not today, before she spoke. The words, the idea, came straight into his head, without thought, without prompting. He pushed himself away from the door and moved towards her.

Helen glanced briefly at the two cars in the drive alongside hers. 'Is she here?' she asked.

'Yes,' he told her.

'Have you given them to her?'

'Helen,' he said, 'come inside. Come and talk to me.'

'No,' she said. 'Make her go.'

He shook his head.

'Tell her to go away,' Helen repeated. 'I'm not speaking to you with her in the house.'

Her gaze, the violent electricity in it, frightened him. But she wasn't trembling, and she wasn't rushing her words. He had never seen her like this.

'I will not tell Catherine to go,' he said. He extended his hand. 'Come inside.'

She stayed where she was. 'Where are they?' she asked.

His hand dropped. 'In the house.'

'You've shown them to her.'

'Yes.'

'Oh, my God.' She looked at the ground, passed a hand over her forehead. 'I knew it would happen one day,' she said. 'You always behaved as if they were yours. Now you've taken them.'

'You can see them,' he said. 'Come inside and look at them. They're safe.'

'Safe from me.'

'Helen,' he said, 'you never wanted them. You always wanted to sell them. As for them being mine, they were left to me. I made you co-trustee.'

'And you always wanted to hoard them,' she retorted.

'That was the instruction.'

'Not to hoard them. To look after them.'

'I've kept them safe all these years.'

'And what changed?' she demanded.

356

He walked to her side, took her gently by the hand. 'Helen,' he said, 'how did you find out they were gone?'

'I went to the bank, of course.'

'To do what?' he asked.

She stared at him.

'You were going to take them,' he said.

She wrenched away her hand from him.

At that moment, Catherine came to the door, saw them and walked over to them. 'Helen,' she said, 'are you OK?' Helen merely stared at her. Catherine's gaze shifted to John, then back to his sister.

'I've come for the paintings,' Helen said.

'You've *come* for them?' John repeated, astonished.

'I want half of them,' Helen said. 'Divide them up however you like. You can give me the ones you like least.'

'Helen,' John said, 'I can't do that.'

'You can even get *her* to decide a fair division,' Helen said.

'Helen,' John said, 'it can't be done. It's not going to happen.'

Helen rounded on her brother. 'This is the only thing I've ever asked you for,' she said.

'Please come inside,' Catherine said.

Helen glared at her. 'I don't want to talk to you, don't you understand?' she snapped. 'I want to talk to my brother.'

Catherine glanced at John. 'I'll be in the kitchen,' she said, and went back to the house.

'That was rude,' John said.

'The lady of the manor,' Helen retorted. 'Already.'

John caught his breath. The familiar pinprick, the

needle searching the muscle. He shifted his weight, as if that would distribute the pain. 'I can lend you money,' he said, 'if that's what you need.'

'I don't want a loan,' she said. 'I just want what's mine.'

'They aren't yours,' John told her. 'They don't belong to us. They're just in our care.'

'Oh, for Christ's sake!' Helen said. 'Why are you so bloody precious about them? Let them go! They're just daubs. Why let them sit in a box somewhere? They could be doing us some good.'

John had been watching her narrowly. 'Where has all your money gone?' he asked.

She stopped short. Colour came to her face. 'That's none of your business.'

'It is, if it means you want the paintings.'

'I never had any money.'

'Your salary?'

'Spent.'

'The money Dad left you?'

'Five thousand pounds?' she said. 'There's thousands upon thousands in those paintings. You could let me have at least some of them!'

John rubbed a finger across his brow. 'We were talking about it . . .'

'You were talking about it?' Helen said. 'With her?'

'We were saying that—'

'You've discussed this with her?' Helen asked, furious. 'What was it? "Give Helen one. Which one shall we choose? One of the little ones. The one even she couldn't recognize when it was put under her nose!"'

'Helen—'

'You superior bastards!'

'It wasn't like that at all,' John protested.

'I want a house,' Helen said. 'I want a place to make a home. Is it so very much to ask?'

'But you can't just snap your fingers and make that happen overnight,' John pointed out. Then he looked closely at her. 'You're strung out,' he said.

'Don't start that.'

'Have you seen a doctor?' he asked quietly. 'Did you come down here without seeing anyone?'

Fury darkened her face. 'Why can't I have what I want?' she said. 'Why can't I have it now? You've set up with her overnight. Look at her in this place. You'd think she'd been here for years.'

'You don't understand,' John said.

'Oh, I do,' Helen replied. 'I understand that you can have whatever you want.'

'I worked for what I have,' John said. 'It didn't just fall into my lap. I built up a business.'

'A very successful business,' Helen said. 'I've heard about all the contracts you've got. I've heard what they're worth. Don't you think,' she said, shouting now, 'that you might ease your stranglehold on those bloody paintings, with all the money you've got? Don't you think, if you had half a heart, that you would just give them to me? To help me? To set me up in a decent life?'

'I'm never going to sell the paintings,' John said. 'And you've got every opportunity for a decent life,' he added. He searched her face, worried. He had heard this kind of repetitive reasoning before. She looked dishevelled. Her hair hadn't been combed; her clothes were creased. As quickly as the anger and impatience had crossed her face, they were replaced with a grimace of grief. 'You don't understand what my life is,' she muttered, 'what it's been.'

The remark floored him. He stared at her, bemused.

Then, before he could stop her, Helen was running for the house. He set off after her. She wrenched open the front door and plunged down the hallway, opening doors as she went, unfamiliar with the rooms. At the end of the corridor, she found the kitchen.

Catherine was sitting at the table, a cup of coffee in front of her.

'What did you say to him?' Helen said. In the next moment, John appeared in the doorway behind her.

'Say to whom?' Catherine asked.

'My brother.'

Helen leaned on the table. Just for a second, Catherine thought that the other woman was going to hit her and recoiled, scraping back the chair, half rising to her feet.

'You can't have these things,' Helen said, in a low voice.

Catherine met her gaze. 'I don't want anything. Only John.'

Helen stared at her.

There was a perfectly still, silent moment.

Then Helen walked past Catherine's chair. John and Catherine looked at each other, with the same puzzled, regretful expression. Then everything happened at once. Catherine felt the chair tugged backwards. Helen grabbed a handful of her hair, pulling her bodily off the chair. Catherine gave a cry of pain and surprise.

'No!' John said.

Catherine was half crouching. Helen was shorter than her. She swung her body to the side in an attempt to dislodge the woman's grip.

'Catherine!' John shouted.

Helen had taken a knife from the draining-board; the pressure of the blade against her throat stopped Catherine's struggle. John stepped towards them both. 'Put it down,' he said softly. Catherine couldn't see Helen's face; she hardly dared breathe. But she saw John's terror. 'Helen,' he said quietly, 'we'll help you. Listen to me. We'll help you.'

The blade pressed harder.

'I know how you feel,' John whispered. 'I know what it does. Let go of Catherine. It'll be OK,' he continued. Catherine saw him edging towards them, inch by inch. His gaze never left his sister's face. 'I can help,' he repeated. 'Let me help.'

Then Helen's voice came as if from a distance: thready, plaintive, a high-pitched whisper. 'You can't help me,' she said, with a flutter in her voice.

Catherine saw John's foot hesitate on the floor; she raised her eyes to his face. His hand was outstretched to Helen, palm upwards, a gesture that she should give him the knife; then, his hand turned. He glanced down at Catherine with something like surprise in his expression. His colour altered. He lost his footing and staggered backwards, clutching at a chair and missing it.

He fell to the floor.

'John!' Catherine cried.

Helen stepped back; the knife dropped.

'John! John!' Catherine scrambled across the floor. She reached his side on her hands and knees. He was lying on his back, staring at the ceiling.

'John,' Catherine said.

The light was behind her, streaming through the open window.

He thought he caught the scent of rose, but it passed. He thought he saw her turning more than once through the green glass, raising her head to look at him. He realized that he had never quite finished the window on the stairs, and the portrait in the glass that looked so much like her.

He opened his mouth to tell her to be careful. To be careful in handling the cracked frames of glass. That the colour should be matched. He had always wanted to match the new stained glass to the original.

It was a difficult tone, a particular tone.

It was the colour of the first leaves and of the water below the cress beds by the weir gates. It was slightly darker than the summer grass. It was the colour of dozens of thinly painted brushstrokes of yellow-tinged watercolour, caught in a mirror where a face was reflected.

It was a shade of green, a shade of green . . .

guides had been printed to show the detail that even a close inspection of the painting might miss: the tiny pale centaur in the bank of clover, the face of Richard Dadd's father in the top right-hand corner; the belts, buckles and lacing of shoes; the deep folds of material; the faint edge of a woman's face reflected in the mirror; and Richard Dadd himself to the right-hand side of the raised axe.

On either side of the painting were all the others, *Songe de la Fantasie*, brought from the Fitzwilliam Museum in Cambridge; and the copy of *The Master Stroke* that John and Helen had owned. *Contradiction*, loaned from a private collection; and *Sketch to Illustrate Melancholy*. One after another the newly discovered portraits from Bedlam, each one full of terrible poignancy, faces of muddled hope and misguided obsessions, sealed for ever in their cages of the 1840s; the *Sketch to Illustrate Jealousy*, brought from Connecticut; *The Crooked Path* from the British Museum.

On the opposite wall, *Devon Bridge* and *Tlos in Lycia*, the dozens of notebook sketches of Syria that John had also owned. And, in the centre of these, *The Child's Problem*, which stopped everyone in their tracks. In the glass cabinets on the other side were all the miniatures, again with the tiny replicas of *Port Stragglin*, *Marius in Carthage*, *Flight of Medea*.

Catherine closed her eyes briefly. The opening night had been almost too much: she had missed John so acutely, so physically, on seeing the completed exhibition. Even Amanda and Mark's presence had not helped. She had felt, bizarrely, irrationally, that she had allowed Dadd to be inspected and exposed.

None of the compliments had moved her; none of the enthusiasm of other collectors, whose own paintings were also here. Everything had become jumbled: the noise of the guests, the questions of the press. She had had to go and stand outside, breathing in the icy air, watching the tourist boats ploughing the choppy tide down to the National Theatre and Cherry Garden Pier, their lights fragmented on the water.

It was two and a half years since John had died.

Two and a half years since the ambulance had come to the door of Bridle Lodge. They had told her he had died almost instantly, but she doubted it. Something of him stayed in that room for a long time, some part of him that had never left her.

Helen had spent the next year in a psychiatric unit. Catherine saw her sometimes, if she came to London, and Helen was the same as ever, sometimes high, sometimes haunted. They never spoke of the paintings, or of John. Robert had worked abroad, in Germany, for the last two years. There had been no contact between Catherine and him.

She walked through Derry Woods every day. It saved her sanity. She had seen two years of seasons come and go; sat sometimes in the summer by herself with Frith in the dark, listening to the deer that still passed along the same route through the valley. Walked in the last weeks of winter, waiting for the spring, to the village by the bridge, and back up again to the weirs below the house; the house that John had willed to her, his last task in the week that he died – the house to her, the paintings to the nation.

Peter Luckham had come only last week and told her that the watercress beds must be cleared again. It had grown as thickly as he had predicted. But the white-beam were lovely when the spring came: John had been right to plant them. Their images were in the stream all the way down to the water-meadows.

John had given her that: made the world different. She couldn't name it, or quantify it. But it was there, changed for ever, a vibrant thing, of joy and significance, that he had shown to her. Even without him, even in the depths of grief, she didn't merely exist. She lived.

It was made for love, he had told her. *To be alive in the world.*

She opened her eyes.

It was enough.

She wanted to go home now.

She took a long last look at the paintings and the crowds, then left and went through the reception area, passing the waiting queues.

On the steps of the gallery, catching her breath in the cold wind, she stopped a moment, closing her hand round the miniature she always carried in the locket round her neck. It was *The Child's Problem*. A piece of John that she could not let go, the only Dadd painting that she had not told them about and given away.

She walked down the steps, her hand closed tightly round it.

THE END

Author's note

Richard Dadd's feelings and beliefs were never actually recorded other than brief observations by doctors at Bedlam and Broadmoor; my creation of them is supposition. It is a fact, however, that many of Dadd's known paintings were lost, and the story of The Girl in the Green Glass Mirror is built around a fictional hypothesis of what might have happened to them. 'The Fairy Feller's Master Stroke' is kept by Tate Britain in London.

A WAY THROUGH THE MOUNTAINS
by Elizabeth McGregor

Ten years have passed since David Mortimer last saw Anna
Russell. Their love affair ended when she disappeared.

Drifting through life ever since, David has never married
and is devoted only to his scientific work and to the book
he has always meant to write about the botanist, Ernest
Wilson, and his extraordinary exploits in China.

But David's isolation is about to change. He receives news
that Anna has been seriously injured in an accident.
More devastating still is the revelation that he has a daughter,
Rachel, whom he has never seen. Both now urgently need
his help – and more than one danger is threatening them.

'JOHN LENNON ONCE SAID THAT "LIFE IS WHAT
HAPPENS WHILE YOU'RE BUSY MAKING OTHER
PLANS", A SIMPLE TRUTH BEAUTIFULLY CONVEYED
IN THIS POWERFUL NOVEL'
Choice

0 553 81338 2

BANTAM BOOKS